D1392005

UNDER CAPRICORN

UNDER CAPRICORN

by

HELEN SIMPSON

WILLIAM HEINEMANN LTD
LONDON :: TORONTO

FIRST PUBLISHED 1937

PRINTED IN GREAT BRITAIN AT THE WINDMILL PRESS
KINGSWOOD, SURREY

BOOK I.

I have read that *Capricornus*, the heavenly Goat, being ascendant at nativitie, denieth honour to persons of quality, and esteeme to the Vulgar. Can a Starre do so by onlie shineing on a Woman in her pangs? Shall *Capricornus* bind a poore man the world ouer, no part, no Land undiscouered, where hee may shake free? I will not belieue it: nor that Honour (not forfeit) can be for euer hidd by decree of this distemperate Starre.

—*A Limbo For Ladies.*

BOOK ONE

(i)

THE year, eighteen hundred and thirty-one. The place, Sydney; a city whose streets were first laid by men in chains for the easier progress of the soldiers who guarded them. This city, growing slowly about a population of convicts and soldiers, had at that date no very penitential air. The harbour water, lively with sun; the many windmills, leisurely bestirring themselves; the ships at anchor, hung with marine laundry, ensigns trailing; the smoke of domestic chimneys: all these things contrived to lend Sydney an air of expectancy rather than despair. Maps show where the habitations were gathered; they were not many, though diarists and letter-writers of the period agree that they were tasteful, and showed up cleanly against the dark universal background of trees. "Not," says one lady, "that I should like it in a *picture* so well as our softer and more rounded perspective, but in a new place, where one likes to see everything plainly, it is very pleasant."

So much for maps and for prose. Poetry of the place and period lacks, or is not much to the purpose. Still, the Chancellor of the University of Cambridge did, in the year 1823, announce Australia as the subject with which his would-be medallists must concern themselves; and since one of the unsuccessful competitors was William Charles Wentworth, born in the new continent, his descriptions must be allowed to possess some authority. After an account of Cook's discovery, with a digression upon the fate of La Perouse, Mr. Wentworth proceeds:

> Lo! thickly planted o'er the glassy bay,
> Where Sydney loves her beauties to survey,
> And ev'ry morn, delighted, sees the gleam
> Of some fresh pennant dancing in her stream,
> A masty forest, stranger vessels moor
> Charg'd with the fruits of every foreign shore.
> While landward—the thronged quay, the
>   creaking crane,
> The noisy workmen, and the loaded wain,
> The lengthen'd street, wide square, and
>   column'd front
> Of stately mansions, and the gushing font,
> The solemn church, the busy market throng,
> And idle loungers saunt'ring slow among——
> Shew that the mournful genius of the plain
> Driv'n from his primal solitary reign,
> Has backward fled, and fixed his drowsy throne
> In untrod wilds, to muse and brood alone.

His account almost fills in the picture, which yet needs to complete it a sense that this new country was no mere copy of the old, but had already taken on a character of

4

its own, defiant, tough, indolent; as though the idle
loungers of Mr. Wentworth's poem were to be viewed
with their hats cocked, pulling in their belts upon hunger
with a laugh, and having a loaded pistol somewhere
ready about them which they were prepared upon slight
occasion to use. There was freedom, derived as usual
from slavery. There was money, derived about equally
from labour, land, and luck. There were social gatherings,
junketings, as there are upon a ship in mid-ocean. And
for the whole company of exiles, bond or free, there was
hope.

It will be seen that Sydney, in the year 1831, may very
well serve as setting for a highly-coloured, improbable,
and yet simple story.

(ii)

AT about five o'clock in the afternoon of December
3rd of that year, a ball hoisted upon the south yard-arm
of the flagstaff at the entrance to Port Jackson showed
that a sail had been sighted, approaching from a southerly
direction. Later, a flag with St. George's Cross was run
up, signifying that the sail in question belonged to a
Government ship, full-rigged at that. Almost immediately after, down came this flag, and was replaced by a
Jack.

Excitement became evident among the boats in the
Pilot's anchorage. At South Head the semaphore

began to function, reporting, in a series of jerks and flickers:

A Government vessel. Between 2 and 3 leagues S.E. of the Head.

To which Fort Phillip, above Sydney Cove, responded in the same lingo:

Report all movements of vessel signalized. Is there much sea between the Heads? State all particulars.

South Head:

This is the vessel expected. Vessel has signalized probable arrival before nightfall. Correct: previous signal should read, vessel does not expect to anchor before morning, owing to lack of wind.

Fort Phillip:

Confirm. Repeat.

South Head:

Vessel does not expect to anchor before morning, owing to lack of wind.

Fort Phillip:

Be more attentive.

Despite this rebuke Fort Phillip was not displeased to have twelve hours' respite. In twelve hours buttons might be polished, arms burnished, the fear of God be put into a guard already drilled to unthinking unanimity. In twelve hours some sort of a reception could be arranged, with flags and bunting, down by the Quay; the citizens' enthusiasm was more likely to show itself freely at the beginning of a hot December day than at a similar day's end. There were speeches to be memorized, beavers to be brushed, children's locks to be put in paper; for all this twelve hours was by no means as much time as could be desired, but it would have to serve. The Commandant sent off runners into the town, to the Colonial Secretary, to the President of the Legislative Council, and the Principal Superintendent of Convicts, then sat down, hooking up his close military stock, to an evening meal with his officers, which ended with the health, drunk in Madeira that had taken a six months' roll round the Horn, of the newly-arrived Governor, Sir Richard Bourke——

"And may he not be another of these prigs that we have to foot out of the Turf Club," said the Commandant as he set down his glass.

The Governor at this moment, in a costume by no means conventional, was lying full length on the deck of that interesting vessel from the south, *Foxhound*, about which the air clung, never stirring. He said to the young man at his side:

"The climate's giving us a warm welcome, anyway."

"It's an omen," the young man returned, "don't build on it. They threw out Bligh, they threw out Darling. For a Governor that's tired of life, I'd say this was a delightful appointment."

"Did you ever hear how they shifted Darling? It was at a Turf Club dinner. They drank his health, all very civil; but when it came to the Jolly Good Fellow that should have followed, the band broke out with 'Over the Hills and Far Away.' Darling looked like a sick hen, one

7

of the soldiers told me that was there; sent in his resignation from the Club, and got out of the country soon after. By God, if they'd done that to me I'd have known what answer to make."

"You'd have whistled, 'Will ye no come back again,' all on your own."

"I might, if I'd thought of it. It will take more than a couple of fiddlers to get rid of me."

"There's some of this Irish boasting we hear so much about. You'll change your tune when it comes to making a nation out of the scum of England."

"I know plenty about the scum of England. If you can make an army of it good enough to beat Boney, you can make a nation."

"Well, be quick about it. I don't want to be half a century out here making my fortune."

The Governor laughed; and looking at the stars, which kept their places upon the chequer board made by spars and rigging, observed:

"I never can get the lie of these upside-down planets into my head, after all these years."

"My idea," the young man went on, following his thought, "is to benefit by corruption. I can't make my fortune any other way; not by fighting, it's too late for that; not by inheritance, I haven't a relative left that's solvent. As for work—true, you can make money working, but it spoils you for the enjoyment of it. And I won't marry an heiress, the pick of them's gone, the only ones left weigh twenty stone or grow beards. I like reading poetry with my feet on the hob, but it takes money, that kind of innocent life. So all that remains for me is to be the Governor of New South Wales's sixth cousin."

"Why can't you write poetry for a living? Lord Byron, I believe, did very handsomely out of his books. You were always a scribbler."

"True," answered the young man with a bitterness which made the Governor turn his head, surprised. "I was always a scribbler."

"I had no notion of being offensive, Charles."

"The truth is never offensive; distasteful, perhaps. I am a good enough poet to write little stuff for the keepsakes. That is the best I can do, though I sweat blood. Therefore, my dear sir and cousin, I won't do it. And therefore, my dear sir and cousin, I propose instead to batten on you."

"I'll disown you once I'm installed."

"I'll lead a faction if you do. I'll invade Government House and rout you out from under the bed covered in fluff, like Bligh." The Governor did not heed him, still staring up, hands locked under head. "Stars! What good are stars to a Lieutenant-General, except to remind him of his damn decorations? Stars are poetical stuff. I'm going below. Are you staying here on deck all night?"

"I am."

"Where's your sense of discipline? Do you think the sailors will think much of a Governor when they can see he has less hair on his chest than themselves?"

"Go to your cabin, young fellow-my-lad, and get some sleep if you can. We have a long day to-morrow."

"Pleasant dreams to your Excellency. Mine, I hope, will be about shameless great bribes."

"I don't have dreams. Good night."

The stars moved steadily as a clock's hands; steadily the water reflected their lights, which wavered now and then and were lost in shining furrows, a shark's fin breaking the surface. The lantern on South Head stared, never blinking. His Excellency regarded all these things in turn as the ship swung about, and fell asleep thinking of Spain, where he had served, and where the nights had something of this quality. His last conscious thought was dredged up out of memories he did not know himself to have acquired; the Spanish word *guardaamigo*, which, as he recollected, meant the prop set under a criminal's chin while he takes his flogging.

(iii)

TOWARDS morning a breeze came up from the south which caught the waiting ship broadside. The captain had been waiting for this, and his Excellency woke to a sound of bare running feet on deck and the shouts of the second mate ordering men aloft. It was almost dawn. As the canvas was set it took shape against the lightening sky, squares, triangles of darkness, soon to be turned a triumphant white by the sun. They began to move forward; the chirrup of water sounded again under the figurehead; and the brown rocky coast, in which as yet there appeared no opening, began to march beside them like a guard of honour. His Excellency stretched, regarded his dominion through a glass for some few moments, then went below as bugles sounded in the soldiers' quarters.

He disappeared as a civilian none too particular in matters of dress. He came on deck a soldier, magnificent in red, with a plumed hat and a sword-belt golden as Orion's, while stars more gaudy than distant Arcturus were disposed about his left breast. His staff in a lesser degree glittered round him, buttons winking their tale of hours of labour, gold-lace only a trifle dimmed by weeks of sea air. Only the young gentleman, Mr. Adare, His Excellency's sixth cousin, appeared at a disadvantage in sober bottle-green, with the paltry chink of seals for accompaniment as he moved, in lieu of a sounding jangle of spurs. But he was not abashed; he criticized the popinjays with his head on one side, and ridiculed the delicate care with which they avoided maritime contacts for their white trousers. They for their part eyed him with the traditional disdain of the military for free agents, and put on formal brisk voices, reporting to the Governor, as though he had been blind, the topography and incidents of Port Jackson:

"Pilot coming aboard, sir. Quarantine station, sir, on the right. Passing the lighthouse and signal station, sir. Shark Island, sir. The fort known as—h'm—Pinch-gut, sir."

All this information the Governor acknowledged with nods, as though he were not as capable as these gentlemen of reading the chart unrolled in front of him. His eyes were taking in other things; a foreshore which reminded him of coasts in the South of France; the many bays, deep water evidently, by the sheer slope of their rocks; the situation of the distant town, not clearly seen as yet; the green of the foliage, uniform and dull as a rifleman's jacket.

"A number of small boats, sir, coming out to welcome you, I imagine."

The staff officer's observation was not at fault. Small boats were all about the Governor's ship as she moved into Sydney Cove, their occupants evidently out for a spree; young men managed the sails, long brown young-sters, watched by their womenfolk from under bonnets trimmed with English flowers—artificial daisies, roses, violets. The boats very skilfully accompanied His Excellency's ship, and from time to time one of their occupants would raise a hand, or a woman would lift a child's brown pud and wave it in greeting. There was no cheering.

"Well, I don't know," said His Excellency to an officer who commented on this fact; "they can't tell yet what they're in for. The Duke used to say he valued the cheers he got after a battle, but didn't give a rap for any that went before."

At the landing-stage, however, things were more
formal. Persons could be seen there, grouped, and
shifting from foot to foot as the December sun bore
down upon their trappings, which glinted in an official
manner and showed in outline all the authentic terror
and exaggeration of the warrior's dress. Those shakos,
tall feathered stove-pipes, had for ancestor the brazen
casque of Paris, whose plume most horribly did dance.
Those epaulettes, jutting from the shoulders, were contrived to awe innocent naked savages accepting them as
earnest of the gigantic deltoids below. Those chains,
studs, spikes of metal terrified by their very irrelevance,
their threat of dreadful purposes not understood. Yet
shakos, epaulettes and the rest of the costume were
comfortable to the eyes of His Excellency's staff, who saw
in them only the norm, and found reassurance in shining
thus familiarly upon a foreign strand.

A naval cutter came out to meet the ship as she
anchored. Into this His Excellency stepped with his
party, and was rowed ashore to receive salutes, cheers,
and a speech of welcome delivered by some civilian
dignitary. A regimental band played "Blue Bonnets."
Against this the Governor heard, behind his shoulder
among the crowd, an echo of "Over the Hills and Far
Away." The whistling ceased as he turned. With a
tightened lip and hands folded quietly upon his sword-
hilt he waited for silence, then spoke. His voice, clear
of any parade-ground quality, yet made itself heard
beyond misapprehension.

"Gentlemen: I am new to your country, and therefore, at this stage, I say nothing of my intentions concerning it. I say only that I am sent by the Government at home to guide you to prosperity as far as the judgment of one man may do so. Your problems are to be my particular study, and your well-being my particular care. I am not unaware that there have been clashes in the past between governed and governors, nor shall that knowledge weigh with me. I am here to perform my duty; which, as I see it, is to promote the order, good feeling, and increased wealth of this Colony. I rely upon your co-operation to attain these ends. I am prepared to work with any man, whatever his station, who will help me to attain them, and to punish any man, whatever his station, who by his conduct imperils them. Gentlemen, I have nothing further to say at this moment, only that I am greatly obliged to you for your welcome."

Mr. Adare was impressed. It was the first time he had heard his relative speak as one who had seen men and cities, served in epic wars, and borne rule in the continents of Africa and America. Other listeners too found this kind of talk to their taste, and the civic dignitary, walking beside the Governor towards the carriage in which they were to ride, made approving comment on it:

"That's the kind of thing we never heard from Governor Darling. Always roundabout; never took responsibility where he could dodge it——"

"I don't care, sir, to discuss my predecessor."

"Oh!" said the civic dignitary, taken aback but not

daunted. "Certainly. The less said of him the better. Well; and what do you think of our harbour?"

(iv)

NEXT morning, having unpacked and distributed his staff (rather a tight fit) among the rooms of Government House, His Excellency said to his cousin, whose decorative idleness he found irritating:

"There is something to be done that you may as well do. Go to the offices of the Bank of New South Wales; introduce yourself as coming from me, and deliver this letter to the Secretary, or one of the Directors. It only concerns me, in so far as I promised Lord Goderich I would deliver it. Talk to the Secretary, and invite him in my name to dine. These fellows know more than Government men about conditions in a country. You might ask him for a little advice on your own account; prospects for investment, and so on."

"I don't view with any gratification the prospect of earning money by work in this heat. His Excellency's cousin may use his nose, I suppose, to find out what sinecures there are?"

"His nose; not my name."

"Sea-green Incorruptible! Or shall we say in deference to the climate, lobster-red? Adieu, adieu. Remember me!"

Mr. Adare put the Colonial Secretary's letter into his

15

tail-pocket and sauntered out into the sunlight. Sydney Cove was on his right, quick with shipping; on his left the trees of the Government Domain proffered a thin shade. He kept to the left, not for this reason only, but in order to beat the marches of the city, of which Macquarie Street formed, at this point, the boundary. His eyes, alert as the infernal brickish dust of passing vehicles would allow, considered houses and people dispassionately, the horses with unaffected interest. They were worth a hunting man's attention. Their unkempt appearance, shaggy legs and manes, could not cheat an Irish judge accustomed to pierce such disguises. Mr. Adare, having seen in the course of ten minutes' walking almost as many rideable horses, began to have a better opinion of the Colony.

As for the streets themselves—he had turned at right angles and was surveying King Street—they were unpaved and damn dirty. They were full of masterless dogs. They offered no picturesque black men, such as Cape Town afforded, no woolly heads adorned with branching horns, or strings of beads, or trophies not easily identified. They resembled, in their undisciplined dusty straight lines, the streets of a manufacturing city at home, save for the depth of the shadows that fell across them, and the height of the Cornstalks who marched along them, trees walking. No colour. No signs of wealth. No signs of pioneering and danger. Why did the place exist?

The answer to that question, at the very moment his

mind asked it, came round the corner of an intersecting street to its own odd musical accompaniment. Against the regular beat of soldiers' feet sounded a shuffling, and above the shuffling a chinking, not rhythmic, never ceasing. Mr. Adare stood, and at his ease reviewed a convict chain-gang as it passed along. Their dress was uniform, spattered with a pattern of arrows; only their caps varied from the fisherman's knitted jelly-bag to beavers not yet wholly devoid of nap. These last perhaps had been worn in London, where their owners exercised those arts for which thieves' jargon found such enlivening terms; smashing of queer screens, shaking of skins, ringing of castors, working the cat-and-kitten rig, or nibbling while Oliver whiddled. Most of them held up their chains as they walked by means of a string hitched to their belts; even so the dulled chinking made itself heard. No man stepped out as a free man may, as the guards did; the chains hobbled them too securely. All kept their heads down against the sun, all shouldered their long-handled, small-headed road-maker's hammers because that was the easiest way to carry them; and the effect of this uniformity was a slavish, hopeless air such as might hang about duppies, those dead men who labour for a witch's profit among Jamaica canes.

Mr. Adare, impressionable, but fortunately volatile; wax to receive, but water to retain; Mr. Adare did not care for the mixed feelings this encounter had roused in him. Pity without the means to relieve is emotion wasted; anger with the human race in general on account of the cruelty or folly of particulars is not to be justified. So he told himself as he walked on towards George Street, while the shuffling and chinking took itself off in another direction. Nevertheless, the generosity in him was uneasy at finding no outlet, and he stared offensively at passers-by who took convicts in chains for granted. A quarrel would have quieted him down by allowing him to translate emotion into action; a translation, in which, as happens often enough, the original impulse might be lost. But he went unsatisfied. No man took exception to his looks, no woman observed him. In a mood still half-truculent, he found the turning for George Street, and entered the premises of the Bank of New South Wales.

The Secretary, whose manner, whiskers, and excellent brown sherry were not to be distinguished from similar attributes of Bank secretaries in England, was glad to welcome His Excellency's sixth cousin. He took Lord Goderich's letter with just the right bow, accepted Sir Richard Bourke's invitation to dine with just such another, and seemed, having given this faultless performance, to wish to take up his labours. But Mr. Adare was disinclined to move out of a pleasant room into the strengthening sun. He began earnestly to talk, to enquire, and the Secretary was obliged to make answer.

"What openings should you say promise best for a young man—for myself, let us say?"

"As to that, it is not easy for me to speak. If you

could give me some notion as to your interests, your capacities——"

"My capacities? Considerable in some directions; riding, drinking. As far as intellects go, I won't boast."

"I referred to the question of money; money to invest. I believe that land in the neighbourhood of this town, for instance, is bound to appreciate. In twenty-five years, let us say, I can very well imagine a capital increase of a hundred per cent in the value of land in certain localities."

"That's a long time to wait."

"Not for such a considerable increase, Mr. Adare. A man does very well, let me tell you, if he is able to double his fortune in that time."

"I haven't a shilling, though."

"Then," said the Secretary, losing that faint breath of enthusiasm which had informed his voice at the thought of a hundred per cent, "it becomes quite another matter."

"That's to say, I've got a hundred pounds."

"Well, Mr. Adare, it is not much, I tell you frankly. It is not much. With a great deal of industry, and frugality, and foresight I don't say it may not be made to do——"

"But I've no wish to work, my dear sir. That's not my intention at all."

A clerk knocked, thrust in his smooth head decorated at the ears with two quills like those of a Secretary bird, and announced:

"Mr. Flusky to see you, sir."

"Pray ask him to wait a moment. Just a moment. Say that His Excellency's cousin is with me just now."

"I won't detain you. Curious name, Flusky. Where have I heard it?"

"One of our most considerable citizens," said the official, rising. "Rich; a landowner."

"No, it's not that. Something, somewhere——" Mr. Adare snapped his fingers at the elusive memory and let it go. "Well; so you haven't any formula for getting rich overnight?"

"The old one, Mr. Adare; only the old one, I fear."

"No good to me. Flusky! Now where the devil have I heard that remarkable name?" He observed the Secretary looking a trifle nervously at the door, which, however, his retiring clerk had shut safely. "Oho! He's a what-d'ye-call-it, is he?"

"Emancipist. Yes."

"I like that. Emancipist—I must get used to it. What was his crime, anything spectacular?"

"Mr. Adare, allow me to give you a warning. Out here we don't talk of the past. The future, sir. This is a country of the future."

"Landowner and lag—yes, I like that very well. Introduce me, will you? Come on, man," as the Secretary looked dubious, "I'll behave myself."

The Secretary, unwilling to keep his richest client waiting yet reluctant to blend him even for an instant with the aristocracy, bowed helplessly and held open the door. A figure in shapeless woollen clothes turned towards them, and Mr. Adare was able to note a flabby bulk, a nose pendant after the Jewish manner above a lip that might have lengthened in Wicklow, and a pair of unwinking mild eyes before Mr. Samson Flusky was formally introduced.

"Mr. Adare," said the Secretary with a nervous laugh, "has come out from Ireland to make his fortune."

Mr. Flusky smiled without speaking and replaced a warm right hand on the knob of his stick.

"I understand," said Mr. Adare, "there's something to be done in land; but I don't want to wait for the money till my beard's as long as your arm."

"Ireland," Flusky repeated, looking at the Secretary; then transferred his gaze to the young man's face. He pronounced the word as no Englishman ever does; his deep voice had a smooth easy quality. "Is that where you come from? What part?"

"The West. D'you know it?"

"I might," Mr. Flusky answered without expression. "So you want to make money. You're not the only one."

"And make it quick," said Mr. Adare briskly. "I don't feel any call to stay long in this country. Not but it has a deal to say for itself, no doubt; only it doesn't talk my language."

"You'll stay, surely, during His Excellency's time of office at least." The Secretary spoke to Flusky: "Mr. Adare is related to Sir Richard Bourke; came out in his ship."

"Lagged yourself for fear the King should do it for you, eh?" said Mr. Flusky disconcertingly. "How much have you? There's money in land, when the Commissioners will let you buy."

"I told him so," the Secretary offered immediately. "Money needs time, as I told him, to grow."

Mr. Flusky seemed to meditate, both hands upon his stick, under-lip shooting out, eyes cast down. Mr. Adare in this moment attempted to sum up the impression left upon him by his first encounter with an emancipist, convict turned citizen. He found himself staring at the thick unmoving fingers, trying them in this position or that; steady upon a trigger, bunched about the haft of a knife, crooking to strangle. He could not fit them to sly tricks with pockets, or skilful tricks with pens. They proclaimed violence. And when, lifting his eyes, he met the mild gaze of their owner he had a little shock, as though a naked man had in the wink of an eye clothed himself. Flusky was saying:

"All the same, Mister, if you've time to listen there's something might interest you."

"My office, gentlemen," the Secretary offered. "Quite at your disposal."

Flusky moved to it, not thanking him. He sat square in one of the chairs, and rested his head upon the interesting hands which his stick supported. He continued to wear his hat. Adare swung himself on to the Secretary's desk to face him, but from perversity or perhaps curiosity, would not be the first to speak;

marvelling, not for the first time, at the power which hedges the man who can hold his tongue, and determined to try his own hand at the game.

Mr. Flusky seemed to have nothing immediate to say. He sat unthinking to all appearance, challenging the younger man's patience. Mr. Adare began to give himself away. He would not speak, but he could not keep still. The manœuvres of a pair of flies were a relief to his eyes, a sudden itching of the nose afforded him a gesture. He became conscious that the situation was a ridiculous one. The flabby fellow with a hat on, the youngster point-device, both with tongues in their heads, and not a word between them to throw at a dog—Mr. Flusky earned his gratitude by releasing a sentence first.

"I don't know how my proposition'll strike you, Government House and all. Maybe I better let it alone."

"Don't lump me with His Excellency. He's not responsible for me."

"Well," Mr. Flusky considered. "But it might be awkward, all the same."

"I assure you I didn't come out here to wear gloves, Mr. Flusky." The mild gaze surveyed his faultless tailoring. "These are all the clothes I have, but if you feel you could talk more freely to a cabbage-tree hat I'll step out and buy one."

"Do you know anything about land out here?"

That was a surprising question, coming as it did with no change of tone or expression; Mr. Adare made frivolous answers as was his custom when taken aback.

"They tie a string to a dog's tail, don't they, and hit him a kick, and when he stops running that's a mile."

"You're thinking of Van Diemen's Land," Flusky said, not smiling. "The man that could kick hardest got best measure. That's how it did ought to be, in a new country."

He went back to his silence. Mr. Adare, amused and a trifle irritated, began to guess.

"Your proposition has something to do with land."

"Well, you see," said Flusky irrelevantly, roused from meditation, "the Regulations are made by Englishmen. You can't run three sheep to an acre here. A sheep to three acres, more like. You got to have room to move stock about."

"I suppose you can get as much room as you want, if you're prepared to pay." Mr. Flusky shook his head, rolling it sideways upon his fingers that were laced upon the stick's knob. "You can't? Why not?"

"No more grants. Land all to be sold at auction, and a Board to see one man don't get more than his share. You come at a bad time for pickings, Mister. August the first, that was the start of it."

"Wait a minute," Mr. Adare bade him. "This is interesting. I was always good at drawing-room games. Don't tell me what you want me to do, let me see if I can divine it——"

"I won't tell you," said Flusky briefly.

"Now wait a minute. Plenty of land available. Correct?" He looked at the white face, took a blink

24

for assent, and went on with his deductions. "Land—
but a Board to see a man doesn't get all he can pay for.
What's the answer to that? If a man were to get someone
else to put in for the land he wanted—am I getting
warm?" He perceived the beginnings of a smile. "I'm
on to it, I believe. Aha! The drawing-room's no bad
training ground."

"A man that puts in for land has to go before the
surveyor and show the purchase-money in cash," Flusky
said without expression.

"What of it? I've got a hundred pounds." A smile
commented. "Not enough? Well, damn it, I suppose
I could borrow."

"You might."

"Perhaps from the man that wanted the land. I dare
say he'd stump up enough to show this surveyor."

"He might, then."

Mr. Flusky, setting his stick between his legs, leaned
back to seek a wallet. He pulled it out, and chose notes
from it, cracking each one, holding watermarks up to
the light. Mr. Adare watched and reckoned the total as
he laid a bundle down; a thousand pounds.

"Five bob an acre," said Flusky, "that's the Land
Board price." He took out another note. "No need to
show this one to the surveyor."

"Fifty," said Mr. Adare, craning to look at it. "Fifty
for a signature, the first day of landing. No need to ask
if this sort of transaction's legal."

"It's not legal. I tell you that flat out."

"But it's the way to get things done?"

"I'm not saying nothing. I'm not asking you, Mister."

The young man came nearer, picked up the bundle, laughed.

"Why, good Lord, for all you know I might put it on a horse." Flusky was silent. "Don't you want a receipt?" Flusky shook his head. Mr. Adare had a qualm. "Are the notes bad 'uns?"

"There's a lot of coves out here haven't forgot their old trade, I'll allow. But those is right 'uns."

"This is the maddest transaction I ever put a hand to, and I've been in a queer rig or two. If I had a grain of caution—but I haven't, thank God. It's a bargain, Mr. Flusky."

"There's nothing on paper, I'd remind you."

"Well, but between Irishmen," said Mr. Adare impulsively, and held out his hand.

How much part in this impulsive decision was played by recollection of the chain-gang, Adare was not able to determine; but he was aware, as he struck hands with the emancipist, of a glow, a release of feeling which might not improbably be traced to that source. The clasp over, he laughed.

"Courtesy title of Honourable!" said Mr. Adare. Then, but to himself: "What the deuce have I let myself in for?"

He was perfectly ignorant of the Colony. The man's statement concerning land might be true or it might not. The bare facts were that he, a guest in the Governor's house, was conspiring with a total stranger to do the

Government. He reassured himself; it was only in principle that the Government would suffer, what could it matter to the Treasury whence came the purchase-money for land; an ungenerous whisper reminded him that the interview had been private, there were no witnesses, no documents—there his thoughts checked sharply.

Mr. Flusky appeared to be troubled by no ironical questionings. He reached out the knob of his stick and rapped on the open door with it. After an interval for dignity, the Secretary answered this summons.

"Business concluded, gentlemen? Satisfactory, may I hope?"

"Mr. Adare wants a word with you."

"I am at Mr. Adare's service."

"He wants," said Flusky, interpreting the young man's quick glance, "to deposit a thousand pounds."

The Secretary bowed, looking from the square flabby man to the thin rosy man. His glance was enquiring. He said, however, nothing of that hundred pounds previously mentioned as the sole fortune of his new client, who began nervously to talk:

"I take your advice, sir, as you see. I buy land. Well, I have seen two foot by four of painted canvas change hands for a thousand pounds, to say nothing of five foot two of womanhood. How far will it go in kangaroos, do you think? By George, gentlemen, I hope landowners in your country have a better standing than they do in mine. They shoot us from behind hedges, like partridges.

27   c

It is not the way a man of spirit would choose to die, winged by a Whiteboy with his dirty coat inside out——"

Mr. Adare prattled on. He found the entire trust reposed in him by this stranger oddly touching, and it was his form of self-defence to talk when silence would have revealed emotion. The emancipist received this patter with no change of expression and said nothing. The Secretary, making out a receipt for the money Adare handed him, observed the numbers of one or two of the notes, familiar owing to certain odd groupings of numerals. He knew to whom he had paid them out. But he too said nothing, having learned that discretion is the first recommendation of a banker, more especially where his richer clients' interests are concerned.

(v)

LIFE in this newest of worlds was patterned in circles upon much the same plan as life in the old. Outer darkness, the convicts, merged into a twilight existence of emancipated men; traders could be dimly perceived, country landowners took the air with a vague grandeur, becoming visible at certain periods, like the remoter stars; but the innermost circle, that which accepted the full light of His Excellency's countenance, wore or had worn uniform. A red coat or a blue one, a wig and gown or the beaver of banking, with an occasional pair of clerical gaiters—this uniformity represented right thinking, and true dogma, and the power to bind and loose. Uniformity prevailed, as might have been expected, at the parties attended by uniforms and their moieties. There would be offerings of wine from Portugal and France; cheeses brought by sea from cool English dales; sugared fruits that had travelled half the world round. These were consumed to an accompaniment of talk well suited to London dining-rooms, but to which the warm Australian air and a pertinacious humming of insects gave the lie. Proverbs turned head over heels in this new uneasy country, and the gourmet's maxim, Tell me what you eat, that I may know what you are, ran in Australia thus: Tell me first what you are; thence I may deduce what you eat, what you wear, the matter of your talk, and the shape of your wife's coiffure; besides making a tolerably accurate guess at your past income, and a reasonable forecast of the income which will be yours in future.

So much Mr. Adare had discovered in the course of a few weeks' sojourn. He wore no uniform himself, but the glamour of the regulation dress was all about him; he was distantly related to shako and sabretache, vicarious spurs chinked upon his heels, and he was received with all the interest and respect due to a bearer of such emblems. However, at the end of a brief period he had begun to weary a little of the uniforms and their wives, and said as much in His Excellency's hearing.

"You're a thankless pup," returned Sir Richard. "They do you well enough, don't they?"

"Well enough. But I'm getting to know all the faces by heart—well, not that; not by heart. By my liver."

"That's something you can't avoid in a small community. The officers in a regimental mess get sick of the sight of each other's faces in peace time. So they do in a man-of-war. It has to be put up with."

"But their smugness I can't endure. Twenty-five, thirty thousand people in this town, and the same dozen self-satisfied phizes at every dinner-table, like wooden nags on a roundabout."

"What else is to be done? You can't mix a society, it gives too much offence. Consequence is all that many of these people get in exchange for exile. Besides, no man cares to drink with the fellow that may have picked his pocket in the old country."

"Would His Excellency's credit be involved, for example, if his irresponsible cousin were to accept this?"

The Governor held out a hand for the letter his irresponsible cousin offered. It was an invitation to dine with Mr. Flusky, signed not by but for him; *per pro.* William Winter, secretary. The paper was good, the writing copper-plate, the wording conventionally civil; only the astonishing address—Minyago Yugilla, Woolloo-moolloo—betrayed the letter's New World provenance.

"Who is this fellow?"

"Rich. A decent sort of an Irishman. Emancipist."

"What was his offence?"

"I can't find out." This was true. Adare's curiosity had uncovered as yet nothing of his benefactor's past.

He repeated the Bank secretary's phrase: "Anyway, what's it matter? This is the country of the future. And besides, damme, isn't there old Uncle Lawrence at home that we can't trust with the spoons?"

"There seems no reason why you shouldn't go. We've got to mellow these individuals somehow before we find ourselves sitting beside them on a jury. Wait a moment. I remember something now about this man."

"So do I, but for the life of me I can't tell what."

"Something about his wife——" The Governor pondered, then dismissed the puzzle. "My dear fellow, do as you please about this, so you don't involve me. What d'you suppose those extraordinary words are?"

"It's where he lives, evidently."

"Yes, but the meaning." He looked up as a youngish civilian entered, carrying a portfolio. "Banks, you know something of the aborigines' tongue; can you tack any meaning to this?"

He underlined the curious address with his thumb-nail and handed the paper over. The newcomer read, and ventured:

"I happen to know—this is the name of Mr. Flusky's house, is it not? The meaning is, Why weepest thou? I have always wondered why Mr. Flusky should choose it."

"The wife, perhaps. A romantic, Byronic, sort of a female might fancy such a name."

The civilian made no comment, but his correctness of attitude, his portfolio, recalled the Governor to a

31

working frame of mind. He dismissed his cousin abruptly, and settled down to consider the Colonists' proposal, shortly to be submitted to the Parliament at home, for a Legislative Assembly of their own.

(vi)

MR. ADARE, thus licensed to accept, accepted; having no least notion of what he was about, or what forces he was setting to work. He was not accustomed to look forward, or to calculate sequels; even had he possessed the highest degree of prudence, he could hardly have read these few polite written words as the warrant setting forth a new course of existence for several people. First, the receipt of his letter produced a remarkable effect in the pleasant capacious dwelling in Woolloomoolloo, which Mr. Samson Flusky had elected to call by so odd a name. (He had no idea of the words' meaning; but hearing the house thus referred to by blacks perpetually encamped in his garden, he had adopted their outlandish phrase, the more readily that he had no wish to preserve, as so many of the other exiles did, any memory of a home on the far side of the world.) Mr. Adare's letter set half a dozen activities taking direction. Miss Milly, a large woman in carpet slippers, upon whom the domestic authority of the establishment devolved; Miss Milly, surname forgotten long ago, who could slap up a dinner, kill a rat, or—as had once been proved to the discomfiture of a visiting clergyman—deliver an excellent impromptu prayer; Miss Milly was summoned, and bid look to her staff, that they behaved themselves and were up to their work on Wednesday week. This order she received with a sniff, and withdrew to convey the sense of it to a mixed lot of female convicts, who, accustomed as they were to fight bloodily, to drink rum when they could get it and eau-de-Cologne when they could not, took philosophically her command to "act ladylike for once." Then it was the turn of William Winter, secretary, a gentlemanlike person doing time for the seduction of a minor. He was new to his assignment; indeed the first task that had been set him was the drawing up of a menu for Wednesday week. He demurred; knew nothing of the resources of the country, what meats were procurable——

"Don't trouble for that," said Flusky easily. "Anything you say, I can get."

William Winter searched his memory. Meals in France; the delicate ridiculous ices of the Palais Royal, wine-dark soup of snails; meals at Oxford tables; méringues, a boar's head whose glass eyes stared from buttered sockets, larks with a bay leaf on their breasts; meals less clearly remembered, by reason of the ladies and wine that had accompanied them. He conferred with Miss Milly, summoned from among her kitchen furies to aid, and between them a programme of courses was assembled, to which William Winter gave French names. When the plan was drawn out he submitted it to Flusky, who glanced at the paper, counted the courses with a moving thumb, and asked:

"Is this a slap-up dinner?"

William Winter reassured him. Everything of the most expensive, everything out of season or reason would appear upon the table, in order serviceable as the bright-harnessed angels of Milton. Flusky nodded, and turned away. Winter stood, wondered, risked a suggestion.

"Am I to show the menu to Madam?"

Flusky stood still.

"To who?"

William Winter knew that his employer must have heard, and did not repeat his question. He was aware that somewhere in the large house there dwelt Flusky's wife, though he had not seen her, and though Miss Milly brushed aside questions. He waited therefore; but he had met his match at that. Flusky took up the paper on which the list of dishes was written, put it away in one of his sagging pockets, and sat down tranquilly to light a cigar such as he smoked perpetually, throwing the butts away before half the smoke was done: his one extravagance. When the cigar was going he gazed wildly through the smoke at William Winter, and the gaze was a challenge. The seducer (who had cut no very gallant figure when pursued by angry brothers on horseback, flourishing long-tailed whips) did not meet it. He busied himself mending a pen, and prepared, with every appearance of earnest attention to business, to receive orders.

These took the form of a command to write out

further invitations. William Winter had not been long enough in the colony to understand how improbable it was that any of them would be accepted, but he was inclined to question his employer's insistence: "Say it's to sit down with the Honourable Adare." Commissioners of this and that, elderly Colonels and Judges, were not, in his experience, lured to dine by the promise of meeting an Irish sprig, aged twenty, of no particular influence or notoriety. But the solecism had to go down, repeated ten times, and a servant was sent off on horseback with the notes, sealed and impressed by the Secretary's own signet ring, a proud crest which he was perfectly well entitled to use.

The dignitaries, unexpectedly enough, found themselves able, pleased, delighted, free to wait on Mr. Samson Flusky at the time he named. Their wives, however, with gospel unanimity, could not come. Flusky took the news with only one comment, a slightly bewildered question to his secretary:

"But don't they know I've got the Honourable Adare?"

They knew it. But they did not want him as sugar coating to the pill of Mr. Flusky's wife, about whom nothing was known, and upon whose respectability they were unwilling to stake that consequence which was their all. William Winter, casting about for a formula which should convey a hint of this to the giver of the feast, observed that individual toss away his cigar, a gesture habitual with him to underline a decision, and heard him declare, without heat:

"Well, but, damn them; she shall be there. Henrietta shall be there."

This was the first time William Winter had heard Mrs. Flusky's name. Its prim ladylike quality puzzled him, for he had added to his vague suspicions a fact or two; cries heard from her room sometimes at night, and rich dresses, torn and soiled, coming downstairs over Miss Milly's arm. The mistress of the house gave no orders, took no walks, ate alone, living a life of her own, meaningless yet apparently content; the life of a goddess without worshippers.

But she was to come to the dinner, and take her place at the foot of the long table. William Winter, setting out in copper-plate on cards the guests' names and titles, looked up at the sound of an order:

"My wife at the foot. I'll take the head. Write her name: Lady Henrietta Flusky."

"But that's—excuse me, sir. That's what is called a courtesy title. It is borne by daughters of nobility. The wives of—private gentlemen—can't claim it."

"Write what I say."

William Winter shrugged, swallowing down further comment, but a little sorry to see how his employer persisted in social error. To atone for the various enormities Flusky had obliged him to commit, he took trouble in composing the table, allowing precedence due, constructing harmonies upon a figured bass of dignity as the Colony understood that word. The Governor's Private Secretary he set at Mrs. Flusky's

left hand. On her right, as a newcomer and the guest
of honour, was to sit the Honourable Charles Adare.

(vii)

THE night of the dinner was hot; nevertheless, most of
the servants kept sober. Miss Milly maintained them so.
She raided all cupboards in the morning, and locked up
any liquor that might conceivably be employed as
stimulus or soporific; marching to the clank of keys at
her waist as to a solemn music, and with her own hand
adding the final glorification of sherry to the turtle soup.
Her eye was an arrow, her tongue a flail. She had all the
attributes of deity, save omnipresence; she could not,
unhappily for the issue, be everywhere at once. Thus
at an hour when the hostess, dressed, curled and becom-
ingly restless, should have been awaiting her guests'
arrival, only Flusky was in the withdrawing-room, standing four-square, never shifting the cigar from under his
drooping nose, nor moving his hands from his pockets.
William Winter's alertness had perceived a kind of scurry
among the maidservants at one period, following the
departure of Miss Milly upstairs, and read a kind of
satisfied thunder in that personage's brows when she
returned, the expression of one justified in an ominous
prediction. But nothing more. There was nobody to
question. He had to make what he could of the fact
that Flusky stood waiting alone.

37

The dignitaries arrived. Flusky, correctly waistcoated and cravatted, received them with an odd dignity of his own, and made his wife's excuses:

"My wife isn't any too good, can't be with us. She hopes another time you'll give her the pleasure."

The dignitaries eyed one another, and at once became more at ease, though it might be supposed that one or two of the married men regretted they would have nothing of interest to tell their wives. Mr. Adare even voiced this regret, saying that a dinner without ladies was no better than a board-meeting. There was laughter, and they went in to Miss Milly's turtle soup.

Mr. Adare and Banks, the student of aboriginal tongues and Colonial conditions, found themselves separated by the empty chair, the glasses and knives and forks, that should have accommodated their hostess. Both looked idly at the card, then quizzically at each other. As the first glass of sherry went down and the noise of gentlemanly talk grew louder, the Irishman said to the student:

"What is she, really?"

The student shook his head, and lifted an empty glass with significance.

"That way, is it? I meant the name, though."

Banks again shook his head, looked for a moment at his host, and shrugged.

"I see," answered Mr. Adare; and felt a moment's compassion for the man who could buy his wife, if she chose, diamonds for her garters, but not keep her sober.

He turned to his neighbour, a soldier, and they fell to
a discussion on the technique of flogging, and the
scandal of Sudds and Thompson, one of Sir Ralph
Darling's legacies to the incoming Governor.

It was just as the dessert was being set on the table;
(walnuts from England; wine darkly glowing, that had
rounded the Horn); at this moment, when the meal had
done its duty, and the gentlemanly voices at last were
loud and easy, their hostess appeared framed in the long
window. She wore the leaf-green skirt of a ball-dress,
with a cambric bodice which did not cover the rising
points of her stays; red hair hung free on her magnificent
shoulders, and her bare feet were shod with ancient red
cloth slippers that flapped as she moved. She looked
like a goddess careless of human clothing, or some
heroine of antiquity run nobly mad.

Flusky did not see her at first. As the heads turned
and the talk ceased he sprang up, with a face which Mr.
Adare saw later in dreams, and put out a hand to keep
her back. She took the hand with a pretty readiness,
smiled, pressed it, and passed on to her place, the vacant
chair at the table's foot. There, leaning on the chair's
back, she graciously bent her head and spoke:

"Pray, gentlemen, excuse me. I was not aware of the
hour. It is not too late, I hope, to take a glass of wine
with you."

Her speech was blurred, the syllables ran together as
though written on damp paper, but the quality of the
voice was not to be mistaken. Mr. Adare, for something

to do, moved back the chair for her. She thanked him, and sat rather suddenly. The guests still stood, glancing under their brows at each other, until Flusky's voice loudly bade them sit down, sit down. Uncomfortably the dignitaries took their chairs, but the talk could not rise, it had been knocked on the head. A sentence or two, and the chink of a decanter's lip against glass, was the best they could do, while they directed their glances so as not to perceive the hostess's bosom or the host's face. Thus every man in the room heard what was being said at the foot of the table, where the red-haired woman was peering into the face of Mr. Adare.

"You have a look of somebody I knew. Long ago. In Ireland, was it? Somewhere——"

"I come from Ireland. Queen's County. Ballaloe. Adare is my name."

"Ballaloe. I remember. Have you not a sister named Alethea?"

She made two attempts at the name; her tongue was thick; for all that Mr. Adare could recognize it and be astounded.

"You know her? You know Alethea?"

"Alethea Adare. We used to ride together. Riding——" She looked at Flusky, and laughed. "Riding's dangerous. How did you leave them at Ballaloe? My father—oh, but I was forgetting. My father died, not so very long after."

At that Mr. Adare fairly jumped in his chair. With a glance at the card, on which William Winter had so

40

doubtfully set out the courtesy title not borne by private gentlemen's wives, he said aghast and aloud:

"Lady Hattie; my God! Lady Hattie Considine, that ran off with the groom!"

"Not Considine," said she correcting him, and kissed her hand, vaguely, in the direction of Flusky's chair. "He married me, you know. Was it not good of him? But he is such a good man. You mustn't believe the things they say."

She rose suddenly and superbly from her chair, swaying a little with the grace of a blown tree; filled a tumbler with port and drank it down, not blinking; bowed one hand on the table for support, and made for the door. Adare ran to open it. As she reached him she paused mysteriously, a hand groping for his arm; the guests heard her whisper, after a backward look of triumphant cunning:

"Are you any kind of shot with a pistol?" He nodded. "Pray come with me upstairs. There's a something, I can't quite tell what, on my bed."

Three minutes later, as the uneasy gentlemen sent port round the table, a shot was fired somewhere in the house. Each halted an instant the movement which engaged his hand—lifting, pouring, stretching—and Flusky made insufficient answer to the question thus mutely asked:

"Finish your wine."

Dubiously the gentlemen obeyed. Whatever their speculations may have been, relief showed itself plainly when Mr. Adare reappeared in the doorway, betraying

41

no sign of a struggle in his demeanour or his dress. He said with simplicity, and as though unaware that anything out of the way had passed:

"She'll be all right now."

With that he sat down. The gentlemen longed to question; they waited for his uprising as for a signal, that they might all depart together and question him on the way home. But he sat on. At last the dignitaries, labouring jokes, and reminding each other of business to be done in the morning, gave up hope of Mr. Adare and departed, aware that the unfinished story would earn them a wigging from their wives. The adieux were cordial; the wine had been sound. At last they were gone, clop of hooves softened by dust, voices rallying and dying abruptly as the vehicles turned the hill.

On the shadowy verandah some blacks and their wives had gathered unnoticed. When the door closed they ran forward, and began to stuff nuts into their clothes, and, like so many monkeys, into the pouches of their cheeks. They sampled the wine, spitting out claret, sour stuff, but gulping brandy down. One of the gins drank from a little vase that adorned the epergne, pulling out the flowers, and looking mystified to find that these had imparted no sweet savour to their water. Another bound up her head in a white napkin. They talked, with sudden bursts of chatter that sounded angry, like monkeys. They were blissful; the cigar-ends and brandy would have been enough to make them so, without the added fun of plundering, which lent savour even to crumbled bread.

Suddenly their leader, a man wearing a brass half-disc engraved with the name "Ketch," signalled for quiet. They listened; then, with a final swig, a final fistful of raisins, scampered off, and were lost in the night. Two men came into the deserted dining-room, and one looked askance at the disorder.

"Never mind that," said Flusky, "it's the blacks. They'd steal your big toe."

Mr. Adare sat down, choosing a chair not damp with spewed claret, and asked his host point-blank:

"Is there anything we can do? Why don't you let her go back to Ireland?" Flusky looked at him. He amended the question. "Make her go back, then." Flusky did not answer, which troubled Mr. Adare. "I don't like this. This isn't right at all. Coming into a roomful of men like that. And then afterwards—I had a pistol on me. I shot her bogy." He pulled a little weapon from his tail-pocket. "Get her away out of this, can't you? For God's sake."

"Her old father cut her off, he's dead, her mother's nothing but an old nanny-goat," said Flusky rapidly and suddenly, and he imitated a kind of Irish country bleat. "Me-e! Me-e! All the time. What for do you say send Hattie back? What is there for her there? She can show her marriage-lines; who cares for that? They'd respect her the more, they'd take her back the sooner, if she'd none to show."

"What started her drinking?" asked Mr. Adare in the merest conversational tone. "They don't

D

get the horrors, women, till they're in pretty deep."

"I was assigned here in Sydney," Flusky answered, after a pause so long that the young man had time to draw his handkerchief through the pistol's dirty barrel. "I got into a piece of trouble once and they gave me up the ladder and down—there's the marks on me yet. Hattie—she'd followed me out. She went to the Superintendent, told him who she was. He made fun of her. She never used her rightful name after that— it's years ago, now. There was a bit of money from some old brooches she'd sold, bits of lace, I don't know what. She lived on it; but the drink got her before I'd got my ticket."

Mr. Adare looked at the flabby man, involuntarily picturing the scars running ladderwise up his back.

"What did she say?" Flusky went on, with a jerk of the head towards the stairs.

"Not much. I shot the bogy for her that sits on the bedpost. She gave me a thank you, and started undressing for bed. It seemed to me time to be leaving then."

Flusky nodded, and after a moment irrelevantly told him:

"I was their groom, ye know."

"I'd heard the story."

"It's her own people she misses. Not relations. Just the sort of women; ladies. Since I've made the money I've taken care to have gentlemen about the house. There's one now, my secretary, that was at some great school in England. She won't look at him, though,

44

squeals when he's mentioned. She don't like the idea
that he deceived some girl. Before him was a clergyman, a very quiet man, a forger. He's got his ticket
now. There's always gentlemen getting into trouble;
I can always be sure of a gentleman, no one else will put
in for them, they can't make themselves useful, ye see;
no offence. But you don't get ladies transported. So
there's no company for her, and she don't take to the
others."

Mr. Adare was silent, unable to reconcile the simplicity
of this recital with the reputation of his host as a man
cunning, mysterious, and blunt to rudeness. As he sat
puzzling, he was aware, as before in the bank secretary's
office, of some compulsion being put upon him. Before
he could recognize whence it came, and draw back to
resist it, the words were out of his mouth:

"Let me have a word with her. Let me try."

"Done," answered Flusky at once, "why not? You're
welcome."

He stretched out his hand across the table. Mr. Adare
for the second time took it, and once again felt a fleeting
wonder at himself. Flusky got up to look for a clean
glass, with some liquid in which to drink the partner-
ship's success. But the blacks had been thorough, every
drop of liquor was either drunk or spilled. Flusky,
surveying the table, found an unbroken horseshoe of
bread, and held it out to the other man.

"What's this?" said Mr. Adare, not understanding.

Flusky smiled, spat on the baked horseshoe, and

tossed it over his shoulder out of the window behind him.

"For luck," said he.

(viii)

NEXT morning, before Mr. Adare had well recovered from his night's sleep, which was apt to lie about him, like mists in a valley, till the sun rose high, a servant knocked to say that His Excellency would be obliged by a word with him. The message had a kind of official peremptory ring to it. Why summon a man to an interview at break of day, whom you can converse with over a meal or a cigar at any more civil time you please? Mr. Adare's mind gave forth tremors. His conscience was not uneasy, but he had fears for his comfort, vague disquiets, blank misgivings. He presented himself, looking neat, within twenty minutes of the message arriving.

His Excellency was in his study, not standing or marching about, as was his custom, but sitting at a big table on which packets of papers lay. He looked up at once, and Mr. Adare heard something resembling, had he known it, his cousin's orderly-room voice:

"Sit down. There's something I'd like you to explain."

He did not add, If you can. But his gesture as he handed over a small paper, half-printed, half-written, allowed those words to be understood. Mr. Adare took, and in an instant recognized, the document.

To the Surveyor-General.

Application of *Donough Charles Adare* of *Government House, Sydney*, for permission to purchase land.

Dated, December, 1831.

Sir,

Being desirous to purchase the following *sections* of land, I request you will obtain the Governor's authority that *they* may be put up to sale at the minimum price determined by the Government, agreeable to the Regulations of the 1st August 1831, viz. :

200 acres in the County of Cumberland, district of Newcastle, sections numbered 17 to 217.

I am free, and arrived in the Colony by the ship *Foxhound* from *London* in the month of *December* 1831.

I have the honor to be, sir,

Your obedient humble servant,

D. C. ADARE.

"Is that your signature?"

"It is, yes. Let me explain this matter, there's nothing to be concerned about——"

"But it is not your writing in the body of the form?"

"No. I can explain that. You see, I am acting on advice. This land will appreciate in value. I shall make money by it if I wait. I can explain the whole affair. It's really a very simple matter."

The Governor suddenly sat back in his chair.

"Very good. Let me hear."

Mr. Adare was still a little drowsy. He had not yet quite understood that here was danger, nor had he, when signing and presenting it, studied the document at all closely. Flusky had assured him it was the merest matter of form.

"I've been talking—you recommended that I should do so—to men of experience. They all have the one thing to say; one must get land. The more acreage the better. This is not like England; small holdings, they tell me, will not do here; one must put in for a considerable acreage, to allow, don't you see, for accidents such as drought or any other kind of bad season. Two hundred acres; it is equal, in fact, to a farm of fifty acres at home. It is all a question of degree. As you know, I have no ideas of grandeur. As Tom Moore says, 'The pride of former days, and glory's thrill is o'er.'" He had done; and humming the tune that accompanies those words, waited more or less indifferently for the Governor to bid him take himself off. His Excellency, however, pondered, tapping the document.

"A farm," repeated the Governor. "Well, I won't insult you more than I'm obliged to, but you are a liar, Mr. Donough Charles Adare. Don't make matters worse, don't make a fool of yourself." (The young man had given an angry start.) "Did you look at the map, down there at the Surveyor's office? You did not, or you wouldn't have offered me that nonsense about acreage and droughts. What you have put in for is town land, valuable land. The price set by the Board runs to five pounds an acre and more. That's a thousand pounds' worth; it's land with the obligation to build, what's more, if your application should be granted. Don't humiliate yourself or me by any more explanations, as you call them. The truth, if you please."

Not easy; for truth was in itself so improbable. Mr. Adare put together something resembling a review of the facts, which included the meeting in the Bank and the loan; but insisted that he had followed his own judgment in the selection of land to buy—"one of these fellows said it was a coming-along district, and I backed the numbers, the two seventeens——"

"But the money; you must have had money to show the Surveyor."

"He lent it me—this same fellow—just for the day."

"What security did you give?"

"He asked none, sir."

"I see. Did you make use of my name, then?"

"I did not."

"I'm serious, this is a serious matter. What did you promise the man in exchange for this money? I must know how you stand."

"I repeat, nothing at all, whatsoever, of any kind, nothing."

"Come; you're this man's bonnet, aren't you? Buying in his name land he wouldn't be likely to get on his own application?"

"I am not, sir."

49

The Governor rose at last, and looked at Adare steadily. The young man cocked his chin and stared back. The Governor gave a kind of quick sigh, then spoke with firmness.

"Your application is refused."

Adare bowed as jauntily as he dared.

"Furthermore, I must make other arrangements for your domicile while you stay in the Colony. This is the sort of transaction——" he flicked the document—"that I can't have carried on from Government House."

"I'll arrange at once, sir. Don't put yourself to any trouble."

"I make no further comment on your conduct. You have a good deal to learn in the way of worldly wisdom; but don't buy your experience at the cost of honour. That's no sort of bargain. I shall be happy to know from time to time how you do. Moreover, some sort of allowance is due to you, in money, I mean. Your parents contemplated your being my guest in the Colony——"

"Excuse me. I shall do very well."

"As you please. I am at your service, should you change your mind."

"Mr. Flusky, I believe, will be good enough to house me until I can settle my affairs."

The Governor at that put off his orderly-room manner altogether and disturbingly. He came round his big desk, took the still young man above the elbow and walked him about as he talked.

"You remember I had something in my mind about this man. So had you; we couldn't hang it on to any peg, either of us. I've got the facts at present."

"So have I, sir."

"All? You know he ran off with one of the Considine girls? And the rest of the circumstances? Why he's out here?" The young man was silent, and Sir Richard halted their march a moment. "The bad part of the business, you see, was this. He shot James Considine dead, that went after them. Shot her brother. They gave him the benefit of the doubt; said James pulled first. That's how Flusky comes to be a rich man instead of a dead one. But it's not a story to associate with; a nasty, bloody, derogatory story. Keep away from it, Charles." The young man stood mulishly; Sir Richard shook his arm with a trifle of impatience. "No chivalry, now. No wild-goose chasing. He's a murderer, and she's all to pieces, by what I can learn. You owe the fellow no debt, and you've done what you could. Give him his money back, and start fresh."

But Mr. Adare was in the grip of that obstinacy which comes from the sense of having behaved like a fool; an obstinacy not peculiar to the young, but more common in them, since their dignity is a new and precious pedestal. This obstinacy did not reveal itself as such to the individual possessed by it. Hastily, it put on the trappings of generosity, and displayed Mr. Adare to his own gaze as a noble figure forsaking the fleshpots, a Quixote. He burst out now with something of all this, much garbled; a new country, old scores should be forgotten, hands of friendship, and so on. Sir Richard listened and lost patience. He too had his dignity; it was not for him to persuade. Two sentences ended the matter.

"Yes, yes, that would sound all very well in a story, my young friend, but we can't afford posturing in a real situation."

"I won't trouble your Excellency with my postures any longer."

A bend of the young man's shoulders. A lift of the Governor's shoulders. The sound of a door impetuously closed.

(ix)

" '——I THINK I can picture you, not working in any way, for that is against your avowed principles, but most pertinaciously and tirelessly watching others do so. Since there has not been time as yet for any letter to arrive, I amuse myself very comfortably, seeing you in this situation or that, without any danger of imagination stumbling over truth. Have you seen any black men? Do they make anything of interest that you could send home? It is tiresome having to abide the bragging of Mrs. Synnott, with a trumpery ensign nephew out in the East, who sends shawls and ivory elephants.

" 'When will this scrawl arrive, I wonder? Perhaps it

may not reach you at all. The ship may go down, or be taken by pirates, who will light their smelly pipes with the best I can do in the way of literary composition. It is not very well worth while writing beautifully for pirates, you will agree, and so I wander about over the paper, on which you may find, I shall be surprised if you do not, the print of a dog's paw here and there. They, Bess and Punch, will come in, and they scramble about so, there is no keeping them in their places. Bess has had a litter since you went away, two dog-puppies and three others. There was the usual talk of drowning, but it ended as usual, with Bess enthroned under the kitchen dresser, and everyone coming to pay respects to the full number of puppies.

" 'What else? Three or four of the women in the village are praying for you, and there was talk of a candle being set up by old Philo Regan. I told her it would do a Protestant no good, she had better keep it for St. Anthony, to find her calf that strayed away. She said, whether a creature went straying to Australia or only into the next parish, it was all one in God's eye, so you may share the petition of the candle between you.

" 'Dear brother, dear Charles, to be serious for a moment, you are indeed very far away from us, and I can't always think with composure of the many months that must pass before you are home again here. Please write. It is not that which you do most easily, I know it, but say to yourself that two poor silly women are fond of you, and will not be easy until they have assurance that you are safe and happy. I will say it again, in red ink if I can find any. Please write. And again, WRITE, in capitals, so that you, who once complained of my "feathery fist," cannot but make that one word out.' "

Mr. Adare paused a moment in his reading.

"And then she signs her name and her love. And that's the end."

"Thank you," said the red-haired woman. She did not ask to see the letter, but Mr. Adare caught her looking at it, not inquisitively, and gave it into her hand. She weighed it between her fingers as though quite unused to handling such things, read the superscription, smiled, and dropped her hands above it in her lap, where embroidery silks, much faded, lay heaped.

"And so, have you written to your sister?"

"Not yet. The ship is only now in, I've not had the letter an hour."

"When you do answer—I have no right to ask this, no right to conjecture what you may do, or forbid it—I hope you will not speak of me."

"Not——? But it is the only thing that will interest her, my one good reason for writing. Why do you forbid it?"

Lady Henrietta did not answer, but began again to load her blunted needle and draw the silk in and out, making knots for the fleeces of a canvas flock. She spoke away from the previous matter, looking sideways at her knot as it flattened:

"This is all I remember of all my old governess taught

me. Shakespeare, the History of England by Question and Answer—all gone, except this."

"Your sheep will thrive," said Mr. Adare, following the needle and the cue. "Milton fed his, you recollect, on knot-grass dew-besprent, and they did well, or so he says. But listen to me; why mustn't I write about you to Alethea?"

She said in a low voice:

"The night you first came to this house, how long ago? Ten days only? That night—I don't clearly recollect it. But I know, because of that night, and because of certain other things, other happenings——"

She stopped. Adare said, sympathetically and easily:

"You mean, because you were drunk."

She stood up at that; the silks and scissors slipped from her knee. The young man unconsciously took a step back, afraid lest she had been wounded by his bluntness, but she followed, putting out her hands to him.

"Do you know that's the first open word that's been said? *He* never speaks. He won't let them speak, or look, not even Milly. I get the bottles. When they're empty I hide them until there's a pile, and then, one day, they're gone. Nobody speaks of them. I do something outrageous, come down half-naked, scream—nobody speaks." She gripped his hands more tightly. "That night, how did I appear? Was I—was I decent?"

"You were covered," Adare answered. "Don't trouble for that. Only you were not quite, we'll say, the glass of fashion."

"Thank God for it. And for you, that gives me the words of comfort I've needed. 'You were drunk.' My dear, you'll never know how I've longed to hear a human creature's voice just saying that."

They stood together. Suddenly Adare began to laugh. She followed the lead a moment later, rocking, half-weeping. Flusky came out on to the verandah from his room astonished at the sound, and stood in the long window of the drawing-room wondering at the laughers, who confronted each other helplessly, their feet upon the fallen silks, and regarded by the round eyes of a scissors that had dropped point downwards to stick upright out of the floor. His wife saw him first, and still catching her breath came towards and past him. As she reached his side she held his arm for an instant and leaned her cheek against it; then went out, swiftly and majestically striding, towards the shades of the garden. Adare remained. Without self-consciousness he wiped his damp eyes, and set about picking up the silks.

"What's funny?" Flusky asked him.

"I don't know," said Adare; for with all his impudence he could hardly confide to this man, who himself never referred to it, the subject of the jest. "Just something or other made the pair of us laugh."

Flusky said nothing, noting the embroidery, which for ten years he had not seen in his wife's hands. He turned away.

(x)

"I'vE been talking with your husband—why didn't you dine with us, cruel fair—as the poets say, the silly fools. How I hate poets! Why don't you ever take a bite with us? We get on very well, but we're a little heavy together, like brandy and cheese. Is it because you're sick of food by the time you've ordered it? I've heard my mother say that."

"I seldom order it."

"I thought the stranger within your gates might have transformed you to a model housewife. What a damnable thing—Venus into Dorcas! Still, you know, it would give you something to do with your time."

Again she was silent.

"Oho! There's something in the way. Now what?" But he did not wait for her answer. "Is there anyone I could kick for you?"

She laughed, and spoke at last.

"It does me good to have you here."

"I know that. I'm little Ferdinand of all the tracts come alive. 'O mamma, pray put that ugly bottle down!' I take my duties seriously, it's a mission I'm on; to restore you to that society, of which you ought to be the jewel and ornament. Let's plan the campaign together."

"How about making your fortune? I thought that was what had brought you here."

"I'll make yours instead, lend myself lustre that way.

Where's pencil and paper? Here we are. Now! Programme of Social Activities, (*a*) domestic, (*b*) in social circles. Lord, lord, those social circles! How I pity you, being obliged to shine in them. *Lux in tenebris*— and the darkness did not comprehend it. All the same, it is your duty."

He looked up suddenly from his absurd task. She was seated in a chair backed by sunset. The noble shape of her head could be seen against red feathers of cloud, dark, calmly brooding. By strong daylight the skin showed thickened and blotched, the whites of the eyes were not clear, and the whole scheme of her beauty appeared half-spoiled, like a great drawing sketched upon some spongy substance. Withdrawal of light gave back this beauty again by lending it mystery. Adare said impulsively:

"You are the loveliest creature ever I saw in my life, I believe—except a mare I once had that died of the strangles."

He laughed at his own conclusion. She did not, making almost passionate answer.

"No, no. I know there's nothing left, nothing——"

"Don't you ever take a look in your glass?"

"There are no glasses here."

That was true. Nowhere in the house had he seen one, except the round small mirror he shaved by, and he now perceived the reason; she could not bear to be reminded of the passing of a beauty that had been sterile, that would light no memories; of which, in this new country, no man would say when she died, "Ah, but Henrietta Considine was the loveliest thing!" Adare was touched with pity. He whipped off his dark green coat, and holding it behind the French window within whose opening stood her chair, made a mirror impromptu, in which as she turned she could see something of her head's outline against the ghosts of cloud.

"Can you see yourself? Enough to convince? I tell you what we'll do, we'll drive together into Sydney to-morrow, and cause a nice scandal, and I'll buy you the biggest looking-glass I can find. It's to stand for your conscience. Every day you must look in it, and say to yourself, Sister Hattie, Sister Hattie, do you see anybody coming? And every day you must answer, I see myself, myself, myself coming back hell-for-leather to make me like I was when I was young."

He took away his coat, swung it on to his shoulders, and when he viewed her again found her head sunk, and her hands at her eyes. She was crying; indeed his own outburst had made a kind of clot come in his throat. He took refuge from emotion in talk, and seizing the pencil again began to make calculations aloud.

"We haven't got far with our plan yet. Activities Domestic; yes, those must be considered first. What the devil does a woman find to do in a house? I have it—back to the beginning of our conversation. One, you must order the dinner yourself."

He set this down, neatly.

"Two, you must take up your needle. I disallow your

59   E

knotted sheep. Embroidery will not do, there is no reclaiming virtue in embroidery, it is frivolous, old ladies in mouldy castles do miles of it, for which nobody's the better. The new world demands something sterner. Socks! Not flocks. I'll give you one of mine to start on, and your husband, I dare say he'll wear out a pair or two to oblige you. Task domestic Number Two."

He set it down.

"What shall Three be? I think I have it. To appear every evening at the dinner you have ordered in the morning. Yes, and eat it, too. I know how it is, you have no appetite, I know that. But that will come along. You must dress for us; you must adorn our table, not leave us to munch together like a pair of bullocks. And you must take a glass of wine with us. How long since you've had a drink in public? Well, that's undoubtedly Three."

She had recovered from her tears he saw, looking sideways at her, and as he wrote she spoke:

"You are talking nonsense, but please go on."

"The first time anyone has ever paid me that tribute. I used to write poetry once, did you know? Brought out—the impudence of me—a book. It even got a critique from the Scotch Reviewers. They said what you said, minus the last clause. Have I to come fifteen thousand miles to find my market?"

"Charles—that is your sister's name for you, isn't it? I will call you Charles, I think. You must believe that I am very grateful."

"My dear creature, I please myself by staying in this house—for I take it that's what you refer to. Indeed, if I didn't stay in this house, I should have nowhere to go. His Excellency the Governor has turned me out into the storm. You are not to thank me for your own charity, taking in an orphan."

"But your plans—you cannot be always talking to me. You have some notion what you intend to do."

"None." He indicated the paper. "Unless it be this. I get the run of my teeth, goddess dear, as Milton has it, in return for the privilege of keeping you away from the bottle."

She said, speaking with difficulty, very low:

"Charles, it isn't only that. That came—because I had lost courage. It is not the cause."

"Cause or effect, we'll get rid of them together. We'll present you to the world, you'll burst upon it like Pygmalion's statue, and the world shall rock, or I'll know the reason why. Lack of company, lack of women to chatter and stitch with—there's your cause, I believe. But my dear, my dear! They are a very deadly set of people, all the best ones."

"I don't want to go among them. Pray don't insist upon that; I have no inclination to society."

"I do insist upon it. I insist upon your staggering all the wives of the Chief Thises and Thats until they go home and beat their uninteresting children."

"Perhaps—perhaps I have staggered them already."

"That dinner party? Pooh, it told them nothing they

hadn't invented beforehand. There must be more dinner parties. There must be races and balls. I'll see to it. I am not *persona grata* at Government House, but I am personable, and a Lord's son, thank that same Lord!"

She was beginning to speak when Miss Milly came in bearing candles. (It had grown dark while they spoke, like a curtain dropping.) The sallow woman came in, peering, for the lights she carried blinded her, and gave the pair at the window a look before she set the two silver branches down. She said nothing, however; licked her finger and thumb to snuff down one of the wicks that was flaming; withdrew.

"That's a nice sort of a family nurse, curse, worse to have about."

"She is kind to me."

"I wonder is she. I wonder does she."

"Does she—what?"

"I don't know." He had been looking intently at the door, but suddenly let his eyes come back to his hostess. "I never could stomach plain women. That's why I like you. The harp that once in Tara's halls might have been strung with your hair. Or the bow of Diarmed. There's a word for what you are."

"There is indeed. There is a word for what I am."

"Oh, not that side of you, not the drinking and the crying and the bogy on the bed. Well, I'll change my tune. There's a word for what you were and still could be. Only I can't find it. Nobody's ever found it. There's a young man, a poet, not long dead, and he said beauty was truth. And there was another man asked once, what is truth; but he never got his answer, not even though he asked God. Nobody knows what they are, truth or beauty. Not even poets; not even lovers. And so that's why I can't finish my little compliment."

"But you are not in love."

"No, thank God. And I'm not a poet."

There was sincerity in that answer. He had for the moment no more to say; and with the unconcern of a young animal clenched his shoulders, stretching, then walked past her chair out into the dark garden. She did not look after him. She sat awhile watching insects that the candles had drawn round them with their silent Ducdame, then stooped to pick up the paper on which Adare had scribbled, idly, the list of her domestic duties. She read it, smiled ruefully, and put it away in her dress.

(xi)

THAT large confused warm room, the kitchen of Flusky's house, was busy after its fashion at eleven of a morning, with gardeners bringing in vegetables, blacks coming to cadge bacon-rind or corks, and occasionally men from the bay with unfamiliar-shaped fish strung on reeds. It was a room drab enough to the eye, but vivid to the ear with women's talk and the ejaculations of the stove. Miss Milly reigned there. Hers was the pair of slippers, embroidered with life-sized sunflowers, that reposed by the door. The nail beside the dresser was hers, on which she hung her apron after carefully, and with a look which the women did not miss, removing everything its pocket might contain. Her taste had directed the embellishments—a string of paper roses in three colours, much blown by flies, a print of Moses striking the rock, and a certificate of First Communion in French, unintelligible, but admired by reason of its illuminated border.

In this kitchen Miss Milly directed the preparation and conservation of food, holding absolute sway. It was the house's first line of defence, and she was entrenched in it. Hence, with a general's eye, she watched and directed activities of all those who came and went about the house. The house-women—one petty thief, one murderess (with extenuating circumstances) and one aged female fence who gave herself airs and talked *ad nauseam* about her former glories—these had friends among visiting grooms and tradesmen, who, for a consideration, would procure them drink. The blacks, too, and the fishermen were channels for the coming of drink into the house. Miss Milly knew and successfully blocked all these courses of supply, so far as her underlings were concerned; they raved at her for incorruptibleness, and drank hartshorn or paraffin, making themselves sick to spite her; but she observed their convulsions unmoved. She obliged her assigned women to work, even taught them something of house-pride and order; she trained

motts and mollishers* to make the kind of wives a rough-
and-ready new world demanded. In the single instance
of her employer's wife her efficiency appeared to fail.
Somehow, into that upper room the bottles still found
their way, and if the flow of liquor sometimes dwindled,
at other times it came in flood. Lack of money could not
settle the matter in a country where raw spirit was
bartered against a set of buttons, a weight of flour, or
even female virtue. Miss Milly, whose powers could
baffle all the manœuvres of the assigned sots, was not
able to discover a tactic which should be effective
against gentlewomen.

Miss Milly, then, spying her ladyship's figure straying
through the garden still young with morning, went into
the upper corridor and looked about her. William Winter
was coming upstairs. She beckoned him sharply.

"Give me a hand here. There'll be something to
carry; I don't care to get up one of the women."

From curiosity only he obeyed, and followed her into
a bedroom whose door he had often eyed, from which in
the night sometimes came whimpers and talking, endless
talking, by one voice only. It was a pleasant room, with a
vast wooden bed. He noted that one of the upstanding
pillars of this bed was scored as though a bullet had
whipped past it. The untidiness of the place was fantastic.
There were clothes spread about the chairs and floor,
enough for a dozen women's wearing; candles everywhere, one guttering still in broad daylight; an ancient

---

*Motts, mollishers = prostitutes, thieves' women.

trunk open, all its contents tumbled. Above the smell of scent was a sweetish pothouse reek of spilled rum.

William Winter was shocked by this disorder. He did not choose to let his eyes reckon it all, but observed instead the view from the window, which looked east, towards spurs of land as yet uncleared shutting out a view of the harbour's length. He could see, down in the bay, one or two craft moving slowly upon the light morning breeze, and a dark fin travelling fast like a tiny sail blown by some ill wind of its own. He did not look at the unmade bed nor the stockings cast upon chairs; he preserved a certain gallantry in his downfall, a corner of civility where he retired when he wished to reassure himself that he was still a gentleman. Miss Milly, too, did not gape about her, but told him sharply to look and find if the madam was still in the garden. He saw the movement of a yellow dress and reported it. Miss Milly, satisfied, proceeded to a cupboard where she bade him attend her, stripping on her way a sheet from the bed.

The cupboard held unnumbered dresses; and among the dresses, hidden below their skirts, wrapped sometimes in a petticoat or a shift, were bottles, all shapes, all sizes.

"Hold this," said Miss Milly, gripping the four corners of the sheet so that it might take a load; and she picked up the bottles quietly, one by one, talking with affability:

"I have to do this while she's out of the way. Not under madam's nose, dear no! That wouldn't do. 'How do they come there? What d'you mean, storing

66

rubbish among my things?' That sort never admits it. Well! Only ten this week—that's having something to occupy her. Mostly there's a couple of dozen. I'm sure I wouldn't have asked you, only I thought there'd be a heavy lot."

"What am I to do with them?"

"Ketch the blackfellow is in the kitchen. He sells them to one of the men in the bay. There's an idea— what do you say? He's making the whole of one side of his house out of bottle bottoms. It's the only good use for bottles ever I heard of. For mortar, he shaves his dog. You need hair for good mortar. Why, one of the old governors, he used to shave the convicts all over; said animals was too valuable. That's how the barracks was built, against the direct command of God. 'Ye shall not round the corners of your head, neither mar the corners of thy beard.' Well, better be going. Madam's not dependable, what I call; may be on us any minute."

They went down together, the gentleman manœuvring his burden awkwardly at the turn of the stairs, and along the passage which led kitchenwards. Passing through a baize door the two simultaneously heard a voice, unfamiliar in that place, speaking clear and high. Miss Milly checked with one hand the steps of William Winter following behind her.

"And why not?" the voice was asking. "This is my house, I will not have you argue with me. Which of you is the cook?"

A murmur answered. Miss Milly, tightening her

mouth, came forward with no uncertain step, and marched in upon the situation. Lady Henrietta stood by the table, facing a pair of women, half-frightened, half-inclined to giggle, who eyed her with most eager curiosity. She held a kitchen knife by its point, rapping out upon the table a drummer's tune with the butt of it. As Miss Milly entered she turned.

"What's the matter with these creatures? Why can't they give me an answer?"

Miss Milly made oblique reply.

"The dinner's settled. It was all fixed last night. You go and take a bit of a saunter in the garden."

Decision swelled in one voice as it fled from the other. Lady Henrietta seemed to stoop, almost to be wheedling.

"Milly, in future pray consult me. It is for me to make the arrangements."

One of the women set up a laugh, uneasy at witnessing an interchange of which she could make nothing. Miss Milly turned on the noisy creature with a gesture which silenced her.

"In future—we must make a plan, Milly, do you hear? We must order the work between us. I've left too much on your shoulders, you are not to blame."

Miss Milly still stood mute.

"In future, I will come—no, that won't do—you shall come to me, in my room, and bring a slate for the orders. Every morning. At nine o'clock. That will do very well. Do you understand me? And we'll settle the dinner between us."

Miss Milly answered at last.

"You'll give the orders, is that it?"

"And I had better—you'll let me have the keys."

They hung at Miss Milly's belt, a dozen of them, their steel rods shining like daggers. She had laid open a convict woman's forehead once with a knock from her bunch; as she walked they rang authoritatively, like spurs.

"Oh, the keys?"

But she did not bring up her hand to unhook them. She went instead to the door, and beckoned in William Winter. He came unwillingly, set down his burden gently. It gave an unmistakable sound for all that, the chink of glass. Lady Henrietta looked at it, and stopped the tune that she had been playing with the haft of her knife on the table. She did not ask what was in the sheet tied by its four corners, nor did Miss Milly make any remark upon it. The convict women met each other's eyes, and one put her hand over her mouth, from which an uncleanly noise came bursting. This time Miss Milly did not rate her. She looked at the bundle, at her silent mistress, and when she judged that the bundle had done its work, with a gesture bade William Winter take it up and away. He obeyed, only once raising his eyes; that single glance had showed him so grotesque a flood of red colouring Lady Henrietta's throat that he could not bear to look again. He heard, as he went out slowly under the humiliating weight of empty bottles, the sound of her step retreating, and found it odious that so much dignity and grace should march away at the threat, the empty threat, he thought, making some sort of forlorn play upon words, of a harridan. It had already caused him unhappiness that Flusky's wife never spoke to him, and shrank aside as he passed her. He had almost forgotten the uninteresting female minor whose reluctance had brought him to this strait, but she was now, vicariously and unknowing, taking vengeance upon him.

(xii)

The dinner that night was neither better nor other than usual. Flusky's wife was not present; the two men found little to talk about. Adare had ridden in to Sydney on one of his host's excellent horses, he had visited the Club and acquired some small change of gossip which he was willing to distribute; but Flusky's dead weight pulled the conversation down, time and again, to silence. He listened, he answered, but it was with questions of the kind which show the questioner to be indifferent. Is that so, now? Did he indeed? Adare, as the walnuts came on, made a last effort.

"Do you see there's an order out forbidding those heads from New Zealand? Who the devil ever thought of importing the nasty things? Human heads tattooed, in pickle. You have queer notions out here of the *beaux-arts*."

"It does them no harm," Flusky answered, sipping water, "the blacks. They're dead enough."

"Well, but," Adare persisted, glad to have struck even this spark, "you wouldn't care for one yourself, would you, as a paper-weight?"

"Not as a paper-weight."

"D'you mean you've got one of the things?"

"Why not?"

Adare hesitated, laughed.

"Well—I don't know exactly why not. I shouldn't care for it."

"You might," said Flusky.

He got up with his usual deliberation, fumbling in one of his wide pockets for keys; opened a cupboard of dark wood that must, in the old country, have held china dogs, shepherdesses and cups; thence took out, *sans* ceremony, an object which he set down casually by the side of his guest's plate. It was a head, somewhat shrivelled and dwindled by the process of preserving, which had turned the longish lank hair a streaky yellow. On the skin geometrical patterns of tattooing stood out, enclosing the mouth, circling upon the cheeks and forehead, dark indigo blue weals upon brown. The eyes, mercifully, were shut.

Adare stared at it. The thing had a kind of helpless and horrid nobility; the individual was undoubtedly dead, the practice of embalming one approved by the ancients. For all that, the young man hurriedly emptied his glass of wine and pushed his chair back. As he did so, he saw Flusky looking at the head, nodding appreciation while he searched for a cigar. This he lit; in the act paused uneasily, and blew out his spill with the guilty expression of a child, offering an explanation that was an apology.

"I forgot. The port's on the table."

And that troubles you, thought Adare. Pick out a human creature's skull and dump it down among the biscuits and raisins; but don't smoke with the port on any account. He was touched by the anomaly of this behaviour. Trying to change himself, thought Adare for her sake, the poor devil. Will she do as much for him? With this in his mind he spoke:

"Her ladyship doesn't honour us to-night."

Flusky looked at him in wonder, mildly.

"Oh, I know she don't as a rule. But to-night I thought possibly—where is she, Mr. Flusky? Let's find her and make her sit down with us."

"I don't know about that."

"Why not? Put that thing away, she sees horrors enough, and I'll fetch her out from wherever she's hiding."

"I don't think so."

"Why not?"

Flusky's eyes, lifted from contemplation of the blue whorls upon the dead man's cheeks, met the live man's eyes for a moment with a stubborn absence of expression. Adare nodded.

"But she was all right this morning. Seemed better. I thought she might keep so. What's been the trouble, I wonder?"

Flusky would not answer. Both stood for an instant quite still, then the young man flung his napkin to cover the Maori head, and went out on to the verandah, quickly down stone steps to the garden. There was a moon coming up. It seemed caught in the thin net of the pepper-trees' foliage, so slowly did it move; on the harbour water, here and there where a gust of air was dying, a star or two danced. Adare looked back into the room he had just quitted, and saw the heavy man, his host, looking down at that dark object from which he had twitched the covering away, the unlighted cigar still in one hand. He had a feeling of hopelessness, of meddling in affairs too big for him, travelling with a poor provision of wits and goodwill through unknown country. Sadness of youth took hold of him, the sadness compact of self-pity, which seeks a listener to whom golden lads and lasses may complain of time's cruelty, secure in the knowledge that the gold is with them still. He looked up at the window which William Winter that morning had preferred to the litter of the bedroom; and, though it was dark, smoothed the set of his curls (barbered that morning by an indifferent and homesick felon) before he called to the square of light:

"Heyo!"

A shadow moved within the room, but no figure showed against the light. He called again:

"Are you there? What's your ladyship doing indoors a night like this?"

She did not answer. He saw Flusky move to open the

French window of the dining-room, obscuring the direct light of the candles with his heavy shoulders, and threw a word back to him, confidently:

"I'll have her out of there." He spoke upwards again, hand on heart, burlesquing: "Your promise, your promise——

> 'Thy vows are all broken,
> And light is thy fame,
> I hear thy name spoken,
> And share in its shame——'

"D'you hear me? What are you at, Lady Hattie? Never mind, come down here, I'm waiting, I've got things to tell you. Come o'er the moonlit sea. That's it! A boat—will you? There is a moon, I've seen to that. Don't miss the moon."

The shadow in the upper room stirred sideways, heaving itself wildly about after the manner of shadows candle-cast, and he saw her come to the window. Her hair was on her shoulders and she was huddling some sort of garment over her breast. She swayed against the window's side, caught the curtain with one hand, and so stood. She did not speak.

"Are you listening? What's the good of roaring to a statue up in a niche? Come down, come down——"

She answered, then. Her voice now hurried, now checked; words were for a moment almost shouted, then smothered; it had the confused quality of shallow water running over stones; the voice of a gentlewoman drunk.

"Didn't order dinner."

"Who's talking about dinner? Who gives a damn for dinner? I won't excuse you. What's become of your promise?"

She muttered something. Couldn't help, Not reasonable, Milly——"

"I can't hear what you say. Come into the garden, it will cool you down. Bring a veil if you like, the mosquitoes are troublesome. I've something to say to you."

He saw her shake her head. Suddenly his eye caught the trick of the shadows behind her. There was one, square-shouldered like a man, which he now perceived to be that of a bottle standing on the table near her candle. A little breeze, shifting the flame, caused the bottle's shadowy shoulders to heave like those of a man laughing, and Adare was enraged by that shrug precisely as though a man had mocked him.

"You won't, do you say? I won't take that. You can't diddle me that way."

Her dark outline changed its position, she was moving away from the window. On the ceiling the bottle-shoulders jerked to the death of an insect in flame.

"Are you dressed? Put something on. I'll give you two minutes, and then I'm coming up the wall."

A tree stood against that side of the house, dark, thickly-leaved. Here and there closed white flowers showed upon it; the scent was heady. Adare took out his watch—no mere gesture, for the moon now rode clear, and he could read the numerals—and with this in his hand considered the possibilities of the tree. It was sturdy enough; it was nailed to the wall and would bear him. While the two minutes lagged by he became aware that Flusky still eyed him. He made a gay little sign with the right hand—Up I go, I must deal with this situation—and spoke towards him in a half-voice:

"Better stand by with the pistol again."

The two minutes were ended. Adare dropped his watch in his pocket, sprang into the first branch of the tree, and made his way up it, rapidly all things considered, to the window under which its main trunk parted. Flusky moved. He went to the cupboard, his illegal trophy's coffin, and took out of it the small pistol which Adare had left behind him on the evening of the interrupted dinner. It was clean, as he discovered by squinting down the barrel. He, however, made no move to load it, but stood with it in his hands, listening to the cracks and ejaculations that accompanied his guest's progress up the tree.

"Lady, by yonder blessed moon I swear—you can't wonder at it. If my tailor could see me now! Ah! Half-way. Why do I risk my neck? That's it, I'm with you. Up and over. And now, madame, if you please——

(xiii)

HE sat straddling the sill, and reproached her.

"Now listen, now listen. I can't have it. What are you doing, making a guy of yourself this way?"

76

She had drawn away towards the bed, against one of whose posts she clung, pulling the mosquito netting over her face as if for a veil. He could hear her breathing hard, great sobbing breaths. Mr. Adare went on, savouring with a sudden little gush of amusement which knocked the romanticalness clean out of him for the moment, his position as the apostle of temperance; climbing into a room like a lunatic instead of walking in by the door, having the chief of a bottle of port inside him that had been drunk in company with a convicted murderer and a parti-coloured human head.

"You were as good as gold yesterday. Have you forgotten what you promised me? I know it's not easy. I know it gets a grip on your vitals. But why won't you take it like a Christian, at the dinner-table? Decent wine, instead of this rot-gut. What is it?" He peered at the humped black bottle. Gin; empty. "Come here to me and let me talk to you. How can I talk if you wrap yourself up like an Arabian, Lady Hester Stanhope in Arabia Felix, Lady Hattie Flusky in Australia Felix? Come along, I won't hurt you, I won't scold you. Bring me that bottle."

He held out his hand. She obeyed as if it drew her magically, came slowly forward, her hair tumbling about her face. But Mr. Adare was determined not to be defied by the hump-shouldered shadow any longer, and he made her pause by the table to take up the bottle. This, when she came near him, he took, and with a fling of his right arm sent it out into the garden. The squawking of roosting birds showed that it had landed in a tree.

"Where d'you get it from?" He took her hand as he spoke, holding her steady on her feet; the hand was damp and very hot. "Henrietta, now tell me. How did you get it?"

"Found it."

She spoke in bursts of sound.

"Found it; is that true?"

"Sometimes——" she made a wide gesture with her free hand which unbalanced her, so that she swayed against him. "Sometimes find them. Never mind."

"Here, in this room? Outside in the garden? Where?"

She answered at random, loudly and suddenly:

"Couldn't order dinner. Sorry. Can't explain——"

At that she slipped out of his supporting arm to the floor, and began a kind of windy crying. He considered for a moment; then pulled his left leg in over the sill, and leaving her where she lay, took up the candle to survey the room. He opened cupboards and trunks. He disturbed dresses. No more bottles were to be seen. When he was certain of this, he returned to her.

"Do you pay for the stuff? How? Who takes the money?"

She shook her head; or rather, swayed her whole body above the waist from side to side. It was not a negation, but a kind of lamentation in movement, a protest against ignominy. She was quite incoherent, and he saw that it

78

would not be possible to draw any answer out of her that would make sense or truth in the morning. He spoke gently, therefore, in another tone:

"We'll get you to bed. Who puts you to bed when you're like this? Milly, is it? I'll ring for her. You'll take cold."

She caught his hand as he went past her and bowed herself to it, kissing it through the mesh of her hair. He felt tears, and patted her head awkwardly with the other hand, as though its red gold had been that of his setter bitch. She let him go when he gently pulled away, and sank against the window, her bare feet sticking out straight from her, green dressing-gown tumbled, hair covering her face, without dignity, awkward as a doll thrown down.

Adare rang the bell. So still was the night that now the sighing in the room had stopped and the birds had settled down again in their tree, he could hear the chinkle of the bell, tossing on its wire in the kitchen fifty yards away, downstairs. He could hear, too, feet coming down the stone steps, slowly, into the garden, and knew that to be Flusky.

It was perhaps two minutes before Miss Milly turned the handle of the door—vainly, for it was locked. Adare went to it, and turned the key, with a flash of self-reproach—why?—that he had not thought to do so while he waited. Only when she looked at him did he appreciate the odd figure he cut, white trousers dirtied and torn by the tree, waistcoat riding up, coat with a feather from one of the cloaks on its shoulder. He said, however, as strongly as he could:

"You had better get Lady Henrietta to bed."

"I'm to put her to bed?"

"Isn't that your work? Send someone else, then."

"Looks more like it's your work." This was spoken very low.

"Oho!" said Mr. Adare, and caught the woman's thin arm. "What's that you said? Say that again, will you?"

She did not obey; looked at the figure on the floor, and back at him.

"None of that, I won't have any of that sort of thing." She eyed him without speaking. "Look here, now. Where does she get the stuff from?"

"How should I know?"

"That's what I'm asking."

"And I'm asking something else, young man. What are you doing here, and her like she is?"

Miss Milly's voice issuing its vulgar challenge made him conscious of squalor. What power had the light of the moon, how could pity itself stand, when there were voices like that in the world, pondered Mr. Adare. He said to the figure on the floor:

"Good night, Henrietta. We'll talk in the morning."

She moved her head from side to side, a sickening motion, abandoned, weary. But she lifted her face a little, and her hair fell away from it. The light showed it shining with tears, lids and lips swollen, cheeks deadly white. From her came a warm reek of drink. Adare was seized by a strong repugnance; but cancelling out, as was his habit, one emotion by the show of its opposite, he stooped to the wet face and kissed its forehead. Then he went out by the door.

(xiv)

FLUSKY's room in which he sat for long periods smoking, or which he paced, slowly straddling, following the pattern in the carpet, three strides this way, two strides that, sideways, turn; this room was the barest in the house. It had the look of an office. There were no books, no flowers save when a branch of creeper, loosened by the wind, tapped on the pane. There was a cabinet, beautifully made of native woods by a carpenter who had been apprenticed to a man who learned his trade in Robert Adam's workshop. This held documents—leases and other papers with the red Government stamp; no private letters that any of his secretaries had ever been able to discover, and no money. There were no pictures, though on one wall hung a map, an outline of New South Wales as far as the discoverers to date had carried it. This map resembled the old cartographers' performances; rivers flowed and ceased abruptly, their sources unknown; hills started up and sank to a mere line of printing; whole tracts were indicated by words— Lofty Forest Ranges, Level Country with Sandy Brushes, Flat Country, Wooded Country, Country Impassable.

Anywhere in the hinterland precious metals might be found, or new pastures, hidden by the interminably folding ranges. The men who pierced to the white spaces on the map might, like their forerunners in America and Africa, seize natural riches, but never any covetable thing made and used by man; no temple, no treasure. The blacks' tenements were frail and airy as those of birds. They made nothing but their weapons. They had so much of the wild in them that they could not even be enslaved and taught to labour. They hunted to live, and when they could not hunt they died. Their one spiritual possession, a pretty liquid language, the invaders had borrowed here and there, but the map-makers grudged space to such words as Warrawolong, Mandoorama, and preferred instead to acknowledge new discoveries under English titles: Parker's Flats, Gammon Plains, Brighton

Flusky looked often at this map, observing how the English names advanced upon it. He had no scruple about dispossessing the blacks; land must belong to those willing to husband it. But though he had no scruple he had pity, as a man may have pity for a useless dog turned out to roam; thus, the aborigines' humpies were allowed to disfigure the foot of his garden. He expected nothing, neither work nor gratitude, from the wretches he harboured, they paid him no tribute, they disappeared and returned to a rhythm of their own like the tides.

Flusky stood now, looking down upon the bark sheds outside which black women sat smoking. Winter sat at a broad table. Miss Milly, nostrils pinched and white, stood just within the door. She was respectably dressed, her apron was spotless; below her meagre bosom two red hands were folded in all decorum. She spoke:

"It's me to answer for it all. If people go behind my back——" She brought her voice to a gentler level. "Now, you see here, Mister Flusky. It's no good, this house won't stand two giving the orders in it. You can't expect the women to put up with that. I know how to talk to them. Madam—do you suppose she could talk to old Sarah, that don't know what you say without you put it into flash language? She's a lady; well, let her sit in her parlour the way ladies ought. I'll do the work, work my hands to the bone for her. But I won't be interfered with, for all she means it well."

Flusky did not interrupt her; walked slowly a few steps right, a few steps left.

"So I'll thank you to tell Madam."

Flusky stopped his pacing as though confronted by a knot in the pattern too intricate to be stepped, and stood, feet well apart, staring down. His hands were behind his back, one holding a cigar. Its smoke trickled up to coil and fan about the room, bringing to the secretary, with a pang of nostalgia, two pictures clear to the least detail; a room at the Mitre in Oxford, the top of a coach in autumn weather. William Winter sighed, caught himself doing so, and bent to his work. The woman's voice insisted, growing louder as though to pierce and end Flusky's continued silence:

"I can't have it, that's flat. She makes work enough

in other ways, excuse me referring to it, without this on top. And I'll tell you another thing." She waited; but Flusky asked no question, and she was obliged to continue without that aid to revelation. "It won't do no harm for you to keep an eye on some of her goings-on. I'm saying nothing more, I'm a Christian woman. I give you fair warning."

Flusky looked up at that.

"I don't say anything without I know. I can hold my tongue." She resumed her earlier quiet way of speech: "Do you want anything more with me? I've got my dinner to see to."

The secretary turned from his table at the window.

"Mr. Adare, sir, in the garden. He is making signs, whether he may come in."

Flusky made an acquiescent gesture, which Winter, rising, interpreted with a beckoning hand. The young man appeared in the French windows. Miss Milly, whose expression had changed with his coming, stood her ground, neglecting the claims of dinner.

"You're engaged," said Mr. Adare, his eyes on the woman. "I'll wait."

"No," said Flusky, and he too looked at the house-keeper.

"You'll speak to Madam, then," the woman reiterated, meeting Adare's glance. "I'll do my work, but I won't have meddling. I won't stand that, not from anybody. I've got this house to see to, there's plenty of it, and I can't get through if there's meddlers about."

"What's all this?" Adare asked.

She ignored him, speaking to Flusky.

"So them as puts ideas into her head had better stop it, for everybody's sake. You can whistle for your dinner, if she's to order it."

She had said her say, there was a righteous pink line along her cheek-bones, the ensign of victory, and she was going at last. Adare said suddenly, smoothly:

"Just one moment. If you please." She opened the door. "Of course, I'll say it behind your back if you prefer."

She shut the door and stood with her back to it, hands flat against the wood as though to press it more irrevocably shut. Her constant strife with tough and insubordinate women had taught her never to let a challenge pass.

"Very well," said Adare. "Mr. Flusky, I'm beginning to get some notion of the situation here with regard to Lady Henrietta. Last night——"

Miss Milly could not resist that cue.

"Yes, last night, I could find something to say about last night if I chose to!"

Adare went towards her quietly, and took her nose between his thumb and finger. She scuffled with her hands to pull his grip loose. He pinched the tighter, reasoning:

"Be quiet and I won't hurt you. It's you who are hurting yourself. Quiet, now. That's better."

"Let her alone," Flusky ordered brusquely, advancing

as though to come between them. "Damn all this cross-talk. Say what you've got to, both of you. Stash the row."

Adare let the woman go at once, took a handkerchief from his tail-pocket and wiped his fingers.

"Well, you see, it's quite true (as Miss Milly so delicately suggests) that I've been meddling in your affairs, Mr. Flusky. I hinted, for instance, to your wife that she should find something to occupy her, even if it was no more than to order your food. I believe she went yesterday to the kitchen, and met some rudeness there. Last night something was troubling her; the dinner, the dinner, she kept repeating. Now, what could that have been, do you suppose? What do you think can have upset her, to do with the dinner?"

Miss Milly did not offer any speculation. She said, beating a ruffle with her fingers against the door to which she had once more retreated:

"He was there in her room last night, and the door locked. There's something for you to put in your pipe. There he was, and her with her clothes half off her. That's where she met some rudeness, as he calls it, and a good name for it too."

Mr. Adare took no notice of this provocation, but repeated steadily:

"You had insulted her somehow. You did some offensive thing."

"I turned her out of my kitchen, and I'd a right to do it, I'd do the same to you. It's none of your business.

If she was at it again last night you best know why——"
She was whipping herself to anger, as sometimes she
whipped herself to prayer. "Yes, and so I tell Mr.
Flusky, I've got better things to do than butter my
tongue when his wife comes interfering, and I tell you
too, Mister Nobody from Nowhere!"

"Excuse me." That was the tremulous secretary, on
an impulse rising and turning from his table. "Excuse
me, I was present yesterday in the kitchen when her
ladyship came in. She did receive an affront." He
hesitated. "I don't know how to describe it, no words
were spoken——"

Miss Milly caught him up, triumphantly seizing her
chance.

"Yes, indeed, you was there, he was carrying a load
of bottles, you know where from, and in he came without waiting for a word and dumped them down in front
of her. Done up in one of her own sheets, too. She
knew what they was and where they come from, and
she turned white like the sheet itself and went out, and
that's your affront for you, if you want a grand word
for a silly start."

The pale secretary caught his breath, turning to Adare
with a cry:

"Sir, you're a gentleman."

It was Flusky who answered that, not moving, shouting from where he stood

"To hell with your talk of gentlemen! Get out of here,
you. Milly, get out. I'll settle this."

"Settle that young fellow first," the woman called, jutting her head forward. "I'm a Christian woman, I don't stay in any house with adulterers. You, young man! Don't cry when you burn in hell, like as you haven't had warning." She began to pray, turning up her eyes, between which her nose glowed, still red: "Oh Lord, pay down upon the nail, after Thy manner, the wages of this man's sin. Let the fervent prayer of the righteous prevail, oh Lord, let not the wicked prosper, nor flourish as the bay tree and tree upon the wall. If Thou, oh Lord, wilt mark iniquity, shall a decent woman endure it? The wicked shall burn, we have Thy word for it, as we may take to our comfort——"

"Oh——" began Mr. Adare; but while he sought an expletive his sense of the ridiculous caught up with him, and he laughed. Miss Milly stopped her ranting, brought her eyes down to the level of his, took a great breath or two to calm the quick pulsing of her blood; then said, in another voice, the voice of the decent servant who has been put upon:

"I'm getting out of this house, Mr. Flusky. I'm free. This very night I go. And you can keep what wages is due me. I'd sooner sweep the Parramatta Factory than lend my face to iniquity."

That, too, tickled Mr. Adare, whose imagination readily played and made pictures with words; Satan the Serpent trying on Miss Milly's face, shaking his head over the fit of it. He sat down upon the secretary's table, wiping his eyes. When he had recovered the secretary and the woman both were gone. Flusky remained in his place, brooding down, and making through his teeth a little sound that clearly indicated dismay.

"You're well rid," said Adare with a jerk of his head towards the door.

"We shan't get on without her any too well," Flusky muttered.

"No, but listen to me. She's been keeping Lady Hattie supplied." Flusky looked up. "I do think so, indeed. A woman like that—do you suppose she couldn't choke off the supply if she put her mind to it? Last night in the room upstairs——" He was aware that any mention of that scene was uncomfortable to his host; but the air had to be cleared. "It's true that the door was locked. She'd shut herself in—you know what for. So it's as well I went up by the tree, though I grant you at the time it looked a silly thing to do. That woman Milly; you can see for yourself she hates me. Now why? Because she thinks there are things I might be finding out. Lady Hattie talks to me, you see." He pulled himself up, and sat back upon the secretary's table. "So you see, it's a good riddance if that's so. Of course, I've no proof."

"No," said Flusky. "No proof of anything."

He suddenly flung away the cigar, which all this while had been burning in his hand. There was a scampering sound on the verandah outside; he cocked his head at it.

"One of the gins. They eat tobacco, give them the chance. Wait hours for a butt." His puzzled heavy expression returned. "I don't like losing Milly. She's been here years."

"But, good God——"

"There's only your word against hers."

"You may accept mine, I think," said Adare dryly.

"What, because you're a gentleman? So's Winter a gentleman. You back each other up. That's what you're taught to do, ain't it? In your schools. Back each other up against outsiders."

He broke off, turned about. Adare watched him, and to check anger told himself that the man had scars on his back, that the man was suffering now, that the man was striking out like an animal, less to cause hurt than to ease his own. He did not speak, and could not, from Flusky's expression, make any guess at what plan of behaviour the man's movements were weaving for him. Flusky stood once more.

"I'd be obliged if you'd overlook all this. It won't be too comfortable, I daresay, with Milly gone. I'd be obliged if you'd stay on."

Adare, who had had no thought of leaving the house, nodded carelessly.

"We'll have Lady Hattie right in a month, once the house is her own. Up with the lark, and to bed with the nightingale, or whatever bird you keep in this country for an example to the slothful. Don't worry your head. Take my word for it." His host's face still was heavy, and the young man, alarmed by any emotion which did not swim to the surface, fired a question, as guns are fired across water to make a drowned body rise.

"You don't take seriously what the woman said? It's so mad I didn't trouble to deny it."

Flusky looked at him with eyes deliberately blank. He might not have heard. Adare could not repeat what he had said; it sounded more preposterous, put into words, than in the silence of his mind. He took a half-crown from his pocket, spun it once or twice and tossed it, resenting even as he did so the obligation which was on him to make movements and speeches, to show himself a target for the emancipist's weapon of stillness. Playing with this coin he managed without further talk to escape into the garden, grateful for once to find himself isolated there.

(xv)

MISS MILLY departed, disdaining all assistance. Her gift for organization had procured from Sydney a cart for the transport of her boxes; they were light, quite certainly no heavier than when, years before, she had arrived to take charge of the house so oddly named, Why are you weeping? Opportunities for peculation, of a kind that the assigned women beheld in dreams, she had been consistent in despising. The money she earned she took; but the shining bunch of keys had been respected by her as the soldier respects his sword, used only to defend the right and to defeat barbarian onsets. She had prepared a final dinner, giving it pious attention. She had scourged the women for the last time with her tongue, so that each utensil shone, no shadow clouded tumbler or spoon. She paid a visit of inspection to each room; checked in each cupboard the list of contents that hung upon its door; detected a gin in an ill-timed foray and routed her; and returning to the kitchen, removed, with the sunflower-patterned slippers, the last emblem of her authority.

There was an interview with Flusky while the charged cart waited before the door. She wore black, as was her custom, with a bonnet on top of such jetted respectability that even the comment of the assigned women failed at sight of it; she bore a reticule jetted to match upon her arm, and in her right hand the keys.

"Here they are, Mr. Flusky. I hope you'll satisfy yourself that all's as it should be."

The master of the house did not take the implements, but nodded that she should lay them down. She did so with a ceremonial stooping of the bonnet, and resumed:

"You won't find a ha'porth missing, whether it's stores or wine. It's my prayer you'll be able to say as much in a year's time—a year! A month's time. I done my duty, and there's no man nor woman nor counter-jumper——" a glance at Winter's back—"dare say contrariwise. Now, Mr. Flusky, there's the matter of my reference."

Flusky rapped on the table for Winter's attention. The secretary found a paper, studied it a moment, and handed it to his employer, who took a pen which he tested upon his thumb-nail, and scored a clumsy signature below the thin elegant script. Miss Milly took the paper and read, her lips moving.

"Very handsome, I will say." She paused; then, more harshly, proceeded: "There's one thing you've left out that might be asked me. Cause of leaving."

"Your own good pleasure. That's all you need tell 'em."

"I won't speak any word that's a lie. And it's a lie, Mr. Flusky, to say I leave you for my own pleasure. I've been here now five years with you, as agreeable as Christian woman could wish. It's no fault of yours, Mr. Flusky. But I won't look on at shameful things, nor I won't be hampered in my duty."

Flusky said suddenly and strongly:

"You don't go putting that about, do you hear? I'm turning you up sweet,* sorry to see you go. None of your yarns."

"You wait and see if it's a yarn. What you want, Mr. Flusky, excuse my saying it, but I've had it for years in mind—you want a woman about you that will see to things. What good's her ladyship——" She spoke that word mockingly, as a woman addresses a troublesome child: My lord.

She stopped as Flusky came towards her. His hands were behind his back, those hands which Mr. Adare had once in imagination seen strangling, and they were

---

*To turn up sweet=to get rid of a person good-humouredly.

straining as though to escape from the invisible bond of his will. She was frightened.

"Oh, very well, I'm sure, if it suits you to have a wife the way she is. I'm not afraid of you nor anyone, the Lord's my guide, and I wish you well, Mr. Flusky. I wish you better luck than you've had, and better luck than you're looking for. And when they ask me the reason why I left this house, you can take your davy I'll tell them."

Flusky said, this time without emphasis:

"You keep your reasons to your nabs. I'm not saying more than that to you."

"Well, good-bye to you, Mr. Flusky. And you can depend I'll petition the Lord to open your eyes."

She held out her hand, genteel in a black mitten. Flusky looked at it, remembered perhaps all he owed to that ill-shaped hard hand—delicate food, cleanliness and order in his household—and slowly brought his own forward to meet it. He did not look at Miss Milly's face, but Winter did, turning for a moment in his seat. In the corners of the Christian woman's small pebbly eyes tears were gathering. It was to hide these that she dragged her hand away before Flusky's grip had time to close upon it in strength, and turned to the door without more words. Flusky stared after her. Winter ventured a remark as he sometimes did—to ingratiate and fend off danger.

"Miss Milly, sir, is really sorry to be going."

"Why quit, then?"

William Winter had his own ideas as to that, but they

were not yet formulated; he would have welcomed a talk with Mr. Adare, a kind of synthesis of opinion concerning Miss Milly's aspirations and past conduct. He answered therefore, after hesitation:

"She has been used to consider this house her own province."

Flusky mused, walking:

"She don't nibble,* though. So what's the objection to my wife giving a hand?"

"Well, sir, she may not have cared to see signs of recovery in Lady Henrietta. I've no proof, sir——"

That innocent expression angered Flusky.

"Proof! I've been tied up for a hundred and fifty before now, without proof. Proof, to hell!"

He picked up the bunch of keys and went along the verandah with them in his hand, to the room where lately, since the first week of Mr. Adare's arrival, his wife had been wont of an evening to sit. She was not there; but at the table whereon her needlework lay Mr. Adare was seated, his legs wreathed about a chair, very fluently composing a letter. He did not immediately hear Flusky, who stood looking in on him, watching with a sort of wonder the brisk whisks and starts of the goose-feather, hearing its cheerful sound upon the paper, a mouselike continuous cheeping. But no man can long be watched and not know it; Mr. Adare in the middle of a sentence looked up.

"You wanted me?"

*Nibble=to pilfer.

95

"My wife."

"She'll be here in a minute," Adare answered casually, dropping his glance again to the paper. He went on, in the toneless voice of one talking and writing together. "She promised a word to my sister under this cover. The *Mary Patterson*'s sailing to-morrow."

Flusky said nothing. He stepped into the room and sat down to wait, idly clinking the keys against his knee. Adare continued to write, strongly aware of that distracting presence. It was putting compulsion upon him to go, and he had to devote part of his attention to repelling the raid upon his will. He wrote, the sentences growing shapeless:

"—and so you see, while I am not yet in the way of making my fortune, I have at least found a temporary harbour. But ships that stay too long in harbour rot, and so I dare say it will not be long before I set out, knapsack on back, to make my fortune—" He struck the repetition out, biting his lip, and substituted—"to find El Dorado."

Not a word further would come into his head. He dipped his pen freshly and began defiantly to write, in broken phrases, of that which he saw when he looked out into the bay.

"The darkness here is not like our darkness. There is a kind of light that comes out of cloudless night—not starlight, dark blue like Byron's seas. You cannot see by it, but you can feel shapes in it. The boats are obliged to carry lights, red, green, and white—I can see only red lights now, which shows the direction in which the ships must be swinging at anchor. Some fishermen's boats are moving very slowly out of the bay, one has a fire on it. That is an aboriginal's canoe, they lay a flat stone in the centre and so carry their fires from shore to shore. It is strange to see a frail shell of bark carrying the most destructive of elements so safely——"

Chink, clash of the keys against the big man's knees, rhythm pointing the strong beats of a tune as a pair of cymbals may do. Mr. Adare's ears were too strong for his eyes, they could not resist guessing at the tune, trying to fit those regular beats to music remembered. British Grenadiers? No, it was not a march; he could not get the hang of it; he resented his domination, which must endure until he had mastered the secret. Looking down again at the paper as though to read over and correct what he had written, he began in self-defence to hum a melody. The chinking beat against him for a bar or two, then slackened, stopped; his host's voice asked what he was singing. It was the first time he had defeated the big man in one of these wordless contests, and he was delighted with himself, with this proof that savage breasts might indeed be soothed, given the appropriate charm. He made answer in song, with the words belonging to that melodic phrase he had reached:

"—and around that dear ruin each wish of my heart
    Shall entwine itself verdantly still."

The door opened; he sprang up gladly.

"Dear ruin, welcome. You're expected, we both attend you most passionately."

Lady Henrietta, coming in, looked first at her husband; and the young man observed with a pang, not of jealousy, the pleasure that came to her eyes, seeing him sitting quietly there. Question succeeded this pleasure.

"Milly's gone." Flusky answered the look, and held out the keys to her. She gazed at them, drawing down her mouth tragically. She repeated:

"Gone?"

And the word rang hollow, forlorn, unnecessarily despairing. Flusky again advanced the keys towards her hand, saying:

"You'll see to things in the morning."

"But Milly mustn't go. It's not to be thought of." Her voice began to hurry and stumble. "Milly mustn't go. I beg you'll bring her back, whatever may have happened. I beg you, Sam."

Flusky looked at her very searchingly. She halted the stream of protest, put her hand to her throat, swallowed. Adare kept his eyes on Flusky, waiting to give the nod which would have meant: You see, I was justified, here's something like proof. But the big man would not look.

"It's her own notion. She don't want to stay. And here's her keys, you see. For you. That's as it should be."

She accepted the keys, sinking teeth upon her lower lip as though to restrain herself forcibly from further speech.

"That's the way. Don't you worry. We'll do all

right." Flusky repeated his reassurance, the only words he could find to assure Adare that he believed no ill, his wife that he had confidence in her. "We'll do all right."

"Perhaps if you paid her more money— She is used to the house, you see, and the women——" The voice relinquished its attempts at calm explanation. "I can't do without her. I must have her back, Sam."

He said no more, but for the first time looked at Adare. His wife could read the answer in that movement of his eyes; Milly's accusations, Flusky's refusal to affront her guest by preferring the woman to him. She abandoned argument, taking the keys from his hand submissively, a symbolic acceptance of his trust. But immediately she held them out again.

"Pray won't you keep them, let me come to you when I need them? You know in such matters I'm apt to be careless."

"Put them at your waist as Milly did. You can't lose 'em; nobody can't get 'em from you, that way."

"No," she murmured. "Very well."

There was a green ribbon at her waist. She untied this now, and threaded the wide ring of the keys upon it. They hung heavily, bearing down the sash to a point on one side. She surveyed them, took a step or two in order to try the feel and sound of them, and smiled with wry tenderness at the heavy man. He beckoned her to him; she came with a lovely readiness. He put his hand at her waist and held her a little away from him; fingered a moment the steel ring that held the keys.

"We must get you a gold one. What's this they call it? To hang at a woman's waist——"

"An equipage?"

"Equipage, hey? Why, that's a coach and horses."

"Not in drawing-rooms; it means keys and scissors there."

"You talk drawing-room, I talk stable. No wonder we get to cross-purposes sometimes; what do you say, Mister Adare?"

He was moving his hand at her waist with the same gentleness and absence of mind that he might have shown rubbing a horse's nose. As he did so he looked mildly but very watchfully at the young man, who under this scrutiny could not wholly command his expression. He knew his own heart very well; he had fallen in love, taking it like a rash, three or four times since he was sixteen; he was no more in love with Lady Henrietta than with Cassiopeia in her chair. Yet he did resent the man's thick hand at her waist, for reasons which he could not at once disentangle. Flusky persisted:

"What do you say?"

"Who, I?" said the young man; and in a hurry unthinking, gave the true answer to his own perplexity. "Oh, she and I speak the same language." He perceived at once that this truth might wound, and went on, picking up his letter. "Lady Hattie, I've left you a good four inches of paper, enough for greeting, not near enough for gossip. Do you write large or small? Mine, you see, is small. I thought once of being one of those individuals who write the Lord's Prayer on sixpenny bits. There is great scope for ambition in it. You begin with the Pater Noster, going on to the Creed; and end up by cramming the whole of the Epistle to the Corinthians on to his Majesty's profile——"

She was still standing near her husband, as though to defend him. She said without moving:

"Then you must write what I have to say to your sister."

He sat down quickly and obediently, sideways on the chair, and dipped his pen.

"I can't go at speed. And I won't answer for the spelling. But my pen, such as it is, waits your command."

She began, looking down at Flusky. He had dropped his hand from her waist, but she still stood near. The young man knew that she too was afraid lest his casual indisputable sentence might have gone home.

"My dearest friend, I may call you so still, I believe, and I do so with a full heart. Your brother will have told you something of my history and situation, but he cannot have told, for he does not know, how gratefully my husband and I look upon him, how happy we are to have him as our guest——"

The young man looked up from his scribbling to bow.

"She will not credit all this. She knows me too well. Tell her more of your own concerns."

"——to have him as our guest while he looks about

him in this strange new Continent. We cannot hope long to detain him, having few distractions to offer——"

"Few distractions," Adare repeated, scribbling, and a series of pictures displayed themselves to his mind's eye; the dinner party; his hostess's entry, plunging among the notables like the figurehead of a vessel in tall seas; a human head among the nuts and raisins.

"Have you got that down?"

"I have. And what a lie it is!"

"Alethea will take my meaning."

"Proceed. 'Few distractions'——"

She seemed to read something of his thought, and could not again catch the thread of her own. The impulse to defend was ended, memory of the words which had set it in motion had begun to die in her mind.

"The four lines are filled up."

"You have no notion of my capacities. I can fit in a Lord's Prayer more, at the very least."

"Then say: I should be as happy to welcome you, my dearest Alethea, did Fate but permit it. I remember you daily, and with affection. Pray write, pray think of me. The time seems so very long——"

The young man wrote, and turned, waiting.

"Long since we met, long till I hear from you——?"

"Whichever you please." But the young man knew that she too had spoken the truth unconsciously, and that the sentence might stand without addition. "I send you from this distant country, hopes for your truest well-being, and my fondest love."

"That takes me to the margin. I have left this corner where you may sign."

She took the pen he offered and wrote in slender sloping characters her full name; Henrietta Flusky. Her keys swung forward as she stooped, and rang against the wood of the desk.

(xvi)

In the morning Mr. Adare woke and looked at his watch. It showed half-past eight. At first he mistrusted it, hearing no corroborating movements below in the house—women's voices, dull encounters of chair-legs with broomheads, the sound of feet on the verandah. But his watch was faithful. He lay awhile listening to those other moving sounds which, with the quality of the light, gave the exile daily assurance of being from home: locusts were choiring, and in the distance, among the woods of the Domain, a laughing jackass mocked the folly of those who willingly exchange old worlds for new. But Mr. Adare could not, as on an ordinary morning, enjoy the kookooburra's good humour. Like other lazy persons, he liked his days to be set in a frame of other people's methodical observance of the claims of time; to know shaving water ready and ignore it; to be made aware of breakfast by appetizing smells at the appointed hour, and turn over again in bed.

He sat up, therefore, feeling cheated by the house's

drowsiness, and began to dress. There was no hot water outside his door. He cursed, but only as a matter of form; the water in his jug was tepid as water may well be after a night when the temperature has kept somewhere in Fahrenheit's eighties, it would serve his purpose very well. He noted, taking out a stock, that his supply of clean shirts was running low, and supposed that the laundress would soon vouchsafe others. The little mirror revealed an appearance as trig as any saunter down Dublin streets would demand. Satisfied, but inquisitive as to the morning's changed routine, he went downstairs. The secretary was coming through the baize door.

"Good day to you, Winter. What's doing?"

The pale secretary flushed, hearing himself addressed in the manner of an equal, and answered:

"I'm afraid, sir, there may be delay. The women took this chance to lie in bed a while longer."

"While the cat's away—hell's delight of a cat, too. What was it happened that other day in the kitchen?"

"I was the instrument of that woman's rudeness, sir. I don't care to remember it."

Pitying him, Adare let it go, and turned to another aspect of Miss Milly's departure.

"Do you suppose we shall get any work out of these creatures now she's gone? I look to you."

"I'll do what's in my power."

"Come with me now, then. Show me the geography."

The bound man pushed the baize door open, standing aside to let the free man pass, and they went through.

Miss Milly had laid down her sceptre some sixteen hours only; Mr. Adare, who had never before entered it, could hardly be aware what great changes had come already upon her dominion. Copper saucepans, scoured the day before, still shone upon one wall; the stove, having no work to do since yesterday's dinner reached a close, still kept its lustre. But the floor was littered with shoes not cleaned, among which a black woman sat, rolling her baby from knee to knee, and coifing it with a colander. A pile of vegetables in one corner had not been sorted; the mould they brought in with them had been trodden in and carried over the floor. Odds and ends of female clothing lay about. There was a smell of grease. The usual noise, too, had changed its quality. One woman sang, one shuffled feet to the tune as she scratched among her hair with a fork; and old Sal the fence, seated by the table snipping rind off bacon with a scissors, loudly instructed the black woman in such English phrases as her experience suggested might come in handy.

"Go on, you heathen covess. Alderman Lushington. Say it after me, the missus has been voting for the Alderman, say."

They did not observe the two men until Adare spoke. He was used at home to something not unlike this kitchen, a place full of noise and irrelevant characters, unknown tongues and something very like squalor, to which, when he had slept disgracefully late, he came to wheedle tea and slices of toasted bread. He advanced, therefore, saying amid the uneasy silence which fell:

"Isn't there anything to eat? By the row, anyone'd think you were laying the eggs for breakfast."

The prisoner women laughed, the black woman wrapped her baby in a cloth pulled from the table, and sidled away along the floor like a crab with her booty. The secretary slipped out of the room again, very quietly. Old Sal rose from her chair, and curtsying, assured Adare that he was just on the nick, that the breakfast would be with him if only he'd give them time——

"Time, is it?" said Mr. Adare, pulling on the vernacular like a glove, "I should have thought you'd enough of that, with what the judges at home gave you."

The recipients of three and seven years' hard labour received this comment upon their misfortunes with hysterical approval, but old Sal possessed a sense of dignity which transportation had ripened.

"I'd have you know," said she, "me lord, that whatever I may of done was from kindness of heart. Don't you go for to put me on a level with these, though I won't say but they're good girls—"

The other two women at once began to recite, looking at each other, and finishing on the old woman's behalf what was evidently a peroration perfectly known to them.

"——for it's my kind heart what brung about my downfall. And what I says is—when a woman follers her heart—she follers the road to ruin."

Old Sal started up, the scissors gripped dagger-wise, to subdue them; but Adare caught her arm, and ceremonially offering his own, minced beside her to where the frying pans hung.

"Madam," said he, "may I entreat you so far to forget your just grievances as to break an egg into that? And as for these other fair females——" who burst out with a fresh gust of giggling——"if they'll demean themselves to fill a kettle we shall soon get going. Now, one more word. Which of you's the cook?"

At once a clamour began, old Sal claiming that by reason of her antiquity and rectitude she had the right to be so considered, the petty thief declaring on oath that she had been the late Miss Milly's pet pupil, apt at the stove.

"I'm no Paris," gravely said Mr. Adare, "but it rests with me to award the apple. Here's what we'll do. Take you each an egg and a rasher, and send them in to me in the dining-room fifteen minutes from now, on three dishes. As for which is which, we'll settle that, if you please, this way." He reached up to the mantelpiece and plucked from its decoration three paper roses, red, yellow, and white, which he distributed ceremoniously. "Each put her rose with her egg on the dish; and whichever sends up a rightly fried egg—not flattened out like a yard of flannel; soft in the yellow, with a milky kind of veil—whichever sends up the best egg shall take the office of Cook. D'you understand me?"

All three ran clattering for bowls and spoons. He halted them:

"Wait. Listen. Her ladyship will be here at ten to

give you your orders. You'll take her orders, do you hear? And curtsy. And call her my lady. And by God, if you're insolent, if I hear there's been the shadow of a shadow of impudence, I'll look to it." He took out his watch. "To work!"

As he left the room he heard another outburst of laughter, but the sound had no malice in it. He went to the dining-room. There Winter, plate-basket in hand, was laying the table with amateurish awkwardness.

"That's a man! Is Flusky down yet?"

"Mr. Flusky was working with me at seven o'clock, sir. He's ridden into the city—some appointment."

"Well now, that's a pity, because I'm going to bring his wife down to breakfast." Winter ceased his laying of forks and knives to stare. "We'll make a day of it. What flowers are there in the garden? Go and pick some, we'll have them by her plate. A little bouquet. Go along now, you've put flowers together to please a woman before. The table's done."

He ran out, and upstairs. Winter obeyed, went out into the morning sun, and gathered slowly, savouring this illusion of freedom, such tribute as the dry summer soil afforded; oleander, a stiff lily gilded with its own pollen. The birds in this garden were more brilliant than the flowers. A troop of visiting parrots surveyed him from their tree, flashing lavender wing-feathers, cocking their heads knowingly to show a spot of crimson on either cheek. They sidled and fluttered, and suddenly swung upside down, the clowns of the air, brightly

habited, grotesque. He went towards the tree, and in
alarm they were off with a great beating of wings, their
colours lost as they became silhouetted against the glare
of the sky. Winter returned to the assembling of his
bouquet, which was stiff and scentless. He tied it, however, with a twist of clematis that gave out the faint
pleasant aroma of lemon, and went indoors to lay it at
the head of the table. As he stood fingering it he heard
voices; and filled with shyness—for though he could
forget his position talking with men, he never failed to
recollect it when a woman spoke—he made his way out
again by the window, and took refuge in Flusky's bare
room with the map hanging on its east wall.

Adare, bringing Lady Henrietta towards the light,
noted her haggardness, the shaking of her hands. She
said nothing, seemed bemused. He told her to sit down,
and putting the flowers in her lap as one might give a
doll to quiet a restless child, went to the dark cupboard
where he knew the decanters were put away. He shook
the handle vainly, and turned to her.

"Those keys of yours—lend me them a moment."

She fumbled at her waist, from which the hand fell
away empty.

"Upstairs. What do you want with them? What are
you doing?"

Her voice sounded almost shrewish. He pondered a
moment, took out his pen-knife and manipulated the
lock, which snapped back.

"I learned that trick young, on the door which guarded

my mother's preserves. And here I am overseas, where all the pick-locks go. The criminal never escapes his due, take warning by my cruel fate——" He was pouring, while he spoke, from a decanter into a glass. She could not see, and her reiterated question had a sharp note.

"What are you doing?"

He turned away from the cupboard, coming forward with the filled glass in his hand. She, looking past him, gave a shriek and sprang up, pointing and retreating. He remembered. The ugly head lay visible, tousled and fallen sideways, as though the decanters had somehow contrived to exercise their dominion even upon death. Adare banged to the cupboard door with his left hand and held it so, while he extended to her steadily, as a man holds food to a nervous horse, the glass filled with brown liquor.

"It's only the trophy—can't hurt you. Here, drink this up, down, whichever way pleases you best. That's it. Now you're steady."

She drank the brandy without gasping, gave a shudder, and set the glass clumsily down as she seated herself. She said, with a half-laugh:

"That thing—I see it sometimes in the night. It opens its eyes at me then. Sam paid ten pounds for it."

"It's hardly a mantel ornament, indeed. Are you better? Isn't that what you wanted?" She looked at the empty glass, at him; then covered her face with her hands. He talked on. "Of course it is. You can't do without all at once. It's like a man with a nagging wife, he feels empty for a while when she dies, for all he's glad to be quit of her. A drop more?" He surveyed her thoughtfully. "I'd say not. You shall have a dram about twelve, if you eat your breakfast like a good goddess."

"Ah, don't, Charles!"

"I'm not laughing. I grant I never saw a goddess go; but she might do worse than walk the way you do, when you're in command. Are you ready?" His voice promised entertainment. "I'm going to ring for our breakfast."

She spoke with petulance again.

"The women—Milly's gone. They won't know, they can't do anything."

"Wait!"

He listened. From the servants' quarters clamouring voices arose, wakened by the bell's thin sound. Adare sat down in his place, and primly, settling his stock, awaited the entry of the kitchen Graces.

Old Sal it was who first marched in, winking above a plated dish-cover. She sketched a curtsy to the lady of the house, set down her burden before the young man and stood back hands on hips, head cocked to challenge. The younger women deposited their dishcovers to right and left of old Sal's, and stood back too, menacing each other with glances. One spied the empty glass by the lady's place, and loudly sniffed; but the moment was too solemn for this impertinence to afford her full satisfaction.

Lady Henrietta looked astonished, then angry, as they ranged themselves.

"What do you all do, trooping in like so many corporals?"

But Mr. Adare gravely rebuked her with his left hand; his right was lifting the dish-covers. This done, he drew back, contemplating with a connoisseur's eye the three fried eggs thus revealed, each nesting upon its concomitant bacon, each adorned in carnival manner with a tattered paper rose.

"Excuse the creatures. They had their reasons for coming all together." He looked up from the eggs. "The roses, you see, might have had the misfortune to get shifted about, unless each one escorted her own."

Lady Henrietta, wholly uncomprehending, gazed at him, at the three platters, and at the three faces behind the young man's shoulder. He, meanwhile, was delivering judgment in detail.

"Yellow rose. Her effort lacks shapeliness. It has a tendency to sprawl; an uncontrolled and (pardon the phrase) blowsy egg. No prize for Yellow Rose. White, now; let me see. Round enough, the veil drawn delicately over the yellow, which yet, I fear——" He took a fork and lunged with it; no trickle of yolk rewarded him. "Ah! The unforgivable sin, the stony-hearted egg. Failed, White Rose. Alas for York! Let's see what Lancaster can do." He raised the third cover, sat back, surveyed. "Lancaster promises well. All the qualities are there; this egg is a very pretty production to the eye.

Now for the test." He plunged his fork; the yolk ran out in a copious flow. "Aha! Lancaster has it—You, what's your name?"

Above the noise that greeted this decision, the voice of the murderess (with extenuating circumstances) could be heard ardently crying:

"Me, Mister! Flo, Mister! It's me the red 'un!"

He hushed them down, beckoned Red Rose forward, and presented her to Lady Henrietta in form.

"Allow me to suggest for your ladyship's consideration this candidate for the high position of cook-in-ordinary to your ladyship. She will do as much as she's made to. She is a bit of a rascal, is Flo. I humbly submit that she has passed with credit a strict examination; not appearing now to great advantage, by reason of a smutty nose and intellects astray, but a willing sort of miscreant, I'd say."

The willing miscreant dropped a curtsy, according to the implications of that traditional verb, with its suggestion of inadvertence and clumsiness. Lady Henrietta, for the moment steadied by brandy, could laugh, and summon enough control to dismiss the women. When the three had passed, wrangling, out of hearing, she said, suddenly dejected:

"I can't. I haven't the power any longer."

"Lord, but I'll deal with them! I'm Grand Vizier to your Sultana."

"No, no."

"What's the matter?"

She answered dully:

"I have been coming to life. It is unbearable. I can't face it." She struck her hand on the flowers, again and again, seeming to take pleasure in belabouring their beauty. "I am useless. Even if I overcome myself I'm useless. The best thing I can do is to die and have done."

"Everyone's in the dumps the morning after. I'll give you another dram."

But she shook her head, and began to torment the flowers between her hands.

"You don't understand me. I'm thinking of him. I've done him wicked wrong, so many, many times. Wrong to love him, wrong to marry him. I was my brother's murderer, and he paid for it." She halted. "No children." The voice rose again strongly. "In this new country I make him a laughing-stock. The only thing I can do now, the best thing I can do, is to die."

"You're the apple of his eye, and you know it," said Adare, out of his depth.

"If I died, he could marry the sort of woman—Milly would do. Poor Milly, with her religion! That's why she put the bottles in my room." She laughed. "Couldn't marry him, you see, with me in the way. Couldn't take a pistol and finish me outright, that would be sinful. So she set about it this way—killing no murder. For years." She shook her head. "But I'm very strong, you see. And then you came, and now Milly's had to go away. All wasted."

"Well, by God!" Adare was standing, flushed, unbelieving. "You knew she was trying to take your place, killing you, giving you drink. You knew what she was at!"

She found his incredulity absurdly out of proportion.

"The only queer thing was her doing it as a Christian. She often said that. A Christian woman. Ha!"

Her laughter was brief. Adare, the morning's gaiety wholly subdued, stared at her. The eggs, the bouquet, alike were neglected. He was at a loss. She spoke rationally and kindly, leaning towards him, the civil hostess explaining.

"So now you see how it is. I am obliged to you, I like you very dearly. It is beautiful, what you have been trying to do for me. But you only hurt me and hurt him. It is not any use."

"Are you saying I must go away?"

She seemed, at that, to come out of her bitterness as from a trance. Her two hands were stretched to him:

"Charles, Charles! It's only because it can't last, having you here, and I can't bear it alone."

That cry of weakness gave him the ascendancy again. He came to her chair and knelt by it, his face very serious.

"Listen. I am no more in love with you than with Britannia on the penny. You know that."

"I know that."

"Nor you with me."

"Nor I with you."

"But I treasure you, Lord knows why. Perhaps because I've never been able to write poetry. I've wanted to, Lord knows. There's something in me—

but it can't get out that way. Nor by my hands. It looks as though I've had to come half across the world to find the way out, my way to beauty. You're the only chance I'll ever have to make a lovely thing. If I can give you back——"

She said, harshly interrupting:

"It's like giving a gold coin to a man crying for water in the bush. I'm useless, useless."

The young man lightly shook both her arms, on which he had laid his hands.

"You'd die for that man."

She cried out:

"Oh God, I would! Only I haven't courage to go quickly."

"But the whole thing is to live," said Adare loudly, holding her arms: "To live!"

"I'm not strong enough. I can't, Charles, I can't indeed."

"I won't let you. I won't have you take your beauty, your fineness, and lay it away underground, like the man in the Gospel. I won't let you break yourself, and that poor devil that the sun rises out of your bosom for."

"Too long! Too wretched!"

"I'm here, I'll stay, I'll help. Day by day, the small things—do you remember the list of duties I wrote for you? Ah, don't, for God's sake, give in, don't let it all go!"

She was silent, eyes closed, head drooping. He laid his forehead on her knees, still murmuring like a lover: "Don't, don't, my dear!"

She gave a deep quick sigh, and put a hand under his chin, lifting his face. They looked at each other through tears. She spoke, gently now, and with a wondering tilt in her voice:

"You and I are nothing to each other. How can you do so much?"

"Friends. That's what you've been needing. Love's too highfalutin for this kind of job, too high-stepping; the chaser in the dray."

"I can say things to you that he would not understand. But for him I'd die, and for you——"

"Darling woman, you're a beauty and a queer one, something out of a fairy hill. But my heart doesn't jump to be like this, holding you. I don't go blind with you."

They were silent, so close that each could see the tears, feel the warmth of the other. She spoke:

"Help me. I'll try."

"You'll try. You swear? Cross your heart?"

She made a little gesture with the point of her thumb upon her breast.

"Cross my heart."

He got up, blew her a kiss, and to ease the tension of their spirits began laughing at himself and her.

"*Amor vincit omnia*. The poets again. Fools, how little they know! All love could do for you was to fill you up with gin. Down with love, and let's have breakfast. Eheu, the prize egg's cold!"

BOOK II.

And *Dido*, that suffered for love of *Eneas*, had done as much for lacke of other Companie. This is the Natur of women: to goe to and fro, and knit up existence as they doe Stockings, a little upon a little. By Fables may a man take them, by steel can he not holde them, in them opposites Rime, their Commandments are writ upon Sand, not tables of Stone. For woman being conceiued in a Sleepe (Adam's I meane) is as dreames uneasie. . . .

—A Limbo For Ladies.

BOOK TWO

(i)

SIR RICHARD BOURKE, Governor of New South Wales, driving with two aides-de-camp on the evening of Patrick's Day, 1832, looked about Lower George Street, pondering:

"Too many drink-shops still. See about it, next time the question of licensing comes up before the Council. Plenty of fingers in that fire; dangerous to nip 'em. That's what did for Bligh."

The senior aide-de-camp, observing His Excellency's frown, took a sighting shot at its cause.

"I hear at the Club, sir, that Mr. Adare has been busy. He's prime mover of this ball, I understand."

"Young Adare?" The Governor recalled his thoughts.

"Well, sir, as an Irishman, naturally. St. Patrick, you know, ha! They don't often have this sort of festivity here——"

The gold-laced Captain spoke the truth. Sydney had in the past honoured Saints George and Andrew thus primitively by dancing; but St. Patrick, as a Papistical saint, had been neglected until the presence of an Irishman in Government House could lend him some tinge of the Established Church, and so entitle him to the ritual tribute.

The matter once decided, two committees had been formed. The ladies, after a succession of tea-parties, produced a strongly-worded resolution to the effect that shamrocks made of paper should be employed in the decoration of the hall. The gentlemen, among whom Mr. Adare was foremost, in the course of a single meeting, determined upon the best supper money could buy, and the band of His Majesty's 4th Regiment of Foot to set the dancers going.

These essentials thus driven like pegs into the social consciousness of the city, further decision and determinations were hung upon them; as, the price and colour of tickets, the place of assembly (Temperance Hall), the hour, and the nature of dances to be rendered by the band. In the matter of this last, a jury of matrons decided unanimously that the licentious waltz must not defile their programme. Country dances were to be the order of the evening, with a quadrille or two by way of proof that Antipodean school mistresses could turn out as genteel and well-drilled young ladies as any seminary at home. This done, the tickets were issued at two guineas a head, and began to fly into the farthest corners of the colony, even to those outer darknesses beyond the ranges registered upon Mr. Flusky's map. Delicate spinsters contemplated without dismay a journey of two hundred miles in a cart, their finery stowed under the seat. Gentlemen, damning the whole affair as nonsense, dipped in their pockets to further it. Clergymen, benevolently smiling, approved "an innocent festivity,

such as cannot fail to weld together in a spirit of fellow-
ship the better elements of our society." Hotel-keepers
along the roads doubled their prices for bait and beds.
All this bustle lay behind the aide-de-camp's innocent
statement that Sydney did not often enjoy such a festivity.

The Governor broke in upon his attendant's polite
babble.

"Do you hear anything more of young Adare? He
has not been to see me. I suppose he is in no difficulties
yet?"

"Well, sir, as to hearing—— Of course, things are
said, but I don't pay attention to gossip."

"You're wrong," said the Governor briefly. "There's
a lot to be learned from gossip. Napoleon thought so."

"Indeed, sir?" The Captain risked a laugh, but
sobered at once, perceiving no echo from His Excellency.
"Well, the fact is, there's a story, my wife got hold of
it; a story that the young man is rather too warmly
interested in a certain quarter."

"Flusky's wife?"

"They say so, sir. I don't heed that sort of thing——"
He broke off, swallowing the disclaimer. "Our housekeeper, you see, was in Flusky's service, and left the
house by reason of this—ah—intimacy. I don't care for
the woman, myself; Milly is her name. However, my
wife vouches for her being sober, and she can certainly
cook."

"What's Flusky's attitude, did you learn?"

"Oh, calm, very calm. Won't hear anything against

either his wife or Adare. So the woman states."

"Adare's to be here to-night, you say?"

"One of the committee-men, sir. Sure to be present."

The Governor resumed his reckoning of the number of grog-shops as the coachman sedately, with no undue use of the whip, made for Temperance Hall.

Temperance Hall was situated at the farther end of George Street, a St. Anthony of buildings beset by public-houses. Eight or nine lay within that radius known to the freer-spoken colonists as spitting distance, and for perhaps three hundred and sixty days in the year they held insolent triumphing sway, regarding the Hall as their wash-pot, and turning out swarms of drunkards to cling about its very pillars. But on the evening of Patrick's Day the Hall eclipsed them. Lights danced in its windows, bunting adorned its doors; and from the hour of seven-thirty vehicles rolled towards it, chariots, gigs, britzkas, four-wheeled chaises, carriages closed and open, raising an impressive dust, and affording the public-house supporters scope for scornful comment:

"Look at she, with the feathers in her hair! Scratch cockie! Snow's* cheap to-day. Watch the old girl toddle, she'd tip over if anyone give her a shove. Hooray for the General, look at his whiskers! He rubs lag's fat on 'em at night."

They had, however, this population of sub-respect-ables, a cheer for His Excellency Sir Richard Bourke when he appeared in his carriage with outriders.

*Snow = clean white linen.

"Bite the land sharks, me lord. Trial by jury, and to hell with the mili-tairy! A leg-up for lags!"

Sir Richard acknowledged these cries civilly, a hand to his hat. He wore evening dress, but uniforms swarmed about him and lent his most ordinary movements, of a gentleman entering upon an evening's entertainment, something of the precision and glitter of the barrack square. He was received by the Committee's six or seven prosperous gentlemen, ten or a dozen ladies in their extravagant best. He shook hands with them all; the clasp offered to Mr. Adare was neither more nor less hearty than that awarded to his coadjutors, but there was a brief exchange of words:

"Charles, I hope you're well."

"Never better, sir."

"A most successful function, judged by numbers."

"And beauty, sir?"

"I have not yet looked about me."

"Wait awhile," said Mr. Adare, smiling. The Governor nodded, and passed on to the dais festooned with flags—no rebel Irish green among them, but someone had contrived a blue-painted shield with a harp upon it, which served as a brooch to hold the draperies of the platform together here and there. He bowed to those known faces in the crowd that made way for him as he walked, noting the while in his administrator's mind:

"Must be a thousand people present. Too much flimsy stuff, too near the lamps. However, plenty of ground-floor windows. A great mix. Many hundreds of strange faces and, by Jove, strange get-ups too. All classes represented. Don't care for shaking hands with pickpockets and resurrection men, all the same. Prejudice, that. Got to end. It will take time, though."

He was on the platform by now. The military band did its duty by the National Anthem: and all the travelled young ladies, all the exiled regimental sprigs; all the publicans and their wives; all the landowners, sheepfarmers, surveyors, physicians and their wives; all the ironmongers, haberdashers, undertakers and their wives; all the supervisors of the Convict Establishment, ticketof-leave men, emancipists and their wives, formed up in line with a view to experiencing the joys of rapid motion under his Excellency's patronage and eye.

They danced to tunes a year or so out of date, with delightful names borrowed from operas and pantomimes: *Love's Frailties*, *A Day up the River*, *The Matron of Palermo*. Hands four round, went the rustic ladies and gentlemen, bustled by more knowledgeable town dancers, back again, down the middle, up again. The experts, clustering together in a set, attempted more difficult fantasies; top lady and gentleman cross over with right hand, back again with left hand, *balaneza la poule*, and *poussette* to place. Corinthian skirts with three and four tiers of ornament swung round the sterner Doric of masculine trousers. There was a pretty chinking of military trappings. Heads, as they bobbed and twirled, revealed ringlets, short hair oiled and brushed to the rich polish of a boot, wax flowers jerking briskly upon springs, natural flowers drooping, ribbons perked into stiff bows, carved combs, and an occasional Prince of Wales erection of feathers. The men's heavy-coloured coats, red, blue, black, stood ranked at times as though to overthrow the muslins; these yielded, fluttered, stooped to conquer, and at length triumphantly advanced upon the uniforms, with which they mingled, obscuring them from view. The sound of the dancers was in itself a whole orchestra; shuffle and thud of feet for drums, violins of voices humming the air, piano-like rattle of speech, with now and then a laugh shrilling out high as a piccolo. The lamps in their holders jumped and flickered, paper shamrocks with their trembling marked the rhythms; gusts of noise, gusts of movement enlivened and belied the character of Sydney's Temperance Hall.

His Excellency was determined not to dance. He possessed a leg which served him faithfully on such occasions, a notorious leg, part of whose calf had been torn away by a bullet in Spain. It did not affect his walk even in rheumatic weather, but he permitted it to debar him from ball-room pleasures, smiling while he reflected that the philosopher may find cause for satisfaction even in an ounce of French lead. The ladies of the Committee, to whom those subtle Mercuries, the aides-de-camp, had made the Governor's disability known, were unanimous in worded pity for it, and unanimous in their inner silent comments: It will make things easier, no unpleasant discrimination, better none of us than a few. One problem remained, and this they pondered, while they balanced their fans, and settled their laces, and furtively shook their heads to ascertain that the three-piled decorations were still in place; glancing at each other, and totting up those noughts added to nought which made the sum of precedence. Who should have the honour of tucking a gloved hand within his Excellency's bent arm on the way to the board? Above their pre-occupation they talked with him, the stately wives, with a fine assumption of carelessness, and echoes of the far great world.

"Really almost gay. Though to one who remembers the social gatherings of London and the Continent——"

"It is our sons, your Excellency, who most feel the lack of superior schools. Do pray, for the sake of us poor mothers, establish something. We cannot expect an Eton here in the wilds——"

"The worst of a new country, your Excellency, all the gentlemen have to work. They have not leisure to be elegant."

"What is the Court news, your Excellency? Is it a fact that the Princess Victoria still plays with her dolls?"

Dear ladies, commented His Excellency's thoughts, dear women, rather; why can't you let the social aspects alone? Why must you carry all the old prejudices and all the old petticoats round your legs in this new country? You are necessary, you are model wives and mothers, but you are deuced ineffectual as fine ladies. I wonder which of these is the creature who has got Charles into her toils? Hard to tell; there's none drunk that I can see.

"—thank you, I am very well entertained, madam, I assure you. I don't move in Court circles to any extent. A soldier, you know——"

Tirelessly below the dais the dancers manœuvred. The clock at the end of the hall, accustomed to record with lagging hand the progress of temperance eloquence, moved briskly towards the hour of supper. The ladies eyed it and each other, calculating chances, and precedence, which in the best of all possible worlds is victorious over chance. Their thoughts reckoned up the other female occupants of the dais, alike and fateful as cherry-stones; Mrs. Advocate-Judge, Mrs. Colonel-Commanding, Mrs. Admiral, Pothecary, Ploughboy, Thief. If his Excellency was aware of the silent contest for his favour he gave no sign, but sat jigging a foot to the twelfth repetition of *Le Garçon Volage*.

The tune was slackening, amid clapping of hands, curtsies, and descending ohs and ahs of regret from the dancers. The Governor's fingers pressed the arms of his chair, he was rising, when at his ear sounded the voice of his sixth cousin.

"I don't know the etiquette, which of you I present to the other. I think, though, you're not altogether strangers."

Sir Richard stood, with an instant but unspoken appreciation of the young man's impudence in bringing the woman along as though he were her husband. Lady Henrietta's red coronet of hair drooped to the representative of the King. Over it he saw for an instant the faces of the ladies whose consequence was legitimate and unsullied, and heard himself saying, while his eye assessed her beauty and the consternation that it was causing:

"We have met already, indeed, but it was long ago."

She answered easily:

"That was in Ireland. There was a bay horse, Cuirassier—but you may not remember."

"A fine performer! I could never forget Cuirassier."

"—you had him from my father. None of us could hold him, he was vicious too. We exchanged, do you recollect? And you by some magic made him into a hunter."

"By Jove!"

Sir Richard's memory was darting here and there, proffering recollections garnered by three senses. A red-haired girl in a close habit, riding with frantic courage and no judgment at all; the smell of steam rising from Cuirassier's shoulders as he pulled up at the end of a gallop; a sound of talking in the open air, subdued, so that no signal from hounds might be missed. The creature! ejaculated the voice of his mind; and whether that expression of admiration might apply to the woman or the beast, he did not at the moment know.

"By Jove, he put me to some trouble. Broke a bone or two. Do you ride still?"

"There is no great inducement in the summer."

"True. Dust, no shade—In the winter, though, something might be done. There was a foxhound pack once, they tell me, when the 73rd were here. I don't know about foxes, but there are dingoes enough——"

The clock's hand was pointing reproachfully to an hour ten minutes after supper-time. An aide-de-camp charged with the mission of voicing public impatience delivered himself tactfully:

"Supper, sir, is ready. When you choose, of course."

His Excellency, so careful of precedent, so discriminatingly aware of public opinion, permitted himself for a moment to appear absent. With the most natural air, talking as though he had not finished what he had to say, he offered Lady Henrietta his arm. So smoothly was the movement executed that the dispossessed ladies supposed themselves beholders of a genuine inadvertence, and with humorous tolerance and cluckings accepted undistinguished customary arms to the supper-room. Only a naval wife, catching Mr. Adare and halting him on the way to supper as a rock may halt a leaf on a stream, loudly put the question they all had in mind:

"Is it true that she's the daughter of an earl?"

For this was the crux. Beauty, after the manner of their kind, they could forgive to no woman; but drinking and a convict husband, with accompanying legends of indecent exposure and brawls—these in a genuine ladyship might pass. Other wives paused, intent to hear the answer.

Mr. Adare reassured them. Genuine old title, Irish, eccentric; genuine old castle, full of shrieks as Otranto; genuine lordly and lunatic relatives all over the

West of Ireland. No deception, ladies and gentlemen.
The wives conferred, deferred, reached a conclusion.

"An earl's daughter, you know, keeps her precedence.
One would not wish, in this far corner of the globe, to stand
upon ceremony. Still, one is aware, one knows one's world,
one is only too happy, one understands how to behave."

Thus the more impulsive and milder ladies. But the
naval wife, in the best bluff tradition of her service-by-
marriage, came out plump with:

"All very well, but I don't see at all why these people
should be above behaviour. My husband was at Palermo
as a lieutenant, he's seen Lady Hamilton's many the time
come aboard half-naked, and half-seas over too. Why
should the wretches have all the privileges?"

Mr. Adare needed only to laugh. The naval broadside
had not done much damage, as he perceived. Ladies,
ladies! He was profoundly happy; more than one pair
of eyes noted and stored the fact away, matter for gossip
at some convenient time. He was too much for them.
He was on top of this small world as a man might be
who has written an unforgettable word, or struck an
eternal posture out of marble. The ladies could not tell
what energy moved him, but were obedient to it; their
thoughts dropped from moral heights to the supper-
table, as eagles readily drop from their palaces of cloud
to a dead sheep fallen under a bush. They were practical
women, as became the wives of pioneers, and to the
practical mind there is no lasting sustenance in the
chameleon's dish.

Adare, needing solitude, found an excuse to depart out of the radius of the ladies' smiles. He went through a door, up a stair, very dark and leading he knew not where, but which had a kind of ventilator pierced in that wall giving upon the supper-room. By this ventilator he stood, peering down, seeking Lady Henrietta with his eyes, and soon finding her. She sat on the Governor's right hand in a dress the colour of a Colmar grape, purple, but having a silvery bloom in the folds of it. He had seen that dress fitted, had advised upon it, she standing laughing, and holding a shawl modestly about her white shoulders. Flusky coming in had seen them thus, and after a moment's contemplation had said something about jewels; how about rubies? They both cried out No, no, with one voice, while the sewing-woman squatting on the floor looked up astonished, muted by her denture of pins. Flusky had said nothing, abruptly going out. Adare recalled now something ominous in that sudden turn, but was not overtaken by any compunction. The man was free to do as he chose, the man might have stayed and laughed with them, and welcome. He had not chosen. He was absent to-night. He is missing something, thought the young man at his peephole, wistfully, that you'd think any husband would give his ears for. Look at her, look at her, my lovely creature that I made out of a drinky slattern, a boozy frowsy poor slut with no friend but her bottle of gin.

She was the only woman wearing no jewels; the only woman with her hair low and smooth on her neck; the only woman who could turn her hands and her head divinely, like the movements of a swan. She bent to the Governor's voice, and it was the stoop of a poplar before wind. She handled her glass, and he thought of that legend of the Queen of Scots, how wine could be seen passing down her throat, it was so white. Her voice he could not hear, but it sang in his mind, a little husky, monotonous and sweet.

All at once he felt limp, as though virtue had gone out of him, and sat down on the stairs with a quick sigh. Finished, the work of art. What of the artist, who the hell cares for him, left empty and purposeless, forlorn?

(ii)

FORLORN! A sound, chiming with that word in his thought, brought him back again to his sole self. It was a movement, a rustle. He said, smoothing hair dishevelled by his own plunged fingers, instinctively tweaking down his waistcoat in the dark:

"Who's that, who's there?"

The sound shifted upwards, a stair creaked. He moved after, stretching his hand before him into darkness, and closed it round an ankle; closed it completely, thumb and finger-tip just meeting. A good beginning anyway, thought the young man, coming out of his melancholy with the rush proper to his age; let us discover more.

"Don't be frightened. Why are you here? This is a silk stocking, it ought to be under one of the tables."

The unseen person gave a brief laugh, but pulled in her breath after it. He went on, fingering the flounces of the dress:

"Muslin. Worked in sprigs. What will it look like after these stairs? How could you use a poor muslin so?"

The unknown retreated a step higher, pulling her dress out of his grasp, and fairly ran upwards, her slippers hardly sounding, but all the petticoats and their frills swishing like the last lap of a wave spreading its lace on a beach. He followed, two stairs at a time, and caught her as she wrestled with a door-handle. His fingers closed over hers, which were cool and rough. He had not expected that roughness, it checked him a little, so that she was able to twist the door open without further interference; when she tried to bang it, however, his foot was in the way.

He looked with interest at his quarry. An oil-lamp swung in the centre of the room—it was an office, fly-blown, its sole beauty the square of window framing stars—and this showed a young girl, short, frail, her dark hair atrociously sown with gum flowers, looking at him resentfully. She had a small pointed face like an animal, much too wide between the eyes, the mouth much too large; she had been crying.

"What did I tell you?" said he, nodding at her flounces. "You're all cobwebs. Mab could dress Moth, Mustard-seed, her whole court off you."

The unknown at this for the first time broke silence with a solitary syllable, disconcerting him:

"Who?"

"The fairy queen; Titania, Mab. Don't they have fairies in this country?"

She looked at him uncomprehending.

"What business have you got sneaking after me?"

Poor child, thought Adare. The voice was rough as her hands when it could be heard in a whole sentence. He said:

"I thought perhaps I might help you——"

"Bender!" interrupted the girl with entire scorn. He could interpret this. The three assigned women, that odd team of harpies which he drove by alternating flattery with boxes on the ear, constantly used the expression to imply dissent or incredulity. Oh yes, I'll make haste—bender. We'll all marry lords—bender.

"I did, though," he repeated. "You were crying, weren't you?"

"What of it?" said the girl, drawing her hand defiantly beneath her nose. "Can't I cry if I want?"

"Not at a ball," Adare said gently. "It's not the thing. No, you certainly mustn't cry at a ball."

"A lot you know," said the girl, again with that laugh drawn in like a sob. She turned her back on him. "I don't want anybody, see? Go away."

Adare shut the door, then came behind her. For curiosity, and because a medley of sentiments were stirring in him that he could not interpret, he took her

wrist as before he had taken her ankle, between finger
and thumb. The finger overlapped this time by an inch
or two. When she shook her arm to escape, he let her
go at once.

"Why d'you touch me? That's gentlemen for you."

"I beg your pardon," said the young man. "I didn't
mean to annoy you."

"Why do you do it, then? Why are you after me like
this? Let me alone, I tell you."

She kept her shoulders turned to him, picking to
pieces, as though she hated it, an ugly flower that had
dropped from her hair.

"Is there anyone I can bring to you?"

He meant any relative, any comfortable person on
whose shoulder, should she feel so disposed, she might
cry, and he was astonished to see the curve of her cheek
turn red as though he had slapped it. She faced him.

"I don't want your charity. I don't want partners."

"Well, then, madam, if it isn't unreasonable to ask,
what do you come to a ball for?"

"Oh, get out," she answered roughly. "I've told you
before I don't want you."

This was no way to address a young man whose spirit
was up; a young man, moreover, beginning to assess
the sullen eyes and mouth at a value by no means
low.

"Are you sure?" said he.

The girl was silent, new to this kind of impudence.
He liked the colour across her cheek-bones; she had the

sallow skin of all currency* women, and the patches of red became her.

"Are you sure you won't let me offer you an arm, and escort you downstairs, and find the wing of a chicken for you? Why do you keep me here among the cobwebs? A bottle is the only right place for cobwebs——"

"I keep you here!" she said, helplessly angry. "*I* keep *you!*"

"Put it to yourself, now, is it likely I'll go away and leave you to cry all alone? Even to be angry is better; more becoming, too. It is my duty to stay here and torment you till you come to a better frame of mind. Besides, I am a committee-man, the success of this ball is my affair, I am affronted when the prettiest of all St. Patrick's patrons runs off in a corner to snivel."

"You don't get round me that way."

"What way, then? Tell me, and I'll march round and round you like those old Bible fellows at Jericho. Tell me how I can make you endure me."

"Very funny," said the girl.

"It was not meant for a joke. It is only my way of talking."

"Why can't you go and talk to all the swells where you belong?"

"How do you know where I belong?" She did not answer. "I believe you know my name. I believe you've had your eye on me all the evening, if the whole truth were told."

*Currency = Australian-born.

"Oh, go away, go away!"

"Listen," said he, changing his tone instantly, "I don't know what's troubling you, but there is something that's certain. If I can help, tell me. If I can't, I promise I'll go."

"You can't. Nobody can."

He bowed without the satirical flourish he had at first intended, and said, looking at her eyes, dark-set, but blue perhaps by daylight:

"Good night, then, madam."

On the words, they both became aware of a change in the quality of those sounds which had run beneath their talk. The bourdon of conversation, human noise, had been steadily sustained; above it flickered, in sharp differentiation, noises inanimate, chinks and clashes of glasses and knives. Now for a moment all these died, a single voice could be heard calling something not to be distinguished. Immediately the human voice rose, again, and another inanimate sound with it, a rumbling of wood upon wood, chairs being pushed hastily back, while the voices took a higher pitch. It might have been only a loyal toast, and the ending of supper, but for some reason neither of the listeners in the office could think so. As they stood, a scent crept to them, carrying warning.

"Wait," quietly said Adare to the girl.

He opened the door. The smell of smoke was not to be mistaken. He went quickly downstairs past the ventilator, through which he caught a glimpse of people moving with the slow urgency of a blocked throng; he reckoned up and rejected this opening as a chance of escape—too small, the drop on the farther side too great. The smoke was thick, he had difficulty in breathing in the darkness, but he reached the door at the stairs' foot and opened it. A blast of fire rushed in upon him, so that he threw up his hands instinctively to shelter his face. He had one thought; I must get back to her. He pulled the door to, shoving his hand through flame, and fled upstairs through the smoke, holding his breath lest he should cough and so stifle before he reached the upper room. He reached the top, gasping, and shut that door too before he looked for her, and saw a white shape at the window blocking out blue darkness.

"Don't," he called. "Wait. Give me a moment—the smoke——"

She turned her head, and to his astonishment, almost his indignation, saw that she was laughing. She spoke out the window:

"That's the way, mister. Set it up, we can drop to it."

A man's voice outside said something, which she answered with a sudden screech of laughter, and a colloquial:

"That's right."

"What is it?"

Adare was beside her, whooping the fresh air into his lungs. Staring down, he could make out a square-covered cart below, drawn by a pony. A man was standing upon its top, setting a ladder against their wall. He could hear the shoulders of the ladder scrape upon bricks four feet or so below the window.

"A danna-drag," she answered. "Are you any the wiser?"

He was not; when a further witticism came from the rescuer, and was answered, still he was at a loss.

"You go first," the girl ordered; "it's nothing of a drop. Hold by the sill."

"Pardon me," Adare answered, humour coming back to him with his breath, "but which of us two is the damsel in distress?"

She laughed again at that—she was excited, the red still barred her cheek-bones—and took the oil lamp from its suspensory ring, holding it so as to illuminate the window; for the first time she looked at her gallant, dishevelled, stock pulled undone, and eyebrows burnt off.

"Looks as if it's you," said she, grinning. "Go on, show the way."

"I'm damned if I do. Women and children first."

"Well," said the girl, judicially, "there's plenty time. Hold the lamp, then."

He took the lamp, holding it awkwardly in his scorched hand. She hesitated, turned half from him, a tribute to modesty, and unhooked, untied, somehow loosed her flounces, which dropped round her feet. She jerked her head at them, advancing to the window.

"Drop 'em after me."

Then with a neat swift movement she was over the sill, and he saw her two little red hands strongly clutching for a second while her feet searched in air. They loosened their grip, disappeared; leaning out, he saw that she was almost down. He picked up the petticoats and sprigged skirt, waited till she had her footing and was looking up, then tossed them. The man on the cart, receiving one soft drift of white, found something jocose to say which Adare, in a puzzle with his lamp, did not hear. At last he put it out, straddled the sill, easily found the ladder and descended to the cart's flat top. There the rescuer, an individual who smelt unpleasantly, could be heard saying, between hiccups of laughter:

"Done for a jump, mister! Well, that's a new one. That's plummy, that is. First time anyone's due to have a medal for knapping a jacob.* You was on toast without it, though; you was, proper."

Adare agreed to as much as he comprehended of this speech, and sought the darkness for his companion.

"Are you quite unharmed?" he called. "Miss ——" but what the devil was her name? "Are you safe?"

"Ha!" commented the man of the cart, with an indescribable weeping snort. "S'help us, her in her kickseys and he don't know her name."

Adare hit him as decisively as darkness and the uncertain footing would allow. The man cursed and fell backwards to the ground, where he lay. Adare leapt down beside him.

"Come, get up out of there. That's for what you said. Here's for what you did."

*Jacob=stealing a ladder. This misdemeanour usually the preliminary to crime, was heavily punished.

"Eh?" said the man, bewildered. "You'd no call to do a thing like that, mister. You was on toast——"

"I know, I know. Where's your hand?"

The man rose grumbling; two half-guineas, the only coins Mr. Adare's pocket contained, were pressed into his hand, and he heard his assailant-cum-benefactor say, on top of a shrill whistle:

"Why, damn it, my fist's grilled like an underdone steak!"

The cart's pony, which during this interlude had budged no more than a sphinx, seemed to wake from a doze and moved forward. His owner, feeling the weight and milling of the two coins in the dark, called out the tribute money can always command:

"You're a gentleman, mister." He added, as an afterthought: "No offence, I hope."

"Where's the lady?" said Adare, peering as the cart moved, and its conductor ran to hook his ladder to the back.

"She won't be far," returned the man, and burst into another laugh. "Fancy, it ain't what I'm used to collecting, by no means, not of a night."

Slowly, clanking, the cart moved off, and Adare could discover no girl behind it. One petticoat lay where it had fallen, but she had assumed the rest of her attire and fled. Adare picked up the petticoat idly, then with a start recollected the reason and occasion of its discarding. Fire, fire! He could hear, coming from the other side of the building, the unmistakable confused echoes that are waked by that cry; and throwing the petticoat over his shoulder, impulsively ran.

Into George Street the fine ladies and their escorts were herding, while from the steps of the Temperance Hall officers cried, in parade-ground voices, reports and reassurances which nobody heeded. In the poor light of coach lanterns and half a dozen street lamps the crowd eddied, unwilling to disperse and leave a clear way for soldiers with pails of water; bound by half a dozen different spells the dancers lingered, by a shawl left in the cloakroom, a husband not yet seen safe, desire to miss no excitement, expectation of some spectacular rescue. Pickpockets, upon whose hopes such a gathering descended like manna, filched with neatness every fob, handkerchief, snuff-box or purse to which Mercury guided their fingers. There were one or two feminine faintings, with masculine bawls of "Stand back there!" Coachmen sardonically looked down from their boxes. In the windows of the circumferent public-houses lights sprang up mockingly, and persons arrayed with no thought for propriety were displayed leaning out. The only thing lacking to this scene was that which had, presumably, set it in motion. There were no flames, though from a window or two smoke listlessly eddied. Voices near Adare were suggesting that the whole affair was a plant of the tinny-hunters.* All at once he remembered Lady Henrietta, his creation, his triumph in a velvet gown.

*Tinny-hunters = persons who avail themselves of the confusion caused by a fire to steal what they can.

"Is everyone out?" he asked his neighbour.

"Everyone, I couldn't say," the neighbour returned, in the sardonic currency voice Adare could never get used to. "The fire is."

(iii)

" 'An event,' " read Lady Henrietta aloud, " 'which might have had unfortunate, not to say tragic consequences, occurred in connection with the St. Patrick's Day Ball, held last night under the auspices of His Excellency and the *élite* of the Colony. Some tasteful draperies with which part of the ball-room was festooned, took fire, owing to the too close proximity of a lamp, and a wooden partition, together with some of the instruments of the band, was wholly consumed. Owing to an early alarm the conflagration was prevented from spreading, and no damage is reported, as we go to press, save to the sensibilities of the ladies, whose evening's enjoyment was cut short in this most alarming manner. His Excellency'—do you really care to hear all this?"

"I know the next part. His Excellency brought Lady Henrietta Flusky to her coach and sent her home, leaving her escort to find his way to Woolloomooloo as best he could."

"We could not find you. You were not at supper. Where did you hide?"

"Answer me a question first. Is it or is it not good manners, *de rigueur*, to return a lady's petticoat?"

145

"Charles!"

"Not in that voice, if you please. Secondly, allowing that such a return is *de rigueur*, how does one deduce the lady's address from a simple tab with her name worked on it in cross-stitch?"

"Suppose you tell me the story."

"How can I? I don't know the half of it. What, for instance, is a danna-drag?"

"Do you really not know? It is the word out here for a night-cart, the men who go about cleaning the privies."

"Ha!" explosively said Mr. Adare. "So much for romance. Now your book hero, your opera hero, would rather expire in a thousand torments than owe his life to such a machine." She laughed. "There, you see, my rescue becomes ridiculous at once. I won't tell you another word. However, I may let you interpret the tab for me."

He produced it, an inch or two of tape on which the name S. QUAIFE was worked in red. Lady Henrietta took it, looking at him as she did so with a question which he forestalled.

"It may stand for Selina, or Susan, or Sarah. I'm no wiser than you."

"But you would like to be wiser?"

He moved his right arm restlessly back and forth in its sling, got up from his chair and moved to the mantelpiece.

"How the habits of posture cling! Here we are with the thermometer at ninety, still I move towards the fire.

It is the Englishman's right, and the Irishman's too, to keep a woman in the cold with his coat-tails when he wants to put her in her place."

She asked no more. He went on:

"It is the merest vulgar curiosity on my part, I assure you. I am not the man to be caught by any sharp-spoken hussy with a heart-shaped face. Yes, that was the shape; her hair grew down in a dip on her forehead, and her chin ran to a point. But if you assure me that one does not return a petticoat, of course I shall not pursue the matter further."

She said after a pause, putting the tab away in a needle-book:

"Let us talk about the Governor. He spoke of you: asked so kindly after you. I told him—something."

"Blackened yourself to whiten me, I'll be bound."

"There was no need. The Governor hears more than we suppose. Charles, if he should make an offer, pray consider it."

"I believe you want to get rid of me." He was naïvely astonished that she did not look up, smile, and instantly deny this. "What? You do?"

"That is not the way to put it. I think it might be as well for you—not to be any longer here."

"I see," Adare answered slowly. In fact, his mind's eye had, upon those words, drawn a picture of Flusky's attitude on the previous evening as they were setting out for the ball, and of a gesture made by him as his wife slipped a hand within his arm. He had put the hand away from him. Adare, remembering, glimpsed for an instant the intolerable burden of the man's debt, unwittingly contracted and now grown too heavy to repay. His poet's imagination for which words afforded no channel assured him of Flusky's suffering, allowed him to compassionate it; but he could find no formula to express the complex situation other than a blunt: It must be hell to owe your wife to another man. Aloud he repeated:

"I see. Well, since that's the case I'll put my pride in my pocket."

She looked up quickly, gratefully, but said nothing. The newspaper lay still on her knee, and she availed herself of the chance it offered to avoid further difficult explanations.

"Shall I read on?"

"Do. I cannot manage, swaddled up like this. I like your voice, besides; your well-fitting o's and i's. How I detest vowel-sounds cut on the cross! I could never love a woman that spoke so. Let me have a list of the goods coming up for auction. I like that best."

She began in all seriousness to read:

" 'Mr. T. Smart will have the honour to offer for public competition on March 30th at 11 o'clock precisely, 1 gross of egg-spoons, a second-hand gig, ship biscuit, baby linen, 1 bass-viol (damaged), castor oil, 3 canary birds, Bohemian glass, a superior Europe feather bed, and the effects of a deceased clergyman——' "

(iv)

THE two men sat after their evening meal (which had been indifferent, a descent from the feasts of Milly's reign) in the silence which had come to characterize their association. Lady Henrietta was with them. She had eaten nothing. The glasses at her right hand all were empty, as were those set by Flusky; only in Mr. Adare's were dregs of amber and garnet still to be seen, and by him stood a pair of decanters. The twilight had none of the calm of an English day's ending; a southerly breeze was relieving one of the hottest twelve hours the Colony had ever known, and clouds the colour of lead and blood were driving before it. The evening had a restless threatening quality, not brooding mischief but marching towards it, as though night were to be the signal for outbreak. All three persons at the table were aware of this uneasiness in the atmosphere, and two at least were glad of it, since it afforded a physical explanation for the apprehensions which beset them.

A cry, sudden and abandoned as the yelp of an animal, made Adare set down the glass he was twisting; Lady Henrietta clapped hands to ears, her mouth for an instant drawn square. Flusky, looking indifferently down towards the bay, said:

"One of the gins. Ketch is back; uses up a lot of wives."

"What use is an infernal savage like that to any one?" said Adare, sharply. "Why d'you let them camp there?

Why don't they gaol all these murdering devils, and keep them in gaol?"

"Well," said Flusky, with composure, "he don't do no harm. He has his uses, Ketch."

Adare was becoming conscious, through his irritation, of the ugliness of the thing he had said. He took some more wine, aware that he did not want it, and that the heat of the evening made drinking unwise, because he was at a loss for a movement to cover discomfort.

"He's come back with a yarn," Flusky went on; then, as if checking a confidence: "but you can't believe all these coves say."

Adare said idly: "I don't know how you make out their yabber. Worse than Irish. What's the yarn, as you call it?"

Flusky took a sip of water; then rose, and going to the window put two fingers fork-shaped to his lips. The whistle carried; it ran down the wind as down a slope. The cooee that acknowledged it sounded robust but far, so that it was astonishing to see, within fifty seconds of its utterance, the black outside the window, greased, and reflecting their table's light from cheeks and shoulders. His face was so marred with confluent small-pox that such skin as had escaped the sores stood up here and there in ridges like scars; his teeth were gapped as the ritual of his tribe prescribed; the whites of his eyes were bloodshot with dust. He stared eagerly at Lady Henrietta, who looked away from him. Flusky, standing square, tossed him a cigar, which the black immediately stowed in his mouth to roll and suck at. Adare had seen enough of the aborigines to find them repulsive rather than strange, and he had no great hopes of the promised yarn. Still, since his chair faced that way, he continued languidly to survey Ketch, whom Flusky addressed:

"You tella where you done been, what you find, Ketch, you sabby tell budgery."

"Yuna bo ta bang wiyunnun tuloa,"* the black began. Flusky interrupted roughly:

"Stow that, nobody sabby's that talk. Piyalla English, you sabby plenty. Say out what you told me."

"Kabo, kabo," the black answered, making placatory movements of his hands. "Ketch bin gone mountain, long, long——" He indicated illimitable distance with a hand pushed forward three or four times. "You gib Ketch lush?"

Flusky poured from the decanter by Adare's elbow a tumbler of wine, stirred a spoonful of mustard in it, and handed it to the black fellow, who swallowed it unquestioning, glared a moment as the mustard bit his throat, then rubbed his seamed chest, nodding and grinning, approving the power of the draught.

"Plenty budgery. Plenty strong. You gib?"

He held out the tumbler again, which Flusky put back on the table.

"That's enough. Get on, talk."

The black rolled his eyes piteously upon the other two white persons, but perceiving that they were in no mood for almsgiving, began his story. It sounded, from

*Indeed, I will speak the truth.

the scurry of the words and the lively movements of the teller, to be one of continuous adventure; sentences tripped over each other, the hands continually eking out their meaning, sketching the flight of a bird, the cast of a spear, the shape of a mountain, the twists of a river. Adare understood nothing of it, and soon ceased the sport of trying to catch words. Lady Henrietta looked at her husband, then past him to the burdened racing clouds.

Ketch at last checked his story, and fumbled among the necklaces he wore, a medley of animal's teeth, corks, and the handles of cups strung on sinews from a wallaby's tail. He found something and held it forward between two fingers for inspection. Adare cast an indifferent glance, then straightened in his chair. The object was a flake of quartz; one side glinted as he turned it.

"God, Flusky," said the young man, keeping his voice low, "surely that's gold?"

"You gib," said Flusky to the black; and when Ketch hung back, made a movement towards the tumbler as though to refill it, at which promise of a bribe he untwisted his treasure.

"It's gold all right," Flusky answered after deliberate examination.

"Ask him where he found it. Ask him if this was all."

"Near the Fish River. Some gully near there."

"You gib," Ketch clamoured. *"Minnung bullin bi?** You gib lush."

*What are you doing?

Flusky filled the glass with the same mixture, while Adare turned the scrap of stone and metal this way and that under the light, inviting Lady Henrietta to admire it. She looked troubled, could find nothing to say in wonder at the white stone veined with gold. The young man at Flusky's side asked for more details with an eagerness he was now at no pains to conceal. Flusky shook his head, and taking the quartz from him, casually returned it to the black with a jerk of dismissal. Adare kept silence while Ketch retreated, imagining this indifference to be part of a plan; then broke out with suggestions and devices.

"There must be more. Let's get an interpreter to question him—no, that won't do, of course, we don't want the whole Colony to know. How are we to get it out of him? How far is this river, has it been surveyed, are there roads?"

Flusky answered soberly:

"I only brought him up for the lark of the thing; something to do. You don't want to take it for gospel."

"But it's gold. It must be gold!"

"It's gold all right." He paused. "Did ever you hear about a cove called Parker?"

"Who, Nosey? Does that mean I'm asking too many questions?"

"Parker was a prisoner, got away from a road gang. When they found him, he had a lot of this stuff, stowed inside his shirt. They took the shirt off him, and the hide, too. He died, not so long after."

Adare stared at the square white face, the motionless hanging hands; looked to Lady Henrietta for enlightenment, but she was frowning; came back to the charge.

"But why? How long ago? Gold means wealth to a country, surely?"

"But it don't mean wealth where it's wanted, see, and that's why." Adare, incredulous, was beginning to argue; the thick hand cut off his words. "Gold's found; as soon as that gets about, what happens? All the population goes after it, shepherds, farmers, useful men out of the towns. It pulls away all the labour. Land's no good without labour. And there's a lot of people here own land. Government included. I go in for land myself."

His explanation ended with that sentence. What followed was in the nature of a commentary. "So, you see, they don't let it get about."

"You mean, this man Parker was killed to silence him?"

Flusky did not answer. A sheet of lightning blanched the room and all three faces for a moment.

"It's coming," said Lady Henrietta under her breath, beginning to reckon on the table with fingers the seconds that heralded thunder. Ten, twelve, fifteen——

"But a private individual—if you were to find it, or I, for instance; they couldn't touch a private individual. Parker was a prisoner. What could they do?"

Twenty. Thunder began to rip and mutter, coming up, like a discoverer blown by storm, along the coast from the south. Adare gave a laugh when it ceased.

"The Government! I don't believe it. It's money in their pockets, too."

"I only know what I've heard. Parker wasn't the only one. Surveyor McBrian found gold in the river up near Bathurst. And there's a road there never got finished; improperly surveyed, they said, and shifted the road gang to Newcastle. I'm only telling you."

"I can't believe they're such damn fools. I'm seeing the Governor to-morrow——"

"Charles! Are you?"

"A message, this afternoon." He returned to Flusky. "Have you any objection to my making enquiries? Discreetly, of course?"

Flusky, hands in pocket, shook his head, and poured out water into a tumbler. Adare called:

"Look out, that's the glass the black fellow used."

"So it is," Flusky answered, rinsing out the dregs of claret and mustard before he filled it again and drank; then said, mildly raising his eyes: "If you want, you could come and look at my map."

The map, a white space on which black symbols indicated the fall of water, lift of mountains, and those places where men had set temporary hearthstones, was coloured by Adare's imagination as a child fills in with chalks the line-drawings in a book. He had talked to men who knew the country, remembering their casual descriptions. He had turned over drawings in the Surveyor's office, and ridden towards the Blue Mountains with some of His Excellency's young men. With pleasure his mind projected the details of a journey. Plains first of all, yellow in the rainless autumn weather, whirlwinds of dust stalking on them, tall as the fisherman's jinn. Then ranges, similar as ridges left upon sand by the outgoing tide, above which crows flew level and eagles soared spiralling. Storms moved high above these hills with an escorting rattle of barren thunder. Winds from the north-west, constant as compass-needles, pointed towards country known as yet only to the black hunters, rich only in their food; grubs, snakes, tree creatures. Beyond this the rivers sank to links of ponds, or failed altogether, the earth gaped in broad cracks ancient and lifeless as craters of the moon. In such country, destitute of everything that gold could buy, gold reflected the sun unheeded; in piles of dirt scratched up by dingoes, in rocks whereon the blacks scrawled with soot and clay the hieroglyphics of their priesthood, in the roots of lean trees overturned by wind.

Adare, gazing at the map, went forward to the beckoning of this imagined thirst-defended gold. Flusky's voice came to him as though from a distance.

"Gold means trouble. Gold don't do nobody any good."

(v)

His Excellency said, looking up from papers:

"Glad to see you, Charles. Sit down. I won't keep you long."

The young man, however, strolled to a window, and looked down across bleached grass to the bay. It was singularly blue, and large ships rode close to shore; deep water there. On Dawes' Battery soldiers in red coats, coifed with tall shakos that left their napes bare to the sun, were changing guard. Not a child watched them, not a dog. Heat prevailed over curiosity.

"Well, Charles?"

"Sir." He turned and came towards the desk, standing by it. "I'm sorry our social endeavours the other night ended in smoke."

"I heard you'd been hurt."

"It's nothing." Adare shook his hand free from its sling. "My own fault. Tell me, didn't you fall in love with my Lady Hattie?"

"She's a beauty, poor woman, no doubt of that. To look at her——"

"To look at her you wouldn't think she was scandalous, and you'd be right."

The Governor did not take up the challenge. He began to seek among his papers, talking:

"You've had three months of this country now. You're acclimatized. I take it, too, you've learned better how to conduct speculations in land."

"You are right, as it happens; there is no speculation in these eyes." He checked. "It was an odd mistake for Flusky to make, of all people. He must have known the applications would go to you."

"Are you so sure it was a mistake?" The young man

stared. "It served his purpose very well; got you out of my house into his."

"He couldn't have guessed you would take it so hard. No, that's far-fetched. He's not such a Machiavelli as that."

The Governor dropped the subject.

"And the poetry? How does that go?"

"Oh, the poetry," the young man answered, inexplicably smiling. "Not so badly."

"Would a project of action appeal to you?" Adare gave consent by his silence, sitting down upon the edge of the desk to listen. "Fortescue is setting out on an expedition with a limited objective——" His Excellency found the paper he had been seeking. "You will hear historians talk of rivers as arteries of commerce. In this country they are life-blood. Mitchell was gone off before we arrived, to survey the Bogan; that was a Government project. Dixon, too, is one of our men. Fortescue is a private person, but he has Government backing to this extent: we will acknowledge his discoveries very handsomely on our maps, and he has authority from me to risk his own existence and that of anyone he can persuade to accompany him. He proposes to take ship along the coast—it is the shortest route—to a spot above Port Macquarie, and thence strike inwards. We know little, as yet, of the river that runs into Tryal Bay; or of the watershed inland, from which perhaps other streams are distributed. Three or four months' wandering, with the chance of giving your name to some mountain, or other conspicuous natural feature. What do you say?"

Adare answered, rather absently:

"Port Macquarie; not near the Fish River, is it?" The Governor did not answer, looking his astonishment, and Adare went on rapidly: "I have heard that name somewhere lately. It stays in my head. Who is Mr. Fortescue?"

"Dine to-night and meet him."

"Very happy." He stood up, half-laughing. "I suppose there would be no objection, if we found a reef of gold on the way, to our bringing some of it home?"

"Gold?" His Excellency looked up sharply. "The first thing every fool hopes to find in a new country."

Adare answered as crisply:

"Why the devil not?" He knew he had spoken with too much abruptness, and turned it off. "Every man hopes to be rich without working. You are an Irishman yourself, we are all of us on the look-out for the leprechaun's crock."

"A lot of good his crock has ever done. Look at the Spaniards, they found it in Peru; and now Spain's choked with the stuff, dying like King Midas. No, no, Charles, be said by me. If your services on this expedition are adequate, there'll be no difficulty about a grant. Get land, don't waste time listening for the tap of the little man's hammer."

Adare was silent. The Governor stood up, offering his hand. "I expect you to-night, then. My regards to Lady Henrietta."

"You made a conquest there."

"She is a fine creature. Very great beauty, great charm."

"Very."

"It is remarkable, for she must be, let me see; yes, she must be over forty."

"Not a doubt of it. The dangerous age."

His Excellency drew back from this thrust and parry, aware that the young man had become defiant for some reason, and put on the official again.

"I will endeavour to have someone from the Surveyor's Office this evening, with maps. No reason why you should not take advice, as far as advice may carry you. Will six o'clock suit you? Till then."

The young man, turning down the left-hand sweep of Government House drive, past a sentry retired into his box to escape the sun, walked by the Secretary's offices, and so by way of Bridge Street to the centre of the town. There in George Street he found a cleanly-looking barber's shop, had his hair cut, and listened to New World gossip as it drifted to him from the neighbouring chairs; prevalence of influenza among sheep up-country, a project of growing tobacco in the Colony—"all right, but how about locusts?"—the recent public execution of a thief. There was no little discussion of this last, until the barber at the next chair pronounced with authority:

"Harper strung him up neat enough, but he had time to kick. It wants what I call the hand. It's something you can't teach a man. There's no call to let 'em kick, not if a man known his job."

Adare, head bent forward to allow the scissors' play upon his neck, recorded this utterance in his memory. To each man his conscience in art, thought he. But he was unprepared for the next comment, which came from a personage with the appearance of a turnkey:

"You'd never ought to have given it up. There's work enough, with men taking to the bush every week. You did ought to have stuck to it."

The authoritative barber shook his head, delicately tilting his client's head sideways with a finger and thumb straddling the nose.

"There's not a living in it. I haven't got only myself to think of."

"Tell me," said Adare, low to his own attendant, "is that individual shaving my neighbour the hangman?"

"Was, sir. Was. Retired a year ago and set up here."

"Does he do well?"

"Well? Yes, sir, nicely, he's got a wonderful light hand. It's a nice connection."

The proprietor looked about him, razor in hand, lacked something, and with the strong crook of his little finger pulled a bell-rope that ended in a loop of twine. Someone entered, pushing aside the curtain at the back of the shop.

"Towels, Sue."

Mr. Adare, idly raising his head, saw in the mirror before him a remembered profile. He sprang up, making a small commotion, sending a brush to the floor.

"It's you! Good day to you. Why didn't you wait?

I lost you the other night. I hope you took no harm."

The girl halted, and a flush brightened her eyes before she looked down at her apron.

"I was all right."

"Who's the gent, Sue?" That was the proprietor, indulgently smiling, but with a steady suspicious glance.

"At the ball the other night." She vouchsafed no other explanation. Adare perceived that the adventure of the escape had been left untold, and might remain so. He was aware, also, that in such circumstances it would not be *de rigueur* to return her petticoat. He repeated, elaborating, his first greeting:

"I hope you took no harm with all the flurry of the fire."

She neither answered nor departed; she was looking at his sling. The other customers stared at them both, and Adare became conscious that once again he presented no very heroic figure, with a towel about his neck and his hair, untutored by any final combing, in disarray. He bowed and waited, unwilling to sit down again until she should be gone, aware of her father's eye upon him. For he had jumped up to greet her with a spontaneous gladness which astonished himself, and the flush that ran across her cheek had gratified something which he supposed must be his vanity. The proprietor strung up their embarrassment neatly and finally; not a kick was left in the situation when he had done with it.

"Towels, Sue. Are you done, Mister? There's others waiting."

Adare accepted the fiat, and did not await the girl's reappearance from behind the curtain. He looked at the sign as he passed out. "Vigors," it read, in letters large and faded; above, inconspicuous, the words "Quaife, late," indicated the shop's present owner, and the value that he set upon his predecessor's good-will.

"That's how I missed it," he thought. This was nothing less than an admission that he had been on the look-out for possible bearers of that curious name. Stung, he moved on, but turned inexplicably after a moment to survey the house again. As he did so, the curtain of a window above the shop was drawn with a brisk clash of wooden rings. He knew why, and stood his ground, looking up. The curtain did not budge again. Nevertheless, putting his uninjured hand to his hat he swept it off, and felt the sun's full weight on his forehead for five seconds or so. Passers-by observed him. He stared them down, resumed his hat, cocked it as well as its width would allow, and strolled on.

(vi)

THE picture composed in the withdrawing-room of the house in Woolloomooloo came within no catalogue description; it was not a conversation piece, nor a genre picture, nor wholly an interior, for two wide windows stood open on to the bay, and the fires of the blacks' camp could be seen from them. Two personages held the eye. One was a woman sewing, holding a thick white sock, manipulating her needle awkwardly, drawing too long a thread right and left to make the web; the lamplight, flaring and drooping, gave her figure primary value. The other, sprawled out of the lamp's range, was that of a man in dark trousers and jacket, bulky, motionless. Hands slid into pockets, slippered feet crossed, he sat still, for sole occupation eyeing the go and come of his wife's arm, into the light and out. A clock, of which both were unconscious, assumed the rôle of a third individual; one who betrays secrets he is never told.

Although in the room no one spoke, unless the clock's monotone might count as a voice, sounds enough entered, each carrying its implication. From the bay came the grating of wood upon sand as a boat was drawn up for the night. The blacks sang like dogs round their fire, drawing great breaths, launching a high note, and dwindling down the scale as their wind failed.

*Morruda, yerraba, tundy kin arra
Morruda, yerraba, min yin guiny wite mala.**

Their curs howled with them. Frogs protested. Nearer, the voices of women in the kitchen never ceased, and upon the path that ran below the window footsteps moved with regular beat; Mr. Secretary taking half an hour's exercise after a long day at his desk.

*The white man walks on the road in shoes,
His feet-fingers are no use to climb trees.

164

"I am sorry, Sam, that the dinner was not good. I have not Charles's knack with the women. They are insolent and lazy, and I can't be at the trouble of perpetually scolding and teaching."

"I'm not grumbling."

"You never grumble."

Silence again, and the clock's insistence: time—time; going—going; gone—sirs; gone—sirs; gone.

"I wish Charles would come home. I am so greatly concerned to know what has happened, the Governor's plan for him. Sam——" the hand ceased its weaving —"you must help me persuade him."

"It's his business."

"You brought him to this house. You owe him, we both owe him very much." A restless movement came from the figure outside the lamp's circle. She resumed her darning and spoke while appearing to give the sock entire attention:

"I have thought sometimes lately that you might be glad if his visit were to come to an end. Was I right, is that true? No, do not answer, I know words make you uneasy. But perhaps it would be better if he were to go."

"Let him stay if you want him."

"Sam, sometimes I wish you would or could be a little more open. I never know what you are thinking and planning. It is my own fault, do not suppose I blame you, it is I who have failed. I have been the worst wife any man ever had——"

"Stow that. None of that."

"No, but I want you to understand that I know what I have done. I have come to know it, and—let me say it, let us clear the air as far as we can. I am very sorry."

"What have you done?" She looked towards his chair, saw him coming towards her, and held a hand to him.

"You know how I have failed you. Publicly shamed you—that dinner-party, I cannot remember, but I do not forget it. It was not the first time. But it shall be different now. I think I have the strength now." She spoke slowly, gazing at her shiny halted needle. "Sam, do you remember what you told me once, how you looked through the window when my father and I were at dinner? You were riding that tall mare, Pope Joan; you could not have seen, otherwise. That was the beginning. How far it has led us!" He was standing by her; she put her hand on his thick arm and heard, coming back from memories, the clock chanting without emphasis its requiem for time. "Both of us to this country, and you to fortune, and me to—I don't know, I can't tell yet. Isn't it a strange thing, Sam, I see what I have been doing as though some other person had done it. That is not the way to change and become better, is it? Not to forget the past; one should remember and be sorry, and build upon it. It was because I had not courage to remember that this all happened, this wretched failure——"

He said nothing, responding in no way when suddenly she laid her cheek to his sleeve. She began to laugh.

"I wish I could train you to talk. I have often wished the same thing with a dog or a horse. What interesting different things they would have to say, seeing us from their own standpoint as they do! I would sometimes like to be able to make words I could understand out of the wuff-wuff you bestow upon me now and then——"

As though in answer to this wish, going away from her and settling suddenly in his chair again like a large dog lying down, he began:

"Milly's gone to some captain's wife."

"Milly! Did you see her, speak to her?"

"Not me. They were talking."

"Who, Sam? What did they say?"

"It's what she's been saying."

"About us?"

"Some of us."

"What does that mean?" Before he could answer she went on. "She disapproved of Charles. I suppose some legends have been started. It will give all the ladies something to talk of. They must be grateful." Flusky continued to look at her, defenceless in her circle of light, from his ambush in shadow. "Charles—I suppose they have made him out my lover. How absurd it sounds! How——" A gesture of the hand, forsaking the silks for an instant to lift and drop, showed better than words could do how powerless over her heart, how preposterous was young Adare regarded as a lover.

"Hush, what's that?"

They had both become accustomed to the secretary's

pendulum swing on the path below the window; the cessation of his steps served now as interruption. They heard voices, one breathless, as of a man who had come fast up the hill.

"You, Winter? I've been down there with Ketch and his pack. They stink prodigious awful. 'However, the poor jackals are less foul (as being the brave lion's keen providers) than human insects, catering for spiders.' "

"I don't know that—sir."

"Byron. I'll lend it you. You can't speak their lingo, can you? Ketch and Company? Never mind. Is anybody up still? There's a light."

The two in the room heard his steps mounting quickly, then an interim of quiet while they crossed grass, then sounding again on the verandah boards. Adare stood at the window, arms stretched wide to support him as he leaned in.

"Domestic peace, salute! Here I come, fresh from Government House. There is a kind of tickling on my shoulders as if epaulettes were growing there. I'm thirsty. Why don't we all have some tea?"

Lady Henrietta nodded towards the bell, Flusky from his ambush observing her face. It was frankly welcoming, the mouth was parted, the eyes bright as a smile half-closed them. Before Adare could reach the bell, Flusky, stretching out an arm over the back of his chair, gave the rope a tug, and they heard a jangling in the kitchen which produced but a momentary effect upon the conversation there.

"That won't get so much as a stir out of them, let alone wet the tea," said Adare.

He turned, and in the darkness ran along the verandah to where the kitchen-window opened, round a corner. They heard a sudden silence from the women, then a whoop of laughter.

"Sam, what precisely is it that Milly has been saying? I laughed, but it is dangerous, perhaps, to let it go on."

"That's right," Flusky agreed soberly.

"Is there anything we can do?"

"Plenty."

"Will you look to it? You are more in touch, more able to deal with such matters than I."

"I'll look to it."

She gave him a little nod of thanks before she began to fold her wools, and they waited silently for the tea. It came, heralded by voices in dispute.

"I never give a civil word to a man at the back door in my life."

"There's plenty of other things you can give to men at back doors."

"Never, don't I tell you! I'm a good girl."

"No doubt of it. Give us a sermon next Sunday."

"You want Miss Milly for that. Sermon! She'd ha' lined her kickseys with hymn-books."

"Pretty thought. Now be off to the back door again. Give me the tray; sell your virtue dear. Don't take a farthing less than sixpence, as you value my regard."

Adare appeared with the tray. He set it down, and

stood negligently pouring the tea, talking the while.

"I begin to depend upon this national drink. Do you observe, in the generation growing up, a yellowish tinge of countenance? In China they are yellow, too, for the same cause. But we absorb beakers where they swallow thimblefuls. We shall be mahogany in two generations, while they can never advance beyond a paltry lemon. Observe, I say 'we.' That is because I am now finally resolved to leave my bones here, after I have done with them. Is this how you like your cup?"

She said as she accepted it, lively eagerness and interest in her voice:

"How went your dinner-party?"

"Fortescue—I told you about Fortescue?—was there. (Flusky, you take sugar, I think?) We did not agree. His Excellency my sixth cousin made the mistake of telling each one of us beforehand what a fine fellow was the other. Result: detestation immediate and irrevocable."

"No expedition, then?"

"Oh, yes. Certainly an expedition, if I can raise the money. But not with Mr. Fortescue. What do you say to gold?"

Lady Henrietta, looking up startled at that word, saw her husband's steady eyes fixed on the young man. Her lamp had been moved to make room for the tea-tray, it no longer allowed him his hiding-place of shadow, and she could read very well the expression which showed for an instant and was gone.

"Gold! Not with Ketch, Charles. Not that gold——"

"And why not, my dear? If, as I said, I can raise the money. Not much; but we want equipment. Shall we say, a hundred pounds?"

He looked at Flusky, as did she. They talked to each other, but Flusky with his silence was calling the tune. He spoke after a little.

"How much?"

"Blessed words!" Mr. Adare set down his teacup. "Does that mean you'll help? I knew it. You're the King-Emperor of good fellows, Flusky."

Lady Henrietta on impulse, on the memory of that single second's glimpse, cried out:

"Sam, no! Don't offer, don't give it him."

Adare turned in genuine surprise.

"What's this? Who's been at me this past month to do something with myself? What's the matter?"

"If you go with the Governor's man, yes."

"My dear, here's a great to-do you're making. Where's the difference between going after gold we have proof of and going after some tomfool river that may not exist?"

"If you go with Ketch," said she slowly, as though in fact she saw events unrolling before her fixed eyes, "he will lead you where he chooses, and leave you to die, walking in a circle in the bush. Then he will plunder your clothes and weapons, and disappear. That is what it is intended should happen."

"Listen." Adare was sensitive to her distress. "I'm not going alone. Listen quietly. There was a fellow there this evening from the Survey Office. Thomson is his name. He detested Fortescue as much as I did. (Priggish, self-satisfied, counter-jumper!) We walked home here in the cool. Thomson is no fool, he is a geologist by nature, and he performs to perfection those mysteries with rods, poles and perches which are Greek to me. In addition he can read—say, rather, he is aware that books exist, and are of a heavenly uselessness. Mr. Fortescue, on the other hand, supposes that books are things kept by double entry, which serve purposes in lawyers' dens. Thomson, like his namesake of the Seasons, is all for binding the nations in a golden chain. At the close of our walk I took him to see Ketch's necklace. He pronounces it gold."

"It is, it is gold," she said, beating her hands together. "That is the bait in the trap."

"Trap?" He turned, following the direction of her eyes, to view Flusky, sprawled in his chair. The big man was smiling. Now, paying no attention to the emotional atmosphere, he repeated his question:

"How much is wanted? How much did you reckon?"

"Two hundred apiece for equipment and food. I have a hundred of my own left. Will you lend me the rest? And take half my share in anything we find. I hope, for your sake, we'll be lucky."

Lady Henrietta came across the room and dropped to her knees at her husband's side. The movement, wholly impulsive, yet had some too dramatic quality due to her height and the sweep of her dress.

"Sam, don't lend this money. I am asking you something with my whole heart."

Adare lightly clapped his hands and went to lift her.

"Bravo! Now for the husband's curse, and the snowstorm of paper."

She resisted the pressure of his hand on her arm, insisting, eyes on her husband's face:

"Sam, I am asking you not to do this. Because of what I now know; I beg you; I will do anything you want."

Flusky patted her shoulder and rose, with a good-humoured nod to Adare over her head.

"Looks to me you haven't got a right notion." His voice was reasonable, kind. "You talk as if I wanted this young fool to go off after gold. I've told him it's not healthy; I'm sick of talking." He pulled her to her feet, and a slow shake of the head responded to her pleading. "You got to do me justice. I done what I could. I told him not to heed Ketch. You take me up wrong. I say it now, I'll say it as often as you like; Ketch is a liar, this gold's more danger than it's worth. He knows that. What more can I do?"

"You see," said Adare, gently adding his persuasion, "I'm only twenty, Hattie. I don't want to settle down to ploughing yet awhile. This is a new country, what's a new country for? Not to sit—no offence, sweet lady—in a woman's pocket. Wait till I bring back nuggets, a beautiful necklace like the one Ketch is wearing——"

"You fool!" said she furiously.

"Hattie! What's come to you?"

Flusky said nothing. He faced the two with a masculine calm that made her agony, expressed as it was in sudden sound and fury, appear a tale told by an idiot. Adare looked from one to the other, mystified. An explanation occurred to him. He lifted, simultaneously, his elbow a little and his eyebrows; Flusky gave a short nod. But she, from the corner of her eye, caught the interchange.

"Charles, no! Not that. I've not been drinking."

"All right, my dear. Sober as a judge. As a whole bench of judges. Of course you are."

The tone, humouring, tender, lent a last irony to her despair. She took a stride forward, tearing her dress; one hand went to her forehead, clutching and loosening the hair.

"Dear." It was the young man's voice at her side. "It's late. Won't you go up to bed? Don't be angry, Hattie."

"Is it no use, then, fighting? Can nothing ever be changed? No hope?"

This was spoken to herself, so softly that the men could take no meaning from the movement of her lips. She opened her eyes. Both were looking at her, and the same expression arrayed both faces; the tolerant masculine look, making allowance for creatures whose balance is less sure, whose emotions are gales which no barometer announces. She ran away from that look with a cry not articulate; ran blindly out of the room.

(vii)

LADY HENRIETTA, sitting alone in her drawing-room in the evening, held a roundel of canvas on her lap at which she did not look. It was the rustic design upon which her fingers had first re-learned industry, Chloe with her flock. Of this last, two sheep remained to be clad in French knots, the grass of the hillock awaited its green, and Chloe's crook its ribbons. She had begun to take up this canvas daily, at the same hour, and to sit with it on her knee. She did not draw the needle through the squares, but threaded it carelessly with any coloured silk that came first to hand, and waited. The hope possessed her that by setting out the inessentials of past magic, she might somehow stir into life the heart of the spell. Her memory found record of an ancestress, Dame Agnes, the Irish witch that diddled a bishop, waiting at cross-roads to command spirits, a peacock's feather held in her left hand. With just such imperative patience Flusky's wife waited, tormented with echoes.

"I'm no more in love with you than with Britannia on the penny."

The words would not take body, they remained echoes only. The voice that had spoken them was sounding —where?

She abandoned her passive conjuration, let the silks tumble, and began to walk the room haphazard. It was late afternoon, rainy, with a wind that made lugubrious music in he-oaks and pepper-trees. The fishermen's boats were drawn up; their nets lifted on poles resembled what she had read of the black tents of wandering Arabs, in Lady Hester Stanhope's life. "Lady Hattie Flusky in Australia Felix." It was the echo again, recurring to plague her; though she could not recollect when the phrase had been uttered, she knew it for his. She looked away from the nets towards the patch of rocks against which Ketch and his company were used to sleep, under piled slabs of bark. The blacks had quitted the place in a body some days after Ketch, with the two young men, had set out northwards. They gave no warning of their movements, but came and went with the unanimity of a flock of cockatoos, according as rumours reached them of plentiful food, or girls ripe to be wives, among those whom they contemptuously called the myalls, wild fellows, living beyond the white man's pastures.

Lady Henrietta, looking now at the patch of rocks which was their habitual rallying-place, perceived a thin and very blue smoke beginning to drift out from it; smoke which towered, then mushroomed, dispersing over the bay. She put her hand with an unthinkingly dramatic gesture to her heart, and watched, quite still, that smoke which was the black man's roof-tree, his standard, and the symbol of his dominion over the beasts. She could see no figures moving, the wind blew away from her any sound of voices there might be.

She opened the window, then, as the air struck cold, ran back into the room to pick up a wallaby skin from the floor. This she held about her shoulders, and, careless for her hair, went down the steps into the rain.

She reached the bottom of the hill and went rapidly on towards the smoke, of which a sweet medicinal gust blew her way now and then, until she could hear voices on the wind.

Their confusion grew louder; as at a signal, stopped. The blacks had seen her.

They were accustomed to the white men's gins, riding through streets, flowers unknown blooming upon their heads, sometimes with gleaming windows fixed upon their faces, to each eye one. These gins when they set foot to ground walked out-toed; they held the arms of men as a precaution against being suddenly struck and carried off; they carried no burdens, and were greeted with bare heads in the sun. Priestesses all, therefore, feeding without labour, eternally dressed and painted for corroborree.

This lubra with the wallaby skin upon her shoulders, her head bare and the colour of that ochre used in hidden valleys to paint their sacred stones, was not of the every-day order of priestesses, they concluded. They looked at her, and as she with questioning glances caught their eyes, shyly turned from her. She began to speak, gesturing between the words:

"You know Ketch?" They looked vacant; she drew with a forefinger on her breast the shape of Ketch's half-moon of brass. They turned from one to the other, and a man said something rapidly. "Ketch, a chief,

went away with two other men, white men——" She
stooped to the fire, picked up a charred black twig
and held it up, two of her own white fingers beside it.
Her fingers began to walk in the air, and the twig kept
them company. The people laughed at this pantomime,
but showed no sign that they took its meaning. "To look
for gold——" She tapped the ring on her marriage
finger with the twig—"One was young with a round
face. Where have they gone? Have you seen?" And she
repeated the airy pilgrimage of the stick and the fingers.
"Charles—Have you heard that name spoken?" She
recollected the curious preference of men for surnames.
"Adare, Adare, Thomson, do you know that? Ketch; you
must know that. You must know something, wretched
people!"

They laughed politely at the white lubra's earnestness,
all part of the play which she was, for some reason un-
guessed by them, enacting for them in the rain. Then the
oldest man, coming forward, touched the wallaby skin,
saying the only words of English that had ever done
him any good:

"You gib it?"

She spoke again, encouraged by this, and pulled the
skin willingly from her shoulders. He took it with
satisfaction as a gift, not understanding that she offered
it in payment for information. It was soft, beautifully
tanned; he bent it in his fingers, appreciating the absence
of crackle, and looked with wonder at her urgent eyes
still questioning him.

"Well? Tell me. Adare. Ketch. Alive? Dead?"

At a loss for a gesture to express the difference, she dipped her twig at the fire till it lighted, and holding it up before her mouth repeated the word:

"Alive?"

They watched. She took a breath, blew. The flame vanished, and a brief trail of sparks fled from her hand. When the twig was black again, once more she held it up.

"Dead?"

They watched as before. They understood nothing, and the old man was walking away with his treasure, paying no further heed to her. She flung out her hands.

"People, have you seen nothing? These men, two white men—nothing? Ketch?"

They watched, interested, as she flung back her head, imploring their secret. They admired and valued her; they were glad to have had her declare these mysteries to them alone, no white person near. When she turned away at last they regretted her going, and called two or three civilities after her, but she paid no heed, scrambling over rocks made shiny by the skid of marsupials' feet.

When she came to the top of the path she stood, for the first time allowing herself to take the full weight of her misery. Exiled from both her worlds, murderer of a brother, bereft by the man she loved of the man who had restored her to some intelligence of life: was not this sorrow? At the word came the echo of a young voice, its natural lightness deliberately clouded, reading aloud:

"Sweetest sorrow . . .
I thought to leave thee,
And deceive thee,
But now of all the world I love thee best."

And that, she remembered, was a verse of the poet, the little apothecary, who had died at twenty-seven. She, at twenty-seven, had been seduced, had killed, had gone for ever from her home, but life held promise, and she would not willingly then have left it. Now only her flesh was reluctant.

She went up the steps, and lightly along the verandah to the dining-room, whose window stood open. Locked, the cupboard door? It should have been, for the women were thievish as monkeys, but as she put her hand to it she felt it obey her. Next moment she screamed.

The Maori head was there, leaning horribly upon the decanter labelled Brandy. She had laid her hand upon its sparse harsh hair, blond from the action of embalming spices. The decanter could not be moved without somehow touching this sentinel. She rubbed her hands upon the wet breast of her dress, but the sensation of touch had been shocked, she could not so easily rid herself of recollection. As she frantically sought to scour the sensation away, the door opened behind her.

"What's doing?" said her husband's voice.

He came towards her, saw the head still on guard, and looked at her long. She muttered that she was ill, felt faint— He nodded, carelessly lifted up the head by its hair, and poured out a little spirit, which he held to her.

"The other hand, the other hand!"

It was his right hand, with which he had lifted the head, that held the glass. He smiled slightly, and changed this to the left.

Even so, she could not bring herself to take the glass, not for horror of the head, but because for ten years and more she had never drunk spirits save alone. Even the cajolery of Adare had not been able to prevail over that habit. She said now, irrelevantly:

"This room is very dusty. I wish Milly were back. Why do you not bury that frightful thing?"

He did not answer; his silence made her aware of his reason, and she spoke it aloud.

"To frighten me. To stop me. Sam—oh, God, can you never take the direct way? Can you never speak and say, I will not have this or that? Forbid me, oblige me to do what you would have done. Don't go silently to make me afraid——"

Mournfully, seeking comfort, she looked in his face, and saw starting at the corner of each eye a tear. He said:

"I have to do the way I can."

"Sam, come here to me." He came, shambling, head down for shame of the tears. She caught him to her. "Sam, you know I am yours."

He said, not putting his arms about her, standing like an animal, forehead dropped upon her shoulder:

"Once."

"Still."

He shook his head, rolling it on the wet stuff of her dress. The movement might have been a negation, it might have been contrived to clear his eyes of tears.

"But that's not enough. There are twenty-four hours in a day."

She stood away from him, hands on his shoulders.

"Will you tell me the truth? I know words trouble you, I'll ask only for a yes or no. We are near now; nearer than we have been for a very long time. Let us use the moment. Will you?" He nodded. "You were jealous of Charles."

It was a statement, but he answered as though it had been a question, with the affirmative of his peasant blood.

"Ay."

"Did you think I had been unfaithful?"

The man said, speaking painfully and very low:

"Not in your bed."

"How then?"

He had not the phrase for that. She had to make what she could of a dozen words.

"Always talking—and you've kept off the stuff—got back your looks. The house, too—ordering the dinner."

"Sam, was it you took a little paper from my work-box? A silly thing, with a list of duties written down?"

"What for did you want to keep it?" She accepted this at its true value: Duties Domestic, Duties Social, destroyed by jealousy, gone. "Him, ordering you about."

"It meant nothing."

"I owed him for that."

She understood that half-statement, too. Where Flusky owed, he paid. The wages of sin—but why should the wages of gaiety, folly, and youth be equalled with these?

"Charles has gone to his death." She contemplated the fact; he did not deny it. "Through you, as my brother died through me. We struck both for the same reason, to possess each other wholly, to let nobody come between. Sam——" she held his left hand to her face —"we're so unhappy, we've brought so much unhappiness about. What good has it done to anyone, our having loved?"

He put both his arms round her at that and clasped with all his strength. The embrace begged her to unsay what she had said; to murmur, in the small voice that like her body was his only, a confession of faith in their need of each other. She could not; nor could he ask in words. He let her go, fetched a brief sigh, and went out of the room. She stood, fingers twisting together. The glass of brandy which she had refused stood on the table a foot away. She emptied it quickly; poured another from the decanter, now deprived of its warder, and drank that. Then, holding the decanter with a fold of her skirt clutched over it, she departed along the verandah, taking care to walk without noise, and looking sidelong to see that there was nobody about in the paths to observe her.

BOOK III.

Now I will set forth a *Parable*, or (not to be Prophane) a *Ridle*. What is that which by giuing encreaseth? One may say, an *Usurer*, one a *Bellows:* a third may make bawdy answer. Not to teize further such ingenious Diuiners I will say, A woman. And not her bodie, for that may fructifie by force, but her immortal part. What of her own Motion she giueth quickeneth, that which she hath of another to give, like a Child's groat of *Sundays*, profiteth not. From her owne Entraills must she endow, bestowe, and spinne out Contentment. . . .

—*A Limbo For Ladies*.

BOOK THREE

(i)

STANDING before the map on the end wall of his room, Flusky erased from it features which had been provisionally marked; Captain Forbes' apocryphal stream, Kindur, the plains Babyran, the burning mountain, Kourada. All these first took shape in the imagination of an escaped convict, who thus endeavoured to lend his breakaway some glamour of exploration; now an expedition had disproved their existence, substituting barren words, Scrub Country, Swamp Country, for the life-giving River Flats. Flusky erased with reluctance, repelling symbolically one more raid upon the white spaces of the map. The attackers had mastered no key position, but only one more of the eternal escarpments by which the country's secret life was defended.

"Ought to be having news of Dixon's expedition soon," said he to console himself. "He's been gone nigh on half a year."

Winter answered, looking up from neat papers:

"No doubt, sir." He added, hesitating: "Of Mr. Adare, too."

Flusky received that with one of his silences. The secretary went on, in a voice louder than he intended, because the words were forced out by his will: "Excuse me, sir. Can something not be done, a search-party be sent out? If we could have some assurance of his safety, I think her ladyship——"

He stopped. Flusky eyed him, bringing his look and his will to bear as a wrestler uses a grip. When the secretary's face was colourless, he spoke:

"Adare's his Ex's cousin. It's for the Governor to move."

He returned to the map. There was silence for a couple of minutes until the secretary once again took courage to address the broad back. It was a new subject, but one hardly less dangerous.

"Sir, is it necessary that I should answer this letter? I have no right to say it, perhaps, I am convinced from— my own observation——" he left Mr. Adare out this time, a measure of precaution—"that this woman is mischievous. It is not my affair. But from what I have gathered, and for her ladyship's sake——"

This time Flusky made interruption in words, catching, as was not unusual with him, at the name which had not been spoken.

"You bloody gentlemen! Your observation, what you have gathered, you and Mr. Adare. Where's this letter?"

Winter handed it, one sheet of paper, written in a hand angular yet unformed.

"Mr. Samson Flusky, Sir, Hearing that there is now no just cause or impediment, and being disengaged, beg to offer myself for the position given up in March last. Will be glad of an answer by return owing to many applications and oblige your respectful humble servant, Milly."

Flusky read it to himself, mouthing one or two of the words soundlessly as he spelled them. When the secretary judged that he had finished he began to make an appeal, hardly audible, which Flusky checked.

"Stow the patter."

"No," the secretary answered, beginning to tremble like a man walking to the triangles. "No. I must not be silent. Lady Henrietta is not yet overcome. She is fighting her horrible weakness gallantly—Sir, if you bring this woman back it will be the end, indeed it will. Milly procured her the means of——" He broke off, with an inadequate gesture.

"What's that? Adare said that, you've parroted it from him."

"No, sir—though he did speak of it to me."

Flusky made a contemptuous sound.

"I go bail he did. What's the idea, Milly getting the stuff for her? What's Milly get out of it?"

"I don't know," the secretary answered, "I don't know, but I do beg you to believe, sir——" Despairingly, flinging himself at the danger in that impassive face, he cried out: "What do I get out of it, come to that? Won't you understand that if I speak like this it's because I can't bear to see a woman, a lady——"

Flusky's gesture checked him, a doubling and withdrawing of the fist. His eyelids trembled, but he stood, gamely enough, to take the blow. Flusky unclenched his hand.

"You talk too much. It's the same with all of you gentlemen, you like the sound of your own voices. Talking shops; that's your fine schools. No good out here. By Cripes, I wish somebody'd tell me what's the good of gentlemen."

The secretary did not answer that. Flusky threw at him Milly's letter, which dropped on the floor between them.

"Write Milly she can come."

The secretary came forward to pick it up, observing as he stooped that his employer was at a drawer where employment and assignment forms were kept. He stood with the woman's letter in his fingers, quite still, like an animal threatened with the last danger. Flusky observed him not at all, investigating the papers with a thumb. When he had found the one he sought he sat down, and began laboriously to fill it in.

Form of Application for the Return of Male Convicts.

To the Magistrate for the district of *Sydney*.

I have to request that the convict named in the margin now in my assigned service, may be returned to government, because

William
Winter

he object to take orders and not trustworthy in house.

I have the honor to be,
Sir,
Your most obedient Servant.

Signature of assignee } *Samson Flusky.*
or his Overseer

When he had completed the formula he looked up. Winter still stood, and was very white; his imagination travailed with the unknown, conjecturing what punishment this defiance might bring. He had no words. His throat was dry with the beating of pulses in it, and a sick twist of his mind translated those pulse-throbs to a beating of hammers on the road, a rhythm of whips descending. He dropped his head and waited.

"Get on with your screeve."

William Winter sat down and dipped his pen. His writing, neat from much recording of Latin verse, bent to feminine curves from much copying of Greek, informed a Nonconformist cook in polished phrases that she might, so soon as suited her convenience, enter again upon her duties at the house in Woolloomooloo. Flusky watched with curiosity the fluent words appearing, folding Form F meanwhile into a square which he put in his pocket.

"I won't send this off yet. All the same, Mister Winter——"

The secretary looked up, a passion of relief in his eyes, and half-rose.

"Sir."

"Don't use your nose so much. Stick to your pen."

He went away. The secretary, in whose mind, a city stricken with panic, no discipline now reigned, laid his forehead on the wet paper while phrases beset him. Nose as sharp as a pen—than a serpent's tooth—thy sting is not so sharp as friends remembered not, friends defended not; not so sharp as the iron of a coward's own fear entering his soul.

(ii)

ENCOUNTERING Lady Henrietta by chance that same evening, the secretary told her hurriedly what had been determined, noting with unhappy eyes that her gait had taken on something of its old swiftness; a gait like that of a very young child, pressing forward in pursuit of its own centre of gravity. She heard his announcement with that old too gracious inclination of the head, but said nothing. He persisted:

"It cannot be agreeable to you, madam, I know. I thought it might be less shocking—that you might be better prepared if you knew to expect it. I spoke against it so far as my capacity allowed."

She said, smiling and swaying:

"Good of you, Mr. Winter. Obliged to you. Mistaken, though. You were mistaken. I have no objection to see Milly back. No longer any objection."

He bowed and could say no more. She did not, however, depart at once. Looking about her, she beckoned him closer.

"Tell me. No news?"

He understood that she spoke of Adare, and answered that so far as he knew there was none. She nodded as though this were what she had expected to hear. He went on, despite a pang of terror which took him at the thought of Flusky, and Form F lying folded in Flusky's pocket:

"But, madam, don't give up hope. In this country —at this time of year, men don't starve. He's making history, perhaps. Five months is not long."

"I know," she answered, as if at random. "He won't come back, though."

She went away along the corridor dirty still with the dust of a storm that had blown two days ago. The women neglected their work; Winter could not deny it, nor that there was waste, food spoilt, disorder everywhere. His common sense could not blame Flusky for wishing to make an end to such a state of affairs.

Two days later, in a spring cart with three neat small boxes stowed behind the seat, Miss Milly arrived.

She found the household sullen. Having learned, by some keyhole method of their own, that the tyrant was due to reappear, the women had taken their last opportunity. By pledging kitchen implements they had obtained a sufficiency of liquor from the fishermen, and in company with their benefactors caroused till a late hour. Towards two o'clock the secretary, tumbling out of bed, had gone downstairs to quell an outburst of noise, and found the wives from the huts engaged in fighting the female servants with fists, skewers and buckets. Being sober and having right on their side they had soon overcome resistance, and marched their husbands off, swearing and singing, to legitimate beds.

But the kitchen betrayed signs of conflict, a splash of blood here, a plate smashed there, and the tin lid of the fish-kettle, which had been used as a shield, was crumpled like a piece of paper. Amid this disorder the three women slept, and woke unwillingly when the sun already was high to find Miss Milly, bonneted, hands on hips, standing in the doorway.

It was her hour. Scorpions lodged in her tongue, her hand was lifted, she overrode protests as an armed man in his chariot. Old Sal, by virtue of her seniority, and having a better capacity than her juniors to hold and recover from liquor, ventured upon an exchange of abuse. She told the newcomer that the Almighty might like a nose,* and have chosen the Jews for his own people on that account, but that she, Sal, could never feel aught but contempt for one. That if there was a thing she could not endure it was a needling,† nailing,‡ manchester-wagger,§ the mere view of whose mug was enough to knap the devil the glim.¶ Miss Milly heard Sal out, folding her lips in upon each other; then without any words struck the old woman on the head with a long basting spoon. She added with a kind of humour, as blood started up along the cut:

"I'm ready for the devil, I'd have you know."

When she had set the rhythm of the kitchen going—it started with surprisingly little trouble, like a good old clock rewound and set—she went over the rest of the

*Nose=spy or informer.   †Needling=swindling.
‡Nailing=over-reaching.   §Manchester-wagger=the tongue.
¶Knap the glim=take venereal disease.

house, noting ravages. It was not only a question of dust. Curtains hung crookedly, with here and there a tear unmended. From furniture in the drawing-room scraps of veneer had been knocked with the broom-head. The beds showed signs of slovenly making, and under them flue lay flaked. She remade the bed in Flusky's room, noting with jealous care an unfamiliar clumsy darn at the back of a sock thrown beneath it. When this room was neat as she could make it she went along the passage and knocked, walking in before there could be any answer.

Lady Henrietta was asleep, though the sun was over her forehead and beginning to shine upon her eyes. This room too was in disorder; Miss Milly, however, had no care for the room. She stood looking at the big woman whose hair strayed to cover her pillow, whose face had grown thinner and clearer in the months since Milly departed. The eyes were hollow, blue-lidded, beautifully framed by their bones. The mouth even in sleep was red. Miss Milly marvelled at this renewal of beauty, hated it, and regarded the bottle upon the table with satisfaction, smelling it for better assurance that it was the right stuff, the wrong stuff, the stuff to do the trick.

"Milly!" She turned, quick as a cat, and slid the bottle down with a hand behind her. Lady Henrietta was awake, gazing at her without surprise.

"It's me all right," the righteous woman answered, disconcerted.

"Ain't you getting up?" She added, maliciously:

"you're not looking any too well. Any news of Mister Adare?"

"He is dead. We are back where we started from."

The woman could make nothing of that last sentence. She answered the first.

"And there's fools don't believe in a judgment!"

"Milly, if you please. Will you take over the ordering of the house as you did before?"

"It's time someone took over. Dirt everywhere, those women selling the very saucepans off the stove for drink and their other games."

"There is some money, I think, in the purse there. Will you take it?"

"I never have and I never will. There's one thing, though, if I'm to take over. The keys."

Lady Henrietta put a hand under her pillow and pulled out the keys on their ribbon, no longer smooth, no longer the colour of an Irish lawn. Miss Milly took them with a disdainful look, and at once untied the ribbon, picking at it viciously with her strong blunt fingers. Holding one finger hitched through the steel ring she swung them, making them jangle like miniature bells for a victory. Her voice was milder when she spoke again.

"You don't need move for dinner. Bed's more easeful when you're not yourself."

"You're kind," Lady Henrietta answered, astonishing the woman by the sincerity in her voice. Easeful; that word came as an echo too. "So very kind."

"I do my duty," Miss Milly answered, folding the grass-green ribbon carefully to put it away, "or so I hope."

(iii)

SAID Mr. Samson Flusky to his secretary, between such pauses as his cigar demanded:

"A letter to the Governor. Put in all the flourishes. Here's what I want said: Government at home don't send out the men we want here. You can't expect it. A sign-painter, say, commits a felony, he's got to be transported same as if he was a useful man. Gentlemen, too, that can't do a hand's turn beyond shove a pen. What's wanted isn't Grammar Schools, or places like this King's School, as they call it; a lot of kids dressed up in uniform to learn Greek. It's schools for teaching trades this country wants. I'm ready to back my words. I'll give the land, and build the school, tell him, if so he'll agree to it. That's the lot. His obedient humble servant, and I'll sign."

The secretary, without replying, chose a sheet of finer paper, trimmed his pen carefully, and bent over the desk.

"Make it plain. A school for men to learn to use their hands. I don't give two chats* for Latin and poetry. Wait; say they'll be taught to cipher. That's got some sense to it, too. Learn 'em to keep an eye on their money when they make it. Poetry——"

*Chats = lice.

He made a contemptuous sound at the thought of that. Winter bent lower, teeth caught upon his lip; aware of himself, not for the first time, as the whipping boy of Mr. Charles Adare.

(iv)

ORDER was returning to the house called Why Are You Weeping? The fishermen came of a morning bearing samples of their catch strung on reeds: mullet, garfish, and bream, and departed discreetly. The blacks drifted no further than the kitchen door, and there were fobbed off with valueless articles, corks, candle-ends, and string, instead of bread or meat. Flo, indignant at being cast down from her consequence as cook, rebelled and went, under the irrevocable direction of Form F, back to Government. A young woman replaced her for whom Miss Milly took almost an affection; a cheesemonger's widow, cleanly, methodical, whose shop had been the meeting-place for certain too noisy partisans of Reform. Old Sal subsided into a Sunday-school sobriety of language. Tradesmen's bills went down. The trays which mounted to Lady Henrietta's room were models of what invalid trays should be.

The house, as it adjusted itself to this outward rule, as its corridors began to shine again and its windows to be neat, resumed the mysterious inner life which had found symbolic statement in its name. The silence that held by day, by night was broken. Once, as in early days, the secretary met his employer's wife wide-eyed on the stairs. He spoke respectfully to her. She looked at him, frowning, shaking her head in an endeavour to focus vision; steadied herself and sighed:

"Pray for me. No. No, couldn't have that, don't think of it. Pray—pray excuse. What I meant."

He answered, as though gentling a frightened animal:

"Won't you let me give you my arm back to your room?"

"Must think of Sam," she said gravely. "Mustn't trouble Sam. I assure you, assure you——" very earnestly—"he's my only thought and care."

She swayed, pursing her mouth, and again looking intently at him.

"Forgotten how it goes. Easeful—something. It torments me." Suddenly clapping her hands to her ears, she cried out: "It torments me, oh, oh! Always echoes, voices. Hurts to think—drink. Mustn't say that. Mustn't drink it—think it, on any account. Tell me the words, the verse."

William Winter, at a loss, recollected suddenly a book lent him by Mr. Adare.

"I can't quite tell what you may be thinking of. Is it a line of John Keats, perhaps?"

Face strained to attention and thrust forward, she had the very poise and stillness of a ship's figurehead, and for an instant he saw her transformed to one, ploughing unknown waters.

" 'I have been half in love with easeful Death.' Is that what you had in mind?"

She smiled wonderfully, the whole posture slackened, a hand was lifted to drop heavily upon his shoulder. She nodded again and again, murmuring:

"Go on. Go on."

"I can't recollect. I'm sorry, madam."

He saw her look over her shoulder, heard some person coming towards the stairs. He had a qualm of fear; it was not possible, however, to withdraw from the hand on his shoulder, or change the posture in which, almost like a lover, he stood looking up at her. It was Lady Henrietta who abandoned him, turning and running unsteadily towards her room. The voice of Miss Milly accosted him:

"What did she want?"

"Lady Henrietta was asking——" But he could not reveal the matter of that plaintive quest. "She was asking the time."

"What made her squeal? I heard it in the kitchen."

"I can't tell why she cried out."

Miss Milly was turning away when Winter came after her, suddenly stirred out of prudence.

"But perhaps you can, perhaps you know."

She faced him, nostrils pinched with a quick drawing-in of breath. "Another of Belial's sons! I do my work for God, and my work for Mr. Flusky, and if there's no complaints from either of them, who are you, I'd like to know? Look out for yourself, mister. The wicked may flourish, but at the last they shall be cut down, and cast into the pit, and be utterly consumed, Amen! You, indeed!" He took a step towards her. "You touch me, you lag! Only touch me, that's all!"

"I am trying to pass you, to get to my work."

"About time you remembered your work. Speaking poetry to her—you did ought to know what comes of that."

"You were listening?"

"Why not, pray? Was you talking so extremely private?" She became the housekeeper arraigning an assigned servant, speaking with a condescension which he found less easy to bear than her shrewishness. "Now you know very well you got no call to be in this part of the house. Be off before you get into trouble."

He went, telling himself that he had been a scholar of Magdalen, that the crest on his ring had been borne by his family since Queen Elizabeth's day, that these humiliations were of his own purchasing. None of the considerations brought comfort. His thoughts were a rack, and where a free man might have tired himself by action, a bondman had no way of escape. He went to the room with the map, and standing under it felt envy of Adare and those other men pressing forward upon its white spaces, giving their everyday names to gullies and flats, suffering distresses which, because free will commanded them, were easily borne. He hated himself because he could not wholly control his indignation nor wholly yield to it, because he was helpless, and because he was afraid.

The immediate task was to check household bills for the past month. Mechanically he ranged upon his desk the ill-written books and the bills, scraps of paper dirty with kitchen stains, speared upon a file. Beside them he laid a paper on which Miss Milly had set down the moneys received by her, and by her paid out during the course of the month. He checked the books by the bills, comparing both with her statements. There was no fault to be found, not a halfpenny which might not be counted to the housekeeper for righteousness. He acknowledged to himself, when he had done two or three of the accounts, that he had been looking for signs of peculation, and that the hope had lent his work unusual interest. The last bill was the wine merchant's, and this he scanned with particular care. If the woman supplied Lady Henrietta, the woman must first obtain the liquor. He therefore gave attention to each item on this bill, which was not inconsiderable. He found only Madeira, claret, brandy in authentic quantities. Some arrangement, his mind insisted, with the merchant; gin disguised as one or other of these wines. Flusky kept the cellar-book accessible in a drawer, though the cellar keys were about his person. Winter searched it, comparing quantities paid for with quantities entered. The dozens matched. He returned the book, folded the wine-bill, and reluctantly made against Miss Milly's figures the V-shaped pencil mark that approved her integrity.

(v)

OLD SAL, seated on the verandah outside the kitchen and plucking a fowl for table, discussed with her less respectable compeer the joys of London life, where persons of the family* all knew each other and traded as friends, where certain pretty skills of the hands were practised, where money was free and manners easy. Old Sal herself had been a fence or receiver; but in her younger days she boasted, tucking her petticoats up to show a leg no longer shapely, that she had been the companion in felony of James Hardy Vaux, most genteel of rascals. How she would cover him she related, while he put down his forks, light as a bird, and brought up handkerchiefs you could have sold to the Archbishop of Canterbury; how he once gave her a ring that he had pinched, he told her, off the little finger of one of the Newgate turnkeys; how he walked like a swell, and talked like a clergyman, and never addressed her in public save as "Sarah, dear love."

Her companion listened doubtfully, recollecting no such days, skills, attentions. She came from a small country town where she had been the chief inn's chambermaid. Finding that her child's arrival coincided with that of lord in a coach, she, not choosing to lose tips or time, smothered the baby and went about her work. She was caught slipping out at night to bury the

*Thieves, and those connected in any way with thieving.

small body, which had the top of an old stocking for its winding-sheet. Her experiences lacked glamour, and for this reason she was unable to believe in old Sal. How came so clever a trickster to Botany Bay? And on a ten-year stretch, too.

But old Sal explained, loudly enough for the secretary to hear at his desk round the corner, that these things were all a matter of luck. You might be fly. You might be up in the stirrups and working well. But you had no protection, she explained, against the dirty devices of traps. These individuals would let a man alone, look the other way, until he committed a crime he could be hanged for—and how, asked old Sal of heaven, could you tell until after you had lifted a montra* whether its value was under the limit or over? £40 was the reward for bringing in a man wanted on a hanging charge. So the traps—blast them!—would say: We don't want him till he weighs his weight, forty pounds, see? This kind of duplicity no man could guard against, and thus it was that the traps had got their claws into James Hardy Vaux and herself.

The younger woman began a little pitiful story of some country constable's astuteness, how he had identified a highwayman by a patch on his boot. She spoke lower, and she was well within the room. The secretary waited for Sal's voice.

It came soon, overcalling the other. The country was nothing, it was easy as butter taking the stuff off country-

*A watch.

men. London was the place, plenty of crowds, London was the place for clever fingers. They all said in London that she, Sal, was as neat of her fingers as a man, more than one had said that. And she dared swear even now with her rheumatics she could lift the handkerchief out of Miss M.'s pocket, given half a chance, except for that one keeping everything on a key; why, she wouldn't leave open not so much as her bowels——

Laughter none too savoury ended the talk by the window. William Winter, accepting instructions from his employer, related what he had heard to what his own enquiry and imagination had discovered. The woman was honest, odiously so; the meagre trunks that came back to the house with her were evidence of this probity, the household books acquitted her. Yet he could not give up an irrational conviction that this was the channel——

"Answer, can't you?"

"I beg your pardon, sir."

"Has that answer come yet from His Ex.?"

"This morning, yes, sir; by hand."

While Flusky slowly read the letter he could escape again to his own thoughts. If the household books acquitted Milly, somewhere there must be other evidence. She was methodical, the expenditure considerable, she could not carry it all in her head——

"Are you hanging it on?* I'm talking."

"Yes, sir."

*Hanging it on=purposely delaying.

"Take an answer. I'll come and see him, say. Obedient, humble, and all the rest of it. Like to see his face if I put Yours, bender! Any of their faces."

(vi)

WINTER, standing in the kitchen to read a list and check groceries while Miss Milly unpacked them, met the eye of old Sal over the housekeeper's bent back. Old Sal had a most pregnant eye. It conceived rapidly, giving facile birth to innuendo or query. Its roll was easy as the turn of a fish, its wink the flick of a snake's tongue. Meeting the glance of Mr. Winter its promise made him in one instant aware that he was about to lose eight ounces of tobacco. This, his month's allowance, he had saved for the purpose of a wager with Sal, which she made sure and jovial anticipation of winning. Praise from James Hardy Vaux and his associates was not lightly given, nor was the skill which earned it readily forgotten. Old Sal's eye, by a deft lowering of the lid, bade the other party to the bet mark what she was about, and admire.

"Candles, wax, 20 lbs," read Winter.

Miss Milly dumped the package upon the scales beside her, calculated the weight and announced:

"Short! Seven ounces. Mark that down."

"Peppercorns, black and white, 2 lbs. Sugar. Four loaves."

"One broken."

In Sal's trade it was customary to work in twos, one party distracting attention while the other employed forks of the only kind not made before fingers. She now allotted to the broken sugar-loaf the former inactive but necessary rôle, shifting towards it step by step. Her left hand was at it: Winter, watching from the corner of his eye, saw how her fingers deliberately rustled the torn corner of paper, and observed Miss Milly look towards the sound. Sal's right hand simultaneously narrowed itself; three fingers went down like prongs into the housekeeper's skirt. He did not see them emerge from the pocket, which they did as Miss Milly in rage examined the other hand for stolen sugar.

"Fed like the Queen of England, and still you lags keep prigging!"

"I never took nothing, Miss M., so help me!"

"Not for want of trying, then."

Later the secretary, back in the room with the map, recognized the whistle of old Sal outside his window.

"Well? What did you get?"

Old Sal answered, aggrieved, that they might both have known the nasty thing never kept a handkercher, too mean, blows with her fingers to save washing——

"But you got something?"

Old Sal had indeed got something, as good as a handkercher for that matter; it had Miss M.'s writing in it, and that showed it couldn't have come from no one else. She brought out of the deeps of her bosom a small black-covered book.

It was all there, two years' expenditure, steadily mounting the sums totted up week by week, month by month, to make an appalling total. Miss Milly, save for the brief period of Adare's visit, had expended almost the whole of her earnings on spirits for her victim. She could not have kept above a shilling a week for her own needs of clothing, and the mild pleasures her convictions allowed. The cost of the stuff was her bribe to conscience, the price of continuing to approve herself. There was a curious little appendix, showing prices obtained for dresses, petticoats and such, and to whom the money had been given; the Temperance Society, the Bible Society, a female orphanage. Nothing of Lady Henrietta's self-despoiling had been used for the purpose she intended. Nor had Miss Milly bought for herself any least credit by these donations. To this, to that, anonymous, the entries insisted. The righteous woman at her victim's funeral might say: with a great price obtained I this freedom.

"Hey, Mister! Didn't I win my bacca fair?"

Winter perceived old Sal again, and paid her off without a word. She went away, grumbling a little, having given her performance as much for the hope of applause as for the price of hire. The secretary began to tremble all over; his knees failed. The fire, which Flusky caused to be lit of a night for the pleasure of staring in it,

tempted him now intolerably. It was newly built of
short logs, piled together tent-fashion; through the
opening at the top the little book might so easily pass
and be consumed——

Flusky came in. The abstraction into which Winter
had fallen had allowed no warnings from his senses to
reach him. Thus the master found the servant sprawled
in his chair, legs stretched out to the fire, studying a note-
book which could by no means be related to any
business of Samson Flusky, Esquire. Winter sprang
up.

"Take it easy, mister. Take it easy."

"Sir, I beg your pardon——"

"Stow that. What's that you got there?"

"A private document, sir."

"Give it here."

"No, sir."

"Do you want to go back to Government?"

Too late to run away. Winter took a breath, trying
to steady his heart.

"Sir, this book does not belong to me——"

"How you come by it, then?"

The secretary had formed, as yet, no plan. Nevertheless even his fears could not hide from him that it was
necessary to speak, because the man would, one way or
another, compel him to speak. He got out the first four
words in a rush:

"It is Miss Milly's." Now, urgently, he was proffering
the book. "Look, her handwriting, you know it. It is

hers. You must believe me. Here is proof. You can't deny it, sir, with this in your hand."

"What's the matter with you? Why are you all of a shake?"

Winter stood, shaking indeed. Flusky took the book, deliberately turned its pages; then leaned out the window, shouting towards the kitchen quarters:

"Milly! Here!"

Turning back into the room he saw the bell-rope, grinned at the gentleman in his employ, and pulled it. Winter said nothing, did not look at the master. When Miss Milly came in, he took a step forward, but Flusky stood still, holding the book out so that she might see it.

Miss Milly looked, recognized the book instantly, and folded her hands high up on her stomach. It was the attitude she took in the kitchen before making some demand with sardonic politeness; "And why, if I may presume to ask——" She did not appear angry or guilty. Flusky asked:

"This yours?"

She did not look at it but at him as she answered:

"It is. And how do you come by it, I should like to know?"

"It's a list of drink bought."

"And why not, pray?"

Flusky at that blinked a little. The secretary said in a low voice:

"She admits it, sir. You see, she admits it."

"You answer me a question. Have I or haven't I got

a right to turn an honest penny by trading as well as another?" She did not wait for the answer, but went on with mounting temper. "Strong drink's a mocker, but it don't make a fool of the man that sells it. Or woman either. You look in that book you make so free with. Look in that, and see how much I've paid into Temperance these last years." As he fumbled with the pages, she laughed. "Liquor making a rod for its own back, see? If I sell drink, and pay over what I make to the glory of the Lord, whose business is that?"

"There's nothing here about selling."

"You've only got the book with the outgoings. There's another, and you shall see it, if you're going to make such a song about what's my business, Mr. Flusky. How you come by that book you got, if you please? I want an answer to that, Mr. Flusky, if you don't have no objection."

"She's lying," said the secretary, still in a low voice, but urgently. He believed what he said; at the same time he could not but see the horrid plausibility of the woman's story. It was in character that her business sense should have perceived the profits to be made from drink, while her religious sense saw no reason why these same profits should not be diverted, converted, made to pay dividends in the Kingdom of Heaven. He repeated what he had said, trying to convince the master by the tone of his voice.

"Now listen," said the woman, advancing on him. "You, I mean, mister. This is your doing. Making mischief, eh? Talking poetry to madam, eh? Don't want nobody with their eyes open about this house, that's about the facts of it."

"You're buying drink for her," the secretary said. "I know it, you know it, the proof's there if only he'd look for it——"

And he had an inkling of defeat coming from the other quarter; as if Flusky would not look, had a reason for not looking at proof. But the woman was speaking again, moving towards him without dropping her hands, which still were folded upon each other tightly, at the level of her waist. It was alarming, as though a statue had walked.

"If ever I took so much as a farthing that's not mine, I'll swallow it red-hot. Red-hot, d'you hear?"

"I don't accuse you of stealing——"

"No, you don't accuse me of stealing. There's one or two things you don't dare do, Mr. Nose. What for should I give her drink? You sneak round this house in places where you've no right to be, saying things you've no right to say, but you can't answer that, and why? Shall I count them pure with the wicked balances, and with the bag of deceitful weights? No, nor use them myself, nor take a penny I don't earn with these two hands——" At that she did move them. Palms held upwards and flat, she shoved her hands at the secretary, as though to show him at once their emptiness and their strength. "What's this you're at? Want to get rid of me, do you? I know why."

"Mr. Flusky," said the secretary, stammering. "I beg

you won't listen to this woman. I've accused her, and brought proof."

"And I say before the Lord, Mr. Flusky, that I've been to you a good and faithful servant, labouring late and early. If you find a penny missing, or so much as a farthing dip, I'll answer for it, if it's gone from this house while I'm in charge. What for should I give her drink? And where did he get that book from? That's what I'm asking."

Her gaze was steady, it held no fear, it demanded justice. Winter, in his consternation, spoke unthinking. The moment the words were out of his mouth he knew that he had committed the final folly, and was done for.

"I swear it's the truth. Ask her ladyship, for God's sake! She'll bear me out."

Miss Milly interrupted him, clamouring:

"That's right, her ladyship, that's good, that is! Ask her, do, Mr. Flusky!"

In those words, that confident cry, Winter heard the enigma of Lady Henrietta's behaviour smoothly and unhurriedly solved; she knew and accepted her fate. There was a thing which remained to be done. Without the warning of an exclamation he ran from the room and upstairs, tearing as he ran at something stitched inside his shirt; a letter. He got it out as he reached the bedroom door, and Flusky the turn of the stairs. There was time, just time, to thrust it under the pillow on which her hair made cat's cradle; to speak one word— "Adare." Then he heard striding feet in the room at his back. Nothing after.

(vii)

"My friend," the letter began. "Or no. Let us observe the formalities. My dear Lady Henrietta, ahem! (You are to suppose that I have tied my stock neatly, and that my hair smells of costly oils. I am a gentleman paying a call by letter.) What months since I've seen you, and what weather we've been having! Actually it is no more than half an hour since I saw you, but I must look forward to the time when Winter will deliver this missive into your hand. He has his orders, to give it you six months from the day of my departure. If I return before that time he is not to trouble you with it. If I delay, then you may need a little light conversation to keep you in spirits till I come back. This is the best I can contrive.

"How do you do, six months from now? Are you standing the test of time, my lady masterpiece? How does a poet, John Keats, say, feel when he turns up the sonnet that kept him awake and sweating blood a week of months ago? Well, never mind that question, there's nobody can answer it. But you might, at this point, take out the little list I made you, and examine your conscience with regard to Social and Domestic Duties. Are you ordering the dinner? Do you go about more? You should have a salon by now, full of gentlemen confidently holding forth, and ladies watching you narrowly.

Are you taking an interest in the garden as you should?
Are you writing home to my sister Alethea?

"I have a sufficiently good conceit of myself to suppose
that you are obedient in all. Ridiculous it may be, but
a young man who throws his whole heart into any
endeavour is unwilling to believe that there will be
nothing to show for it in the end. If I did not think
that you were safe I would not leave you. (Confound it,
we are back in the present tense again. No matter.)

"And now for a scolding. It is the matter of your
attitude to this departure of mine. Why do you talk,
look, protest as if your husband were trying to murder
me? You cannot rationally suppose it. I grant there was
uneasiness once, but we have talked that out, in so far
as talking is possible with him. (He has a scunner, by
the way, at gentlemen.) He is a man almost too simple
for us to understand, who are sophisticated creatures.
His manœuvrings are those of a child, and like a child
he cannot speak out what he means, has not the words
for it. Nor do I believe he always knows what he intends
to do until it is done. He must do his thinking and talking
by deeds. This money for equipment, this fifty pounds,
is an *amende honorable* for having at one time suspected
me. There will be a new dress or a trinket for you, on
the same account. It is not our way of doing things, but
we are not for that reason to condemn it. Wear your
trinket, as I take the money. He is a creature people
could love if he would let them, like a sort of rough
cantankerous retriever dog. I begin to see in him what

you saw, the day you ran away with him out of Ireland.

"And that reminds me. Do you recollect S. Quaife of the petticoat? I saw her yesterday (damn these tenses) and I am taken with a sort of heartburn at the thought that it will be a good many months till I see her again. If she were not whose daughter she is, and had not a voice that I don't care for, I should be in danger of falling in love. What a phrase, falling in love! I could do you an extravagance à la Touchstone on the various degrees of falling—the slip courteous, the tumble with circumstance, and so forth. My adventure, despite that petticoat which might seem to witness the contrary, comes under fall number three, the trip modest. An odd thing, that while your beauty and tenderness could not touch me, S. Quaife should set me off like tinder. Perhaps it is not so. Perhaps six months hence, when this is in your hands, I shall have forgotten her. But it is too soon after seeing her to think so now. Will you, then——

"I can't ask it. The hangman's daughter! No, no. I have still some feeling for the proprieties left, Lady Henrietta. (My hands go under my coat-tails, and I make for the fireplace, that rostrum of the domestic preacher.) I have still some regard for the decencies, and therefore I do not ask your ladyship to go in person to a small barber's shop—clean, though—and enquire for S. Quaife. I only say that the shop may be discovered by the curious somewhere in George Street, not so very far from a stationer's, and that the lady in question may be recognized by her having a face shaped like a heart, dark hair, blue eyes, and a mole at the corner of her mouth.

"That is not a description by a man in love, is it? Unemotional as those Wanteds by which criminals are made known, only the touch about the face's heart-shape, which will not quite do. Omit that, and the rest may stand for proof that I am not a lover yet. Remember, I have asked nothing of you.

"I had thought to leave half a dozen of these missives with Winter, so that you might have them delivered regularly, every fortnight. But that would be to take for granted that I shall be absent longer than six months, a depressing consideration. There is only this one letter, therefore, to hold you in talk till I can come and button-hole you myself. You looked heavenly with the light on your hair an hour ago. Why am I not over ears in love with you? Do not forget me."

Lady Henrietta ceased to read. She was at that stage of her trouble when the perceptions take on a momentary delusive acuteness. The people lately thronging her room had been definite in outline as paintings, every detail of colour and texture clear. While they raged a bird flew past the window. In the half-second of its passing she had perceived the set and colour of every feather, and the expressionless roundel of its eye. So sensitive was she that her flesh had seemed to reflect the whole scene unquestioning, her blood, restlessness stilled, quicksilver on glass, served to record those movements which her mind could not interpret. The young man, grey in the face, who rushed in to thrust a paper under her pillow she had seen fall without any concern. Milly's triumphant look had neither escaped nor interested her. And she had answered nothing to any questions, lying still, mute, half in love with easeful death.

Only when they were gone did she remember the single word Winter had spoken, and move a hand to feel for the paper he had hidden under her head. This she read, simultaneously seeing and hearing, as though someone were speaking the letter aloud while her eyes followed the strokes of the pen. It meant nothing to her, entranced as she was. The letters and syllables were distinct, their meaning absent. She felt, however, a warning very subtle and far off, the kind of warning dreams give of some real pain to which the dreamer must wake. Raising her head she looked about her at the confusion of the room, and imagined herself dressing, moving with purpose amid that confusion. She saw her own fine nose, thickened chin, tousled hair, and surveyed them, while an echo gravely informed her that all love could do for you was to fill you up with gin. She could not at once discover what the purpose was that sooner or later would set her moving about the room. Her eyes closed again, her head sank back. Unconsciously her will imposed a duty upon the first finger of her right hand, which traced and retraced upon the counterpane two letters, S. and Q. unrelated to reality, but like abracadabra somehow giving assurance of protection.

She woke three hours later and remembered what she had determined to do. Also she was ashamed, as on that night when Adare, climbing up by the magnolia tree, had found her drunk. She touched his letter as a talisman, making no attempt to read it again. A clock struck, and now her ears were strained to number the sounds which three hours earlier had descended on them loud as a hammer on iron. It was six o'clock. She pulled the bell-rope.

It was Milly who answered. She came in bearing a neatly-dressed tray, shining, tempting, the very tray to wheedle an invalid out of indifference to food; set it down on Lady Henrietta's knees with an encouraging, "There now!" and began to remedy the room's disorder, talking as she stooped and folded.

"He's out of the house, Mr. Flusky said I was to tell you. I wouldn't have his back, this time to-morrow. Rushing in like that to a lady's bedroom! That's the end of Mister Winter."

There was no answer from the bed. Miss Milly went on, drawing a stocking over her thin red hand, turning it, seeking for holes before she rolled it up.

"Accusing me, he was. But Mr. Flusky stood by me, and always has. We're better off without these young fellows that think they're somebody."

The stocking showed no imperfections. Miss Milly rolled it with its fellow and gave the compact light bundle such a pat as a mother in good humour will give her child's bottom before she tucks it into bed.

"Now we can all settle down, no mischief-making, everything like it was. Try and eat some of that chicken.

And I brought you a little draught the doctor ordered."

Miss Milly was in command again. No longer did she show as that sour and raucous spinster who had watched Charles Adare and routed William Winter, but as the good servant, plain-spoken, who would run any house like a palace if only she might have her way. Lady Henrietta, eyes following her, knew that the purpose which informed this woman was stronger than her own.

When Milly departed, she made an effort, as a diver turns his hands upward and kicks himself towards the light. She got out of bed, and went to her work-box, feeling through its pockets, recognizing by touch those silks which should have clad the flocks and garlanded the crook of her shepherdess. She found a needle-book in which, one evening, she had hidden the scrap of tape with the name S. Quaife cross-stitched on it in big letters. When she had it in her fingers she could not remember what she had intended to do, and so went back to bed. She slipped the tape into Adare's letter before (Miss Milly's draught powerfully aiding) she fell asleep again, to dream urgent reasons why she should live, and to find herself clinging to a hangman's noose as to a rope of salvation.

(viii)

MR. SAMSON FLUSKY, crossing his hall to the front door where a vehicle waited, was astonished to hear his wife's voice:

"Sam, will you take me in to the town?"

He looked at her. She was dressed neatly enough; her gloved hands were clasped together in a gesture excessive for the request she was making; but then, that was her way.

"No reason why not."

He surveyed her again, more closely than before; this time perceiving that she clasped her hands because they quivered, and that she was haggard in the cruelly clear morning light.

"If you've got some notion about Winter, it's no good. He's been rumped* by this."

"Winter?"

And her voice held genuine surprise. She had forgotten the secretary. Winter was a messenger, a walking gentleman, who played a little part and now had made his exit unnoticed from the stage of her mind; in him she had never divined an ally. She frowned a little at the word which she knew meant a flogging and answered:

"He's gone, hasn't he? Milly said something."

"He's gone all right." Flusky's scrutiny satisfied him. His voice was genial. "Well, you feel able for it? Step out, then. If I drop you in George Street, will that do?"

She sat beside him, while the groom let the horses' heads go and sprang up behind, the toe of his boot treading for an instant one spoke of the moving shining

*Rumped = flogged.

wheel. Lady Henrietta sat up straight enough, but did not speak as Flusky pointed out new buildings with his whip; she was fighting nausea. At the turning by Hyde Park Barracks he seemed to hesitate; the horses' feet stopped their clatter, and the sound could be heard of St. James's clock striking ten. Flusky grinned, gave a brief whistle, and a cluck that sent his beasts off straight forward down King Street.

"Now, which of the shops d'ye want?"

She could only think of the name Quaife, and the vague direction, "by a stationer's."

"You have an appointment, perhaps. Don't consider me."

"Appointment," said he. "I'm late for that, anyway."

"With whom?" she asked idly, for time to gather her powers of invention. It was long since she had been in the town, the names of the shops were strange to her, the soldiers ludicrous in their shakos and tight coats; a striding black fellow in a flax-fringed cloak seemed less perturbed, took the bustle more for granted, than did she. "With whom is your appointment?"

"With His Ex. Dick Bourke," Flusky answered. "It won't do him any harm to wait half an hour."

He looked at her, but she did not make the appeal that might have been expected; ask him for news, ask him what will be done about Charles Adare. S. Quaife was the idea regnant. Little speculations flitted about the initial S. Did it stand for Selina, Sarah, Susan? Thus she had no comment to make upon this appointment with Sir Richard, unwonted and interesting though Flusky's glance proclaimed it. It did not occur to her to ask the question, nor would he volunteer the answer unasked. They drove in silence until she, desperately spying about her, perceived the sign of R. Bourne and Co., Family Mourning, Millinery and Baby Linen, and touched his arm.

"This? How long will you be?"

"An hour—more—I don't know."

He looked at the draper's shop; a public-house neighboured it. He leant over as if to speak, pulled back, gave a shake of the reins and a nod, and so left her. It occurred to Lady Henrietta as she stood in the street that there was no reason in the world why she should not have taken her husband into her confidence about S. Quaife. But somewhere in her half-sleeping spirit a vigilant personage warned her against explanations, against any use of the name Adare. She stood for a minute abstracted, until she saw a man in the doorway of the shop look inquisitively at her. She smiled at him, asked (for something to say) where was George Street. He put her on her way, and returning to his counter conjectured, grumbling:

"New out. You can always tell, asking for George Street, as if there wasn't as good shops in Pitt Street or King. They learn, I suppose, if they live long enough."

Lady Henrietta began to walk. She felt ill; there was money in her purse, and drink offering at every street corner, under emblems of fertility, patriotism, and caprice; "The Wheatsheaf," "The Trafalgar," "The Cat and Mutton." She walked faster, until loungers with broad hats tilted over their eyes began to stare after her. It was a hot day, her dress of the kind they were accustomed to see floating a foot or two out of the dust, smoothly, to the rhythm of hoofs. She had, besides, a characteristic step, very light and free. The loungers, nonplussed, found outlet for their oafish bewilderment as usual in laughter. But she was concerned with her own growing faintness, and with the need not to miss the sign of a small barber's shop—"clean, though"—somewhere near a stationer's.

To the right lay the barrack square. Vaguely she remembered spectacles other than purely military ones that were to be witnessed there; a wall on the south side had iron rings set in it, just a little higher than a man's head, to which were tied the wrists of those about to be flogged. Upon instinct she turned left, and almost immediately discovered the inconspicuous sign.

Quaife's customers waiting their turn stared at her, halting conversations to do so. She stood rather helplessly, aware of activities behind a half-drawn curtain, men's heads swathed in towels, a voice holding forth:

"—when you can tell me why the duty on home-made rum should be ten and tuppence, when it's only three bob on other spirits——"

"Easy. Rum's cheaper to make."

"Who says?"

Lady Henrietta stood still, looking about her for some

means of summoning attention. One of the waiting customers, with a wink at the others, got up, made an elaborate bow, and asked what he could do for her. She murmured that she wished to speak to Miss Quaife. He misheard her and called to the inner room:

"Boss! It's your lucky day. Lady here wants you."

Lady Henrietta saw the curtain jerked back to admit a large man holding a razor in his right hand, from which, without looking at it, his left fingers drew off and flicked away soap.

"We don't attend to females here," a voice told her, the same that had demanded enlightenment concerning the duty on rum.

"Your daughter—I don't know her name, I fear— might I speak to her?"

The quality of the voice surprised the barber. He stood aside, motioning with the hand that held the razor for her to pass through the shop, where his clients turned grotesque faces to watch her go; eyes red with soap swung above snow-men's cheeks to follow her progress towards the inner door. The barber pushed this open, and bade her go straight up. A clamour of questions and soft whistles arose as he turned back to attend to his business.

The girl was mending towels. She sat in the window, a sliver of sun lying across her cheek, feet tucked up on the bars of her chair. In this attitude, like some forlorn heroine at the beginning of a fairy story, she sat for a moment gazing at the visitor. When she decided to get

up, surprised though she was, she did so slowly, blinking
a little as though to free her eyes from the sun, and said
abruptly:

"Who is it?"

Having said that, from sallow she became deadly pale,
and Lady Henrietta saw recognition in the blue eyes.
Yet she had never, to her knowledge, seen the girl before.
Charles's description was a good one, however, the girl
represented his words come to life. Immediately, and for
no reason, she felt a rush of hope. Her knees weakened.
The girl said nothing, did nothing.

"I will sit down, if I may."

There was only one chair. The girl pushed it forward
and stood looking straight at her visitor, while her hands
busied themselves folding the towel as her father had,
without giving an eye to it, cleared his razor of soap.

"You don't know who I am. But I am here because
of somebody you do know; Mr. Charles Adare. He has
asked me to call on you—" ridiculous word for a visit
to a barber's shop—"to give you a message from him."

"Is he back, then?"

Eagerness sharpened the voice, languid, with slurred
vowels; the sort of voice he could not care for.

"I have had a letter."

"Oh, you had a letter." There was resentment in that;
the girl looked at her sombrely.

"In which he asked me to say——" But he had asked
nothing. "To find out if you were well."

"What's it to do with him?" said the girl uncompromisingly, and left to be understood the pendant to her question: Or with you?

That should have ended the conversation. But Lady Henrietta was becoming each moment more strongly conscious of reassurance in the girl's presence; she would not investigate the reason for this feeling, lest there might prove to be none; but the vigilante who had argued while she gazed unseeing at Family Mourning told her that here was an ally. At the back of it all, confusedly, ran a feminine syllogism: This girl is alive to Charles, Charles to her, therefore Charles cannot have died.

"I came also for another purpose. Pray don't be surprised, or think the request very strange. It was only this, to ask if you would come to my house."

"I don't do hairdressing."

"Forgive me, I explain myself badly. As a guest."

"Me?" The girl laughed, awkwardly, too loud for the room. "I don't see what you mean."

"Nor do I, altogether," said Lady Hentietta, apologetically, softly. "You must excuse me." The girl heard the difference in their tones, her face became alive with positive anger.

"What are you getting at? I don't know how to talk to ladyships—honourables either, for that matter. I know when a person's on the cross, though. I'll keep where I am."

"My husband was a felon," said Lady Henrietta without hesitation or emphasis, surprising herself. "He has been whipped before now, perhaps by your father, down there in the square." The girl stared at her, wholly taken aback. "So you see, I cannot put on airs, I am not on the cross, I am not teasing you. I am asking in good faith. Will you come?"

"But I don't see what for."

"Will you?"

The girl, striving to make difficulties, outmatched by her own curiosity, did not answer. She regarded the visitor, gave again her uneasy laugh, and looked about the room. It was poor, too sunny; the loud talk of customers, the smell of soap, was ascending to it all day long.

"Charles wrote to me," Lady Henrietta said after a pause, "that you had a face shaped like a heart. It's true; the way your hair grows on your forehead."

The girl shifted her feet, looked down at them frowning, and was understood to say that she was fly, had to be, she knew his sort. Then, lifting her head and looking straight at her visitor, she asked clearly:

"What would you want me for? I won't say anything without you tell me what you want me for."

It was the vigilante who spoke, above physical malaise which could no longer be fought in that hot small room.

"I want somebody to be with me that I'm not afraid of, or sorry for."

With that she drooped at last. The girl forgot to be wary, to detest the woman she had last seen on the Governor's arm from that peephole on the stairs where, lacking partners, she had gone to cry. She knew sickness

when she saw it, George Street being a place where the
ills of the flesh came often enough under the casual eye.
Coming close suddenly, with a strong hand she forced
the visitor's head towards her knees, calling out at the
same time in no ladylike simulation of a shout:

"Dad! Here, quick!"

There was suddenly silence below, and her father's
voice:

"What's up?"

"She's gone off. Fetch water."

There was rumbling talk. After a moment Quaife
appeared in the room bearing a glass half full of brownish
liquor.

"Water, I said."

"This'll do her more good."

He advanced it to Lady Henrietta's mouth as his
daughter, shifting her fingers, lifted the bowed head,
remonstrating:

"She'd ought to have salts, or something—a lady."

But Lady Henrietta took a mouthful and swallowed
it. Quaife winked at his daughter, tilting the glass. A
few drops ran out of the corners of her mouth, but she
continued to swallow as though the stuff had in fact
been the water with which convention supplied fainting
ladies. When it was empty she gave a little cough, wiped
her lips, rose; and in her beautiful voice said with dignity
to the barber:

"Your daughter has been good enough to promise to
pay me a visit. I hope you will allow it."

His daughter, incredulously looking from the empty glass to the lady, and inwardly from the lady to a young man in a beautiful waistcoat, found nothing whatever to say. She nodded, however, to her father's glance.

(ix)

"WE need a school of this kind," said His Excellency, "no doubt of that, Mr. Flusky. Here I have grumbles from men all up and down the country, that can't get a wheelwright or a carpenter for money. Look at this list of trades among the latest arrivals; a comb-maker, a man-milliner, two soap-boilers and a teacher of dancing. Who'll put in for that last individual, do you suppose? And if nobody does, what good will he be at breaking stones? We are like shipwrecked men on this deserted continent, we must take what the sea brings us, and be thankful. So far it casts up ten gauze bonnets for one good barrel of pork."

"I've been out here longer'n you," said Flusky. "You can't tell me."

"I don't like the assignment system," Sir Richard mused; "allotting craftsmen out of a hat the way we do now. I write to the Colonial Secretary once a month or so. He writes back: What alternative do you propose? And I have none. But if we can supply free men, trained, then I can say to him, keep your prisoners in the gaols, where they belong."

"You'll have the landowners agin you," said Flusky. "They don't care what a man's trade is, so long's they don't have to pay him."

"They care, though, whether he can do his work."

"No," said Flusky. "They think they can learn him with a whip."

"Are you saying the magistrates flog without cause?"

"I'm saying nothing," said Flusky.

The Governor looked curiously at the square man in his misshapen suit of Botany wool, so like in cut and colour to the convict's slops, and thought he saw the fellow's reason for wearing it. Once I wore this dress because I must; now I please myself, and by Nick I'll wear it still, and your best tailor, Mr. Maelzer of George Street, he shall cut the trousers like as to leave room for irons. To hell with the past! Or else wrap it round you like a flag. And His Excellency recollected how once, before the justiciary of his mind, he had arraigned the uniform ladies for their hankerings and flutterings after the past, their England, distant and for ever gone. Flusky, an unwilling migrant, yet had a better title to this new country than the uniforms could show.

"To go back to this matter of the school."

"Ay, well, what I say——" Flusky frowned, endeavouring to put into words just what he did say, when he collogued with his own thoughts. "What I say: in a country where everything's to do, the hands has a chance to put themselves equal with the head. A gentleman, a scholard, will do pretty poor thinking without a roof to his head or food in his belly."

"I don't know about that," the Governor answered easily. "I've had to think fast many's the time in Spain, with never a shelter and my stomach touching my backbone. Wellesley didn't take excuses."

"That's soldiering," Flusky answered. "We don't have to reckon for soldiers here. We have to reckon for peace. That's a thing what people here don't understand, they're new, it's all new——"

"People that know not their right hand from their left; besides much cattle!"

"That's about right," Flusky answered, nodding. "That about hits it. Only it had ought to have been sheep."

The Governor laughed, glanced at his clock, and put papers together, hinting dismissal, while he summed up the interview.

"It's understood, then. I'll see that the land's allotted for your technical school. Government has reserved an acre or two here and there within the town. It must be easy of access for the kind of young men we want to catch. Leave that to me, I'll do my best for you."

"Good enough," Flusky answered.

"Shall I bespeak the services of the Colonial Architect?"

"Give me a note to him. I'd like to say a word or two about the plan. He'll want to waste money; rams' skulls carved on the pillars. I'll get him some real skulls if he want to nail 'em up."

"The Greeks, whose Corinthian style Mr. Lewis imitates, did just that, I believe. Real skulls."

"Showed their sense."

He rose, obedient to the Governor's lightly tapping fingers; Sir Richard sat for the three or four seconds during which his mind was divided; get up for a damn gaol-bird? It's your business to make these fellows self-respecting. But I'm the King's representative, by God, and he's—— That's past; to hell with the past! Sir Richard stood up, offered his hand.

"I'm obliged, Mr. Flusky. You shall have the letter to Lewis."

"Thankee."

"Lady Henrietta well?" Before Flusky could answer he went on: "I have a message for her—for you, too; you too will be glad. They have found young Adare. In a bad way, but still—where's the letter from Dixon?"

The secretary, starting forward, found and handed a thick budget. His Excellency sought among the pages, talking:

"A messenger came in this morning. Dixon, you know, has been exploring the source of the Bogan—ah, here's the passage. But you'd prefer to read it to yourself."

Flusky took the sheets as though they were weighty, and laboriously, under Sir Richard's eye, perused Mr. Dixon's message.

"As I was reconnoitring this spot for the purpose of making out the camp, I came suddenly upon a party of natives, one of whom giving a short cooee first made me aware of the circumstance. I went towards them with a branch, which always serves as an assurance of peaceable intentions. They seemed by no means disturbed at our appearance, and an old man coming towards me pronounced an unusual word which I repeated after him as well as I could understand it. He continued to speak in their language, several times pointing to my beard and eyes. For the most part they point to articles which they expect, or hope, will be given to them. I therefore could make nothing of his gestures, on which he repeated the former word, taking pains to articulate it. What was my astonishment to recognize in these syllables the name 'Adare.' I repeated the name, therefore, pointing myself to my eyes and beard, which are something the same colour as Mr. Adare's. He seemed delighted to be understood, and taking my sleeve endeavoured to pull me in the direction of their camp, to which I yielded, only requiring Burdett to hand me my musket and load his own.

"The camp consisted of some forty persons of both sexes, including children, and there, not to spin out the suspense, I found Mr. Adare. He was in a most pitiable condition, though the blacks had done their best for him, in a high fever, and not able to give any account of himself. I proposed by signs to the chief that the invalid should be transported to my camp, offering in exchange a clasp-knife and the skins of two wallabies we had shot that morning. This was agreed upon, and we made a litter of blankets and poles which served to convey him thither.

"Happily the encampment was near good water, and we were not short of provisions, owing to the supply of game we had encountered, and which, no doubt, accounted also for the presence of the blacks. Mr. Adare continued delirious for a further twenty-four hours, after which our broths and brandy seemed to revive him. He owes his life to his youth, for I hardly suppose that an older man could have survived the hardships he has since described to me——"

The Governor's voice broke in upon Flusky's reading; reckoning at the speed of an educated man's scrutiny, His Excellency misjudged by two pages the progress of the slower eye.

"Adare, you know, is a sort of cousin of mine. This is as good a moment as any to thank you for what you tried to do for him. He made no secret that you had advised him, as did I, against this adventure. If he survives now, it is not for want of prophecies to the contrary."

Flusky made no comment.

"Dixon says nothing, you see, about any gold. It's true he has not been able to get much out of the boy yet in the way of information. But I interrupted you; you hadn't finished."

Flusky shook his head, restoring the letter.

"Well, it is briefly told. He is leaving Charles behind at the house of a settler, who will look after him until he is fit to travel. We shall not see him in Sydney before December. I don't know how it takes you, Mr. Flusky, but I have a kind of weakness for young men who won't do as they're told. It is the thing I like best about this country, none of the currency generation will do as it's told. Charles is a misfit in England, in Ireland he is lost in the crowd; but in New South Wales he may do very well if he lives."

Sir Richard's clock struck eleven. The interview had lasted nearly an hour, and His Excellency was fatigued by it. He respected Mr. Flusky, he proposed to help Mr. Flusky to the full of his powers, he had faith and hope in Mr. Flusky; all the same——

"Talking with this fellow is like beating a bale of wool with a blunt cleaver; you tire yourself out, and devil a thing to show for it. He's off at last, and best of luck to him, but for all that, thank God!"

(x)

DOWNSTAIRS Flusky sat at the desk in his room, a lamp by his elbow, papers under his hands, which moved among the written sheets as awkwardly as their owner through a drawing-room confused with ladies. The room was warm, and his cigar-smoke scented it pleasantly, lazily twisting in the upper reaches of the lamp's light. Windows shut against a mizzle of rain prevented the usual inroad of voices from the kitchen. No sound came from the blacks' camp, their songs about dingoes, rainbows and food were being howled to other stars. Even the fire no longer spurted, but lay quiescent, glowing with the pink hue of burning cedar, more like light than flame.

Miss Milly came in with tea. He did not look up or thank her, but gave a grunt, fumbling still among the papers. She said, watching him:

"Can't I give you a hand, Mr. Flusky?"

He sighed suddenly, and became aware of her.

"Putting in for another secretary. No more gentlemen, though. Can't any other sort of a man read and write?"

"No, we've had enough of them," Miss Milly agreed. "Look, I've made the tea just how you like it."

Flusky took the cup she poured out for him, stirred it and drank. She went on with a kind of domestic calm and naturalness:

"I shall be wanting another female soon for the kitchen. That woman's due for her ticket any time now. Going just as she's begun to be useful."

"Keep her, why don't you?"

"Now, Mr. Flusky, she's not worth wages, not when we can get help free only by asking. Help, do I call it? Hindrance, more like. I won't have you pay out your good money just to save me a few weeks' trouble.

He said nothing to that, so that she was obliged to make her own complimentary acknowledgment.

"I like managing, always did. Why, even nowadays I don't have all I can do. Work's my holiday."

She poured tea into the empty cup he held out, sugared it, and with a grotesque little coquettish move-ment stirred it for him before she returned it. He observed none of this, and she saw with vexation that he used the spoon as freely as before. She sat down on the edge of a chair by the fire.

"Will you excuse me if I have a sit-down? It isn't that I'm tired, but—well, the fact is, I can't have any what I call conversation, so to speak, in the kitchen. Ladyship's comfortable, I've seen to that."

"How is she to-night?"

"Why don't you go up yourself and see, Mr. Flusky?" He did not answer. "I know you don't care for to see her the way she is sometimes." She added, after a brief pause: "We shall all be able to have a bit of peace now that Winter's gone, with his nose poked into all your concerns. My concerns too, for that matter. But you're a just man, I can take that to my comfort. Him to say I was keeping her supplied! What for, I should like to know? He couldn't answer that. No, nor anyone else."

She settled back into her chair, and taking from her pocket (guarded now against depredations by a brooch made of bog-oak) a stocking and wools, began to occupy her hands as was her custom. From time to time she looked into the fire as a cat will do. The atmosphere of the room was tranquil.

"Of course, as you know very well, Mr. Flusky, she's taking brandy. The doctor won't have her deprived altogether; might go out of her mind if we did that. It's against what I think right, but I give her the dose, and I measure it out like as if it was poison—which it is, for that matter."

He had finished his tea, and now stood lighting another cigar. She said irrelevantly:

"You always stand on both your feet at once. Excuse me. I was thinking of that young fellow, Mr. Adare, that always used to be lounging and leaning about." She began to match wool against the stocking she held. "This house is a very different place from what it was with him here. Winter, too. You're like me, Mr. Flusky, penny plain as they say. We can't do with fal-lals."

She smiled as she bracketed herself thus with her employer, and looked about the room, neat, warm, her own creation.

"You've come on, Mr. Flusky. Since I came here five years back, you've come on like the righteous man in the Psalms, of whom it says: wealth and riches shall be in his house. You'll be able to leave off working one of these days. There's a funny thing to think of; not to have to work any more." The voluntary briskness left her for an instant. "It would be acceptable, very."

"How much are you giving her?" said he to the smoke of his cigar.

"That's something I won't speak about, Mr. Flusky, excuse me. Still, it's true she's gone down hill since that young Adare went from here. There's no good my denying what you can see with your own two eyes. He kept her going with—well, I say other interests. Now she don't care."

"What does doctor say?"

"Oh, him! They can't afford to what I call dot their i's. It pays a doctor to be cheerful."

She put out her left hand towards him; the grey stocking drawn over it made the attempt at a tender gesture ridiculous.

"We've all got to go, Mr. Flusky. You'll feel it, but it's got to be. It's the best thing in the end for all, and that you can't gainsay. One go, another come, it's the Lord's plan for the world. But there's one will stand by you——"

Who this might be, the Almighty or Miss Milly herself, was left indeterminate. Flusky in any case paid no attention, disregarded the hand, and moved abruptly away towards his map, taking the lamp with him so that Miss Milly was left without light to darn by. She dropped the sock in her lap and sat quiet, doing nothing at all, savouring the funny, the acceptable delight of leaving off working, while he stood tracing with his eye the distance from the Fish River to the Bogan, and reckoning, with breath whistled in, the ranges, flats and forests between.

(xi)

SUSAN QUAIFE, turning up out of the blue with a small hair-trunk at the house in Woolloomooloo, had her first encounter with Miss Milly on the doorstep.

"Ladyship's orders. I'll just see about that."

Miss Milly closed the front door, and the girl heard the key turn. She was frightened enough, out of her depth completely, and would—or so she thought when she first descended from the cart—have been glad of the chance to run. But that click of the key angered her. She sat down upon her trunk. Miss Milly returned.

"There's been a mistake. Ladyship says she never heard of you."

"I dare say," Susan Quaife answered. "Nobody can't hear if they're not told."

"Perhaps you'll give me a little more information, if I might presume to ask. *What* do you say you've come for?"

"To visit."

"Oh, indeed! Very good. Come to visit! Whose invitation?"

"Hers."

Miss Milly gave a laugh; then, composing herself and putting on her manner of the trustworthy and decent servant, leaned forward:

"Ah, I see. Very sorry, Miss. The fact is, Madam— she's not always what I call herself. By no means." She paused, making a slight lifting movement of one hand, which recalled to the girl instantly that emptied tumbler of rum. "She don't always remember what she's said or done. That's how it is. So here's what we'll do. Come in a minute, and I'll have the cart got ready to take your box. A young girl like you! She's never done such a thing before, to my knowledge."

She stood aside, and the girl walked, hesitating, into the hall. It shone darkly, it was cool; it was the biggest apartment, churches and the Temperance Hall apart, that

Susan Quaife had ever set foot in. Her defiance found its match in the order and spaciousness about her rather than in Miss Milly's assurances, and in the silence, intimidating to one used to the clatter and eternal voices of George Street.

"In here," said Miss Milly, opening a door, "I'll bring you a nice cup of tea after your ride."

She withdrew. The dining-room was more alarming to Susan Quaife than the hall. How deep was its carpet, thick as lush grass! How the handles of the sideboard gleamed! They were elaborately cut in brass, swinging between pairs of lion heads, of which every hair and hollow shone. The pictures were darkly impressive, the inlay upon the table nowhere was dulled; the marvelling eye of Susan Quaife counted twelve chairs exactly of a pattern. Nowhere was there anything unsymmetrical or out of place, nowhere a speck of dust. The room silently but with conviction offered a testimony to the character of Miss Milly which the intruder could not but accept. She had not been offered one of the twelve chairs, and did not like to take one. She stood, feeling a fool.

The cup of tea did not come. She could hear no sound. She began to move about; stood at the window, and so escaped for a little the room's insistence that Miss Milly was to be esteemed. It occurred to her that Adare had sat at this table, on one of the twelve chairs; she turned back to stare at the furniture, imagining him with a glass of wine in his hand. But she could make no clear picture of his face. Her practical mind enquiring sardonically what was the use, she abandoned this effort of imagination and resumed her blank attitude of waiting.

The tea did not come, there was no clock in the room, no sound in the house. She fidgeted with her nails, which were a little ragged, and allowed herself to be beset by the notion that somehow it would be satisfying to cock a snook at this too righteous room. A cupboard in the corner tempted her. It might, from its appearance, hold salt which could be spilt, pepper to be artfully shaken out near the door on the chance that Miss Milly would catch a whiff of it and sneeze with the tray in her hands; a satisfying cataclysm. Susan Quaife, with a grin that was pure George Street of the gutters and the docks, gave the handle a twist and a tug. The cupboard opened; she saw among decanters a leaning, sleeping human head, its hair stiff and yellow as straw, the patterns on its cheeks standing up like flesh under a whip.

She did not cry out, nor at once shut the door. She continued to look at the head, while in her mind the evidence of the calm polished room, the orderly hall, strove with that offered by this new silent witness. She was not shocked by it, she had lived too long by the barrack square to be squeamish, but she was angry to think how nearly Miss Milly had bluffed her. Any house that casually kept such a curiosity in a cupboard was not innocent, however its brass might shine, however cool might be its rooms. That defiance mounted which had impelled her to sit on her trunk before the shut front-door; the recollected click of the lock dictated her next move, to turn the key of this room, thus momentarily disconcerting Miss Milly.

She slipped out on the verandah, remembered that her enemy's footsteps had marched one way, and stole in the direction opposite, peering in at windows as she moved. There was a big room with a pianoforte in it that looked forlorn, though spotless as the other. This monopolized three long windows, and the verandah went no further. She climbed down on to grass, and stood looking up at the windows above. A sound reached her, knocking and rattling to which she could assign a cause; she listened pleasurably, her eyes busy the while, assessing as a good bet a window with green curtains showing behind white ones. She hollowed her hands and called softly towards it:

"Cooee! Ladyship!"

There was no answer, and she could hear that the struggle with the locked door had been abandoned. She lifted her strong little hands to the first branch of a magnolia tree that was trained by the wall, easily found a footing, mounted towards the window. She caught at the sill as scolding voices broke out on the verandah below, whose roof concealed her now that she was above it. She put both hands upon the sill of the upper window, heaved herself up, lay flat across it for a moment, then tumbled into the room, panting. As she lay, the voice remembered from yesterday, which she loved unwillingly for its likeness to that of Charles Adare; this voice spoke, a trifle blurred with laughter, from the bed.

"That will be the first thing for you to study; how to come into a room."

(xii)

"WHAT's these other places laid?"

"That's for Ladyship coming down, with a visitor."

"What visitor?"

"Well, that's it, Mr. Flusky, I've been waiting for you to come in. Of course, I'm only a servant." She paused. "I'm not consulted, quite so. It's your orders she's to do as she likes within limits. But it's my opinion this goes beyond. You may well ask what visitor. It's Quaife's daughter."

"Whose?"

"You know very well, Mr. Flusky. The hangman that was. Now, what do you say? I done my part, laid the table and all, it's for you to say whether you'll sit down to it. It's not my business. 'Be not curious in unnecessary matters,' says the son of Sirach."

Flusky, surveying the table conventionally set, gave a cluck with his tongue.

"Where's Ladyship now?"

"Drawing-room." Miss Milly gave a laugh. "Old Quaife's daughter in a drawing-room. You'll excuse me, but it does look what I call comical. All things considered. Drawing fowls is more what she be used to."

Flusky went out by the open long windows, and

turned in to that room which S. Quaife on her exploration had summed up as forlorn. His wife sat in a low chair, dressed, her hair tossed up and held by yellow tortoise-shell combs. A dark girl sitting awkwardly, her legs slewed sideways, was looking towards him with all the silent insistent appeal of an animal compelled to take part in nursery games. She got up and stood as he entered, while Lady Henrietta told her husband that this was a guest, giving no further explanation. He did not offer to shake hands, nor did the girl. He said to his wife:

"You'd ought to be in bed."

"Later." She went on smoothly: "It is very good of Miss Quaife, is it not, to give me her company?"

"Is this what you——" He stopped. "I suppose it's all right. Dinner's nigh on ready."

He went out, and almost at once a gong sounded. S. Quaife, intimidated by the thought of those twelve identical chairs and by the secret of the cupboard, which she had no business to know, hung back a little; but Lady Henrietta's hand was on her arm, that fine slender hand, untouched by the circumstances whose power her face acknowledged. They moved forward together.

At table began a period of uneasiness for S. Quaife. She was in two minds; the defiant mind which knew itself as good as anyone else or better; the mind more timid, which wished to melt into its surroundings and felt safe there. She contemplated the mahogany and silver with an eye which her will kept from widening; inwardly the most astonishing thing about the table was the discovery of her own legs under it. This mental see-sawing preoccupied every minute while she sat; with each dish, almost each mouthful, a decision had to be made—whether to eat fish as was the custom in George Street, to the tune of I'm as good as you; or to take up unfamiliar implements such as Lady Henrietta was using, and be safe in sameness. She had an odd sensation of embodying in herself the two other people at table; for if Lady Henrietta handled her forks delicately, she used them only to break and leave the food, while Mr. Flusky, selecting forks at random, and shifting them from hand to hand as convenience dictated, managed to make a very good dinner. Questions asked themselves. Ought ladies not to eat much?

"Better try a glass of this, Hattie. Madeira wine; just a toothful."

"I think I'd rather not."

But he filled her glass and poised the decanter.

"What about Miss?"

"Oh, certainly. Miss Quaife, you'll take some?"

So it was all right to drink wine, Miss Quaife understood. She swallowed her glassful in one or two gulps, being thirsty, which was one of the only two reasons she was aware of for drinking. The sweetish nutty burning taste disconcerted her, and increased her thirst; somewhere under her ribs warmth began to diffuse, as from a small brazier secretly lit. Her host had barely spoken to her, she observed that, so far as he was concerned, the decanter existed for show. "He has been whipped, perhaps by your father——" and yet here he was, could buy up her father's shop and never miss the money, hob-nobbing with His Ex., and married to a ladyship. Currency declared at once and hotly that excellencies and ladyships were naught, but was obliged to recognize that to rise to them from the puzzling-sticks* in the barrack square must be reckoned something. For currency was shrewd; knew that while there was nothing like five shillings' worth of silver in a dollar, yet a dollar bought five shillings' worth of goods.

The meal ended amid these confusions of thought, with a slight inviting bow of Lady Henrietta in Susan Quaife's direction, once the decanter had come to anchor in front of the host whose glass held water only. She observed that the hostess had not touched her wine. Her mind's eye set an empty tumbler beside this spindle-shanked glass, compared the quantity and power of the brown liquor in each, but could not make a sum of it. Again, they were in the drawing-room together, and the awkwardness of S. Quaife's legs became evident once more. She made conversation to distract attention from them.

"Who's that let me in to-day?"

"It would be the housekeeper, I imagine."

"Do you like her?"

"She is useful. Very economical."

"But you don't have to look at money both sides."

Lady Henrietta lifted a hand, smiled, was going to answer—

"I don't like her," said Susan Quaife in a rush,

---

*Puzzling-sticks = triangles for flogging.

"she tells lies, too. Said you knew nothing about me."

"Nor I did. Nor I do."

At that, which seemed to herald some sort of questioning, the girl blushed suddenly and violently, and knew why. She could not say it, but she was in this house by reason only of Charles Adare, copying a way of holding forks in his honour, enduring for his sake a hundred blank misgivings, irrational fears, and scoldings from her currency conscience. She did not turn away, nor attempt to cover the blush. Lady Henrietta's eyes dropped first, and she spoke, looking at her hands:

"You must have wondered very much that I should come the other day and speak to you. You may hear them say—Milly say—that I am not always very well. That is true, but you must not think that I did not know what I was doing." She saw an expression—"Milly told you something like that?"

"I locked her out, anyway," said Susan Quaife, evading the question.

"There's something I want to show you. It will make us known to each other better than anything I can say."

She took a paper from the long swinging gold bag upon her arm, and held it out; the girl backed a step or two.

"It is from somebody you know. Won't you take it?"

The girl said, the blush burning away under her eyes till they shone:

"I can't read. Not writing."

"I see," said Lady Henrietta with simplicity. "I'm

sorry. Would you care for me to teach you while you're here?"

Before the answer, Miss Milly came in quietly upon them both.

"Time you was in bed, ladyship, if you please. We don't want you tired out. It's been a long enough day."

It was the abrupt but devoted servant speaking, but she handled her keys as she spoke, beating with the bunch upon the palm of her left hand, a gesture which had its own significance for the girl. Men with just such keys went about their business in the gaol quarters, and spoke jovially to her father, beating time to just such a commanding measure. She owned an antipathy to gaolers, who, rather than judges and juries, made felons out of free men. She answered Lady Henrietta's question, not choosing to observe Miss Milly.

"I'd be thankful."

"Very well," said Lady Henrietta; but the acquiescence was spoken to Miss Milly first, her eyes sliding up for an instant towards the righteous woman's face before she smiled at the girl.

"To-night?"

"There's only one thing Ladyship's doing to-night, and that's bed. I'll bring you up your little something when you're settled."

Lady Henrietta's eyelids flicked once or twice above her smile.

"Perhaps it would be better. Perhaps, just for to-night. I'm a little tired."

"Tired! So you'd ought."

Miss Milly said no more, but she tightened and elongated her lips. The girl, coming out of her own excitement, saw that in fact her hostess did look deathly ill. On impulse she went to her chair.

"She's not used to you," said Miss Milly; and that sentence, too, might have been addressed to either of the hearers. "Here, you let me."

She pulled the girl aside, and taking Lady Henrietta behind the elbows, pulled her up. Her hands looked unpleasant against the white skin, but they were strong, they knew their business, and Lady Henrietta obeyed them. She went out to the clink of keys. Once again S. Quaife was left, alone and ripe for mischief, in an unfamiliar room.

She walked about it. No mittened governess had told her not to finger. She had the illiterate's pleasure in things that may be handled, and the young creature's delight in novelty. She fingered, therefore, such novelties as china shepherds whose knee-breeches were beautifully patterned with French lilies; small oval pictures in which each hair seemed separately painted; boxes made of tortoiseshell with designs in silver nails; and a fan whose ivory sticks, held against the light, showed lattice work and little climbing Chinamen. This last she was holding before her face when a shadow across the lamp lost her the Chinamen.

"By yourself?" said Mr. Flusky. "Where's my wife?"

"Bed," S. Quaife answered briefly and rather rudely, because he had surprised her spying on his possessions.

He did not take the tone amiss. They spoke on equal terms.

"How did she get hold of you?"

"Came and asked me. I didn't know her. I thought it might knock up a lark. She spoke very nice."

"What's the idea?"

She spoke, with difficulty hardly surmountable, the name of Charles Adare; something about a letter.

"What's he got to do with it?"

"He told her to——" She stopped; but in fact, that was all there was to say.

"Ay," said Mr. Flusky as if to himself. "All right. You're very welcome."

He went out with that, and left her again to the toys. But she could no longer give them her attention, so engrossed was she with the spectacle provided by herself moving about in this house, its question awake and dinning in her ears.

(xiii)

THE mornings came, greeted by locusts. Gradually the air thickened with the scent of hot grass, and clouds which floated above Sydney's hills at the sun's rising sank below them, leaving the sky clear and very pale. This was a month of hot days.

Susan Quaife was beginning to know that true horror of being suddenly pitchforked from one way of life to another, the difficulty of discovering a new endurable routine; lack of occupation beset her, like a foe fighting by the clock, from seven until twelve in the morning. Had it not been for certain expressions in Mr. Adare's letter which she had come to decipher she would have packed up her hair-trunk and gone back to the hot rooms and never-failing occupations of home. Her boredom was such that she had even truckled to Miss Milly, begged for dusters, and received a refusal too civil by half.

"Oh, I couldn't think of it. Ladyship's guest—oh, no. Servants is quite another matter. Unless you was complaining of the dust anywhere. If that's so, point it out, I'll have it seen to, gladly."

Miss Milly had not forgiven the locked door and the evasion. S. Quaife had not forgiven Miss Milly's attitude at their first colloquy, nor her: Ladyship says she never heard of you. It was as much the wish to give battle, as the desire to come within the shadow of Adare, that kept her in the house. She watched Miss Milly with young eyes that missed nothing and did not know their own cruelty. She tormented her in such ways as suggested themselves, George Street ways, imitating her strut so that the kitchen women could see from their window and laugh, seeking out beetles to put in her slippers. Miss Milly knew well whence the offences came and was silent, taking no measures beyond locking her door, and resolutely wedging her window shut.

Skirmishing thus, Susan made for the kitchen quarters, feeling the sunlight lift and fall like a series of soft blows as she passed one by one the thick wooden supports of the verandah. She looked in at the kitchen window from outside; Miss Milly was not there, old Sal stood by the stove toasting herself a bit of bread, the murderess sat at ease by a basin of water and a heap of potatoes. It was an agreeable picture, and the girl envied both women their air of belonging to the environment, their occupied hands. They spied her head at the window. Old Sal whipped away the bread into a fold of her skirt before she recognized and laughed.

"Cat's away," said old Sal jovially.

Susan accepted this as an invitation to enter and make one with the kitchen garrison amid its unladylike activities and smells; she began to help with the potatoes.

"You put me in mind of that young gent," said old Sal, lavishly spreading dripping. "He was a proper nib, what's this his name was, gone off with the blacks somewhere—Adare, that's it."

"Adare," echoed S. Quaife, halting her knife. "What about him?"

Old Sal, rocking with pleasure, told how Mr. Adare would come into the kitchen and take a hand in what was going on. Many's the time he had accepted from her just such a slice of nice dripping toast as that which she was preparing. And she recounted the adventure of the poached eggs, pointing in proof to the fly-blown decorations from which three roses still were missing.

S. Quaife looked long at the gaps, and encouraged old
Sal.

"Go on. What more did he do?"

"I tell you one thing he did. Got her out of the
house."

Old Sal indicated with her head the slippers, Miss
Milly's emblems, now restored to their place. " 'She
getting your lady the lush,'* he says to the master. 'If
ladyship's on the lush I know who she gets it from.' He
was sharp, Mr. Adare, he was fly to her."

"What did Mr. Flusky say?"

"Oh, she took herself off, but she left him with a flea in
his ear. 'It's not the lush,' she says, 'she's off the lush,' she
says. (And so she was, while Mr. Adare was here.)
'That's not what you got to look out for,' she says, 'it's
her dab† you want to keep your eye on.' Have a bite of
toast, duck?"

S. Quaife, understanding and taken with a horrid sick
qualm, yet could not resist the temptation to know
more.

"What happened then?"

"Oh, after that ladyship come and give the orders.
Him too, Mr. Adare come. 'Madam Sarah, would you
give your attention to the bacon?' he'd say. 'Just a glance
from those eyes as you dish up, that'll curl it proper.' He
was a nib."

"Was that right, that about——"

*Lush=liquor.
†Dab=bed.

She could not finish the question. Old Sal, however, understood, and rolled her eyes sentimentally.

"Ah, I don't blame nobody. When a woman follers her heart——"

"No, but was it?"

"He never," said the murderess unexpectedly from among her potatoes, "for all Mr. Flusky thought so. I was housemaid, used to make the beds then, and I'd take my oath——" She stabbed ferociously with her knife in the direction of the slippers. "It was her. She want a man herself, for all her tex's. She didn't care for to see ladyship getting right."

"Nor didn't Mr. Flusky, come to that. Well, he was jealous, oh, something terrible. Put me in mind of Mr. Vaux one day when I'd been out with a friend, one of the family—But I won't say he had any reason. No, you don't catch me talking ill of the dead, it's unlucky for one thing."

"Who's dead?"

"This Mr. Adare's dead, you wasn't listening. Mr. Flusky, he fixed up a rig with Ketch the black, and this poor young feller Adare, he was a go-alonger, why you could gammon him a penny was a dollar by daylight——" Old Sal sighed sharply, and sucked dripping off her toast. "Off he went."

"But Ladyship's had a letter. She's read it to me. He's all right——"

"Well, she may. I don't say no. But Mr. Flusky, he's not one to put his hand to the plough—chah, I'm talking

256

like Milly. He's not one to slip up. If he says croak,* croak it is. Ladyship or no ladyship, letter or no letter, Mr. Flusky didn't want him, and he's gone. Same as that Winter." She ate her toast luxuriously, dipping the crust in a cup of water to soften it. "But it's Milly at the bottom of it. He gets his way, so does she." Old Sal winked above chumping jaws. "You'll see, once Ladyship's gone, somebody'll be in her shoes."

At that, her sharp ears catching a warning jangle in the passage she thrust the remains of her bread into the fire, smeared her mouth with the heel of her hand, and became attentive to a seething pot. Miss Milly, entering, observed Susan Quaife by the table and ignored her.

"Ladyship's tray. Ladyship won't be down to-day."

Susan Quaife had learned a good deal. One of the things learned had sunk already below the surface of her mind, where it ached—Adare's presumed death, and the reason for it. A violent anger, the alternative to tears, possessed her, together with a feeling of powerlessness. She dropped her potato knife deliberately, and went across the kitchen to where Miss Milly's slippers, stately twins, reposed under their chair. She picked them up, dressed her hands in them, and made them scamper ridiculously over the chair-back.

"Pardon me. That's my property you're making so free with."

Susan Quaife did not answer, beyond obliging the left

*Croak=die.

slipper to perform a pirouette. She heard behind her back one of the women snort.

"You heard what I said—miss." The right-hand slipper gave a kick and came down in the fifth dancing position. "Will you kindly put them shoes down? I'm asking you. I shan't ask twice."

Susan Quaife, letting her shod hands fall by her sides, turned to face Miss Milly.

"If I don't, what'll you do?"

"Never you mind."

Susan Quaife laughed offensively at a retort which revealed that the threatener had no further plan.

"Who are you, I'd like to know, coming into my kitchen and taking up my property as if it belonged to you?"

"You've got to call me Miss, anyway," Susan Quaife answered, clapping the slippers against her thighs.

"And a right Miss you are, too. Jest not with a rude man, it is written; nor girl neither. I know my place, if you don't know yours."

"Why don't Ladyship come down?" Susan Quaife asked, defiantly.

"Because she don't choose. She's took ill again."

"Whose fault's that?"

"Ah, there I wouldn't like to say." Miss Milly put off the shrew, and chose another manner from her armoury; that of the preoccupied housewife, too busy to attend to children. "Now you put down them slippers and run along. And keep quiet."

Susan Quaife hesitated a moment, dropped the

slippers, and marched out. It was not the retreat of a
beaten army, but rather of one outmanœuvred, which
must seek another position, more favourable, before
challenging again.

But at two o'clock as usual, most punctually, Lady
Henrietta did come down; restless, her hands quivering,
she descended to the drawing-room and the lessons
began, Susan sitting at the desk, her legs gathered ladylike under her. She worked a while to the pointing of a
pencil, then observing how the other's hand now and
then dropped like a dead creature, said in a burst:

"Don't go on. You're sick."

"A little nervous," Lady Henrietta admitted. "It's
because I wouldn't take my medicine."

"You'd ought to take it, then."

"I don't think so," said Lady Henrietta, smiling, but
uneasily. "I do better, I believe, without it."

The lesson proceeded. Reading from the Bible, and
from a book called *Tales*, by Miss Edgeworth, whom
Lady Henrietta had known in Ireland. It was the phrasing
of these pages, perhaps, that touched Susan Quaife, or a
description of one of the young men, or the voice of the
reader; for after a page had been stumbled through, when
Lady Henrietta read it again aloud, to show how it should
go, she broke out of a sudden, jumping up from the low
chair:

"What's the good?"

Lady Henrietta closed the book, seemed to gather and
reserve herself, sitting completely still.

"What's the good, what did I come here for? I knew it was silly, I knew that the first day."

"Has somebody been unkind?"

"I don't care what they say, it's not that."

"If you're not happy—— But it is such a pleasure to me to have you with me."

The girl did not speak, only looked sulkily and long at her feet, as during their first meeting.

"You are so much younger, it is dull for you. I forget that at seventeen one wants to have done with schooling."

The girl hesitated, and went forward, breasting her trouble.

"That letter—you know."

"Yes? The letter?"

"Oh," said Susan Quaife loudly, "what's the good? It's cruel, I call it, when you knew all the time he was dead."

Lady Henrietta heard herself speaking the truth, slow and hollow, a voice out of a wall.

"I did not wish to know that."

"I was a proper softy," the girl went on angrily. "A proper flat. Lessons——" she spurned Miss Edgeworth. "As if it would ever have been any good."

Lady Henrietta said:

"It was for myself. To keep Charles alive in myself. I can't explain wholly. You are too young."

Susan, astonished for a moment, went back to her anger and the jealousy that drove it, of whose existence she was not so much as aware.

"Young, am I? Don't you trouble for that. I know all I need to. It was your husband sent him away, wasn't it? What for did he do that?"

"You've been listening to kitchen talk."

"That's where I belong, the kitchen. That's where I'm best off. I'm not one for drawing-rooms, never could be."

"His letter——"

"His letter, yes, written just the way he and you talk, so's a person like me can't understand, so's not to mean anything. Rude about my Dad, about my way of speaking——"

Susan Quaife's anger was coming close to tears. Lady Henrietta stood up. She spoke low.

"I have become very fond of you. I never had a child. But you are free, of course." The girl did not look at her, fighting tears. "When I brought you here it was because your existence, your face—so like as he described it— gave me some kind of assurance that he was not dead. I cannot explain my thoughts very well. Only you must be sure I did not mean to make you unhappy."

The girl turned away, took up the ivory fan out of its box; the lattice-work was blurred to her eyes. Behind her, painfully, Lady Henrietta's voice went on:

"You spoke of my husband. I don't know what they may have told you. But here is something that I will tell you. Years ago, in Ireland, I shot at a man and killed him. My husband took the blame for it; transportation for seven years, and other punishment besides. I spoke to you of that. So you see——" The voice failed, and resumed more strongly: "You may think of me what you please. But when you say my husband sent him away, was responsible for his death, that isn't true. That is a thing nobody must say."

Susan Quaife muttered:

"I never said it was his fault."

She felt that Lady Henrietta had come behind her; a dry fine hand closed over hers that held the fan's sticks together. She said sharply:

"Don't do that."

Susan began in good earnest to cry, with a first rasping sob that surprised and dismayed her so that she could make no further resistance. She had a vision of her own hand ridiculously prancing in an embroidered slipper an hour ago, now for no reason brought out of its sphere to lie between these two ivories. She wrenched it away; then, awkwardly turning, with her head sought the comfort of the other woman's warmth. She wept standing, hands by her side, one still clenched upon the fan, while Lady Henrietta held and very gently rocked her, not speaking.

When the tears ended, and she was drawing away ashamed, Lady Henrietta said, not as a question:

"You won't leave me."

"Not if you want."

"I do. I do want."

(xiv)

No secretary, pallid from five months' voyaging under
hatches, was despatched by the Assignment Board to the
house in Woolloomooloo. Whether Flusky's refusal to
take gentlemen stumped them, whether among the comb-
makers and dancing masters was none who could handle
a pen, Winter's place was not filled; and Miss Milly,
coming in to the map-room of an evening with tea, was
accustomed to find the master deep in papers, moving
lips as he slowly and heavily ciphered.

"It's too bad, Mr. Flusky, as if you hadn't got enough
work of your own, with this new school and all."

"I'm not much of a screever. What's that, tea?"

It was tea every night, and every night he asked the
same question. Miss Milly poured a cupful as he liked it,
strong, with plenty of sugar.

"Isn't there any writing you'd like to pass on to me?"

"You got your own work, plenty of it."

"It's not work so much as keeping an eye——" She
sat down; another nightly custom. "But of an evening
like this I've nothing to do. What's a pair of hands for
only to work? Of course there's some thinks different."

It was as near as she could come to a hit at Lady
Henrietta and S. Quaife, idling out their afternoons over
poetry, or stitches on canvas no use but to frame. As
though Flusky had understood her true meaning—and
yet it was his nightly question, invariable as that about the
tea—he asked:

"Ladyship all right?"

"Well, Mr. Flusky, you seen and heard her yourself at dinner-time." But she had something of her own to add. "She's not taking what the doctor said she should take."

He swallowed his tea, frowning, and put down the cup near her to be refilled.

"You know my views, so to speak. It's not for me to force brandy down anyone's throat, without it's a matter of life and death. Still, I got to speak for myself. She'll be getting the horrors, we'll have her howling round the house like a kangaroo dog, and it's me that'll have to settle with her, not that bit of a girl, and not you neither."

Miss Milly checked and went on, holding the filled cup out to him:

"Mr. Flusky, what's this girl here for? Ladyship's sick, and I'm paid to put up with her, whatsoever she may do. But there's a thing I won't put up with. Immorality I won't put up with. That you know. And, if I make no mistake, we've got some more of that young man's leavings here."

Flusky with an impatient movement of his big hand tried to possess the saucer; she held to it, a frail bridge. He took up the cup without it, and walked away to the end of the room. She followed.

"Why, that young Adare before he left, it seems he had this girl's petticoat off of her. I heard them laughing, her and Ladyship; a petticoat, fancy that!" She halted the upward lift of her voice. "Wait on Ladyship, yes; she's your wife, Mr. Flusky. Wait on Mister Adare's leavings, no. Dead though he may be."

She was ineffectual and knew it, standing with a blue saucer shaking in her hand, addressing a back that would not turn. She caught at self-control, knowing that to play her old card was to throw up the game, and spoke in another tone:

"Excuse me. I was going to say, come what may, I'd never make trouble for *you*."

"Ah," said he to the map's sterile white spaces, and turning, put down his cup upon the saucer which she automatically held to take it.

(xv)

ALL her life Susan Quaife had worn without self-consciousness Botany wool in winter, prints in summer; in all her life she had donned one grand dress only, that with the gum flowers in which she had appeared at the Patrick's Day ball; and this, even, had been a loan from the gad-about wife of a sergeant. Now it had been determined, after study of the fashions in such collections as La Belle Assemblée or The Ladies' Elegant Souvenir, that Susan should endeavour to possess a waist, bosom, shoulders; in one word, a shape. She had no true in-clination to this, appreciating the loss of liberty inherent in a shape; yet the prospect of for once being fine was not without temptation for her. Currency (be under no

obligation) striving with natural vanity, lost the encounter.

The establishment kept by R. Bourne was chosen. The
proprietor recollected Lady Henrietta and set out his best
on the counters, pleased to find his own prophecy come
true. They learn, mused the proprietor, that there's shops
as good as George Street; they learn if they stay long
enough.

Susan, out of a kind of shyness, the desire not to seem
too eager, hung back a little from the preliminaries. She
heard, however, the shopman's question:

"Would it be for self, madam, or daughter?"

Lady Henrietta, smiling at the girl over her shoulder,
answered clearly:

"For the young lady. You must not show me pinks or
browns."

"The colour of the eyes, madam, blue, quite so. I have
a periwinkle here, very suitable——"

Susan, drawing nearer gradually as a bird to crumbs,
put out a finger and thumb. There was no rasping sound
as she rubbed the stuff; idleness had brought her finger-
tips to a softness correct for such ladylike purposes as
feeling silk.

"Miss prefers that shade? Very sweet, very much the
young lady——"

Susan restrained the muttered denial: No young
ladies here. The shopman draped her, casting extravagant
silks upon her shoulders like some Eastern potentate
adorning an odalisque, rapturously bringing out his most

treasured blandishments, standing back, darting forward:

"Certainly, madam; harmonizes if I may use the word—new out from England this last week—nothing at the price to be seen in Sydney, don't care where you look—if His Excellency had a lady, she couldn't do better—three shades, periwinkle, sea-green, white—— And the styles, madam, have you any, so to speak, notions?"

They discussed the styles; shoulders widened with lappets, three flounces or four, not so much lace being used nowadays, beautiful piece of Limerick on madam's gown, nothing too elaborate, nothing conspicuous, nothing in the way of a spencer, Sydney very warm, quite so.

Susan, standing apart, heard this polite interchange of shopping jargon with contempt, yet felt a pang of fear. Silks and muslins, with the behaviour necessary to and consequent upon silks and muslins, set bonds invisible upon their wearer. No walking in dust, no impromptu meals, no running out hatless for any young lady cased and billowing in these materials. They implied too complete acceptance of a new way of life; the road to escape was closed by them, George Street cut off, invisible behind their sheen. She came behind Lady Henrietta to say:

"It's too much, too many. One's enough—I don't really ought to have even that."

The shopman, silenced by this interjection unique in his experience of young ladies, heard Lady Henrietta make an answer which rendered the situation less intelligible still.

"My dear, allow me this indulgence."

"I'll never be able to wear them."

"We'll get plainer things for morning."

"For mourning?" The girl took the word at its sinister value, stammered out something about having no right and turned away. The shopman, shrewd, puzzled, stood looking from one to the other. Lady Henrietta rose quickly to go to her.

"I didn't mean that. Indeed, I think you have a right—But I meant, dresses for the day."

"I couldn't wear those at home, it would look—they'd laugh."

"But you'll be with me."

The girl's look denied that and dropped. She hated herself for seeming ungracious, all the while a vision of George Street closing frightened her.

Lady Henrietta said no more, leisurely returned to the counter.

"Be so kind as to put aside lengths of those colours I have selected. The matter of the style and making I prefer to leave for the present. We have other establishments to visit."

She called to the girl, bowed pleasantly to the shopman dashed down from his heights, and went out. He, bowing, ruminated:

"There's a queer start. Smooth, the lady, very smooth. A girl jib at silk dresses, that's new. That's never her daughter, I'd tell my oath; speaks too rough. Something up there. A madam picking up a girl? That's like it, getting her in her clutches, price of shame, eh? My silks——"

And he regarded them, turning to do so; had some momentary idea of making a noble scene when the madam came back, as she would surely do, having paid; relinquished this on second thoughts as not being business; and contented himself with watching from his door and shaking his head at the progress of the two figures down the street.

The figures were arguing:

"You said——"

"I know."

The heat had increased while they were withdrawn in the shop; it was now insistent. Dust suddenly lifted above a crew of cur dogs darting from a side street, and hung after they had passed, drawn up almost like vapour by the power of the sun. The flies were pestilent.

"It is of no use, then, to go to other shops?"

The girl answered by catching at her companion's arm; a vehicle had almost run them down while they marched thus blindly, voicing alarms and persuasions. From this vehicle, unexpectedly, a voice first and then a gentleman descended.

"Lady Henrietta, surely! Do, if you please, give me the pleasure of taking you up out of the dust, and your companion too."

They halted, and within the next minute Susan Quaife, elated (for which she reproved herself), had shaken hands with His Excellency. She kept her mouth shut while her companion and this legendary being exchanged amenities.

"We became tired of our shopping, and there is an hour before the carriage meets us."

"I might offer you a chair at Government House; but I believe we should all be cooler in Mrs. Macquarie's seat."

"Oh, by all means. That would be delightful."

The vehicle turned, making for that pleasant road three miles long which a Governor's wife had caused to be made within the Government Domain. One rocky point near the shore still was known as her Chair, and no place could be cooler on such a day. As the horses swung, the harbour water shone like pewter between the trees; it was too windless a day for colour. At the Chair they dismounted, the Governor scanning his watch.

"It so happens that I have an appointment half an hour from now. Wilks shall set me down and come back for you. Meanwhile, let us be easy. It is this matter of your husband's school, by the way, that takes me from you."

Lady Henrietta bowed, after an instant's hesitation. She was smiling, and appeared to the sidelong eye of Susan Quaife untroubled; not the same woman who, in the dust of King Street, had almost tearfully pleaded. Sham, thought Susan; stalling it off; but she envied this armour of manner, so supple, so readily donned, proof as her own silences could never be against social ambush.

"This country must stand on its own feet, says your

husband; breed and train its people to its own conditions which are unique, rather than depend upon the caprices of English crime for craftsmen. At present the malignancy of individuals at home is such that you cannot catch them in misdemeanours; all the farmers and carpenters and builders that we need are resolutely respectful of the law, they will not be criminals, the law cannot transport them. Meanwhile our horses here go unshod and our houses blow away. It is a state of affairs which Mr. Flusky designs to alter."

"Are you telling me that my husband has *said* all this?"

"Well——" His Excellency laughed. "Mr. Flusky believes in deeds rather than words. His view is that you cannot mistake the meaning of a blow or a five-pound note, whereas you may listen to a lawyer for hours and be never the wiser. But I don't need to interpret Mr. Flusky to his wife."

He addressed a remark to Susan Quaife:

"I believe that deeds alone will not do for young ladies, though. They like something more poetical."

"Miss Quaife was born here," said Lady Henrietta quickly. "She knows the value of performance very well."

"Does she? Then she is something rare among young ladies. I had one refuse me once because I could not read a charade for her." His Excellency went on, staring at the ships lying like logs, their ensigns drooping, down in the airless bay. "Someone like Charles Adare; there is your real ladies' man. He has other stuff in him too, but it has been overlaid with chat and agreeableness. It remains to be seen what this country will do for him."

There was no answer to that. His Excellency, looking round at his audience, perceived that both faces were perfectly white, and that the elder's eyes were fixed upon him. Swiftly he recollected the gossip that had prevailed before Adare's departure. Some truth in it, then? Well, no harm done if there were. He went on, through the silence:

"Six months of wandering may have taught him something other than how to cross a drawing-room. He has paid for the lesson, though. I daresay Mr. Flusky told you of his illness after the rescue."

"What?" interjected Susan Quaife. The word came out like a shot fired among the rocks of the Chair, loud enough to echo. The Governor looked at her, a quick questioning glance.

"My husband told me as much," said Lady Henrietta in a voice level as the water in the bay. "It has been a most cruel experience."

"They found no gold. I'm glad of that, at least. A young country, like a young man, should not start life with too much or too easy money."

"What is your latest news of Charles?"

"Why, there is nothing beyond what I gave your husband three weeks ago, that Dixon's messenger brought. The next, I hope, will come from our young man in person. He will be in time for Mr. Flusky's foundation-stone-laying, where——" His Excellency took out his watch and rose—"where I shall most certainly meet you again."

"Most certainly," she echoed, and gave him her hand, not rising.

"Good luck to your purchases. Wilks shall return for you both."

Susan was looking at him without moving, mouth open as if to speak; then, suddenly, she thrust out her hand and he felt it cold through the silk glove. Another of them? questioned his Excellency's eyes. Not Charles, surely? Odd company for her Ladyship. A pretty creature, though.

The horses went off at a languid trot. Susan Quaife took a quick deep breath, and let it out, half-whistling, looking after the carriage. She stood with her feet apart like a boy, and surveyed Lady Henrietta as she sometimes watched Miss Milly, cruelly alert. She said, obscurely:

"Well. So that's all right."

Lady Henrietta did not budge. Her head was leant backwards, her eyes had closed, as though she were recollecting or intently listening. The girl went on:

"I never shall get what your game is. You knew all the time—all this time." Silence; no denial. "Why isn't there nobody that will talk straight?" She paused, forging jealous suspicions, then voiced them. "Was it to show me up? I know how I look by you. You talk right, I don't. Knives and forks and reading—all that. If anyone saw us together it's me would look the fool. In spite of everything, all that brandy what the doctor ordered. Fond of me, bender! I'm off home."

She stood a moment, gave a little stamp like a horse, and set off, almost running, down Mrs. Macquarie's road.

(xvi)

THE girl walked fast. The hot roads seemed short to her; the dust, though she blinked at it, was powerless to annoy. She was on a pinnacle of anger up above it all. Her young pride puzzled away at its wound like an animal at a thorn. She was white in spite of the day's heat as she turned in at the doorway under the barber's sign.

Half-way across the shop on her way to the stairs she stopped. A nose that she incredulously recognised was between her father's fingers, his razor was clearing soap, together with some very fine fair hair, from a lip more familiar in dreams than in fact. She stood; and for the first time in her life the thought came to her mind: How do people feel that are going to faint, going to die? Then Mr. Adare, one cheek white, the other ruddy, was beside her. She held to him instinctively for an instant.

"I'm back, my dear."

"I see you are," said she; pitiful translation of all that was in her heart.

"Can I speak with you?"

"You better let Dad finish," said she, her eyes on his soapy cheek.

"Damn Dad. (No offence, Mr. Quaife.) Where can I talk to you? Let's go and walk somewhere."

Mr. Adare impatiently wiped the soap off with a handkerchief. She said nothing, steadily looked at him. She heard her father's voice:

"No going out of my shop like that, like a half-clipped prad.* No, you don't, Mister."

Susan pushed open a door that led to the kitchen. The customers waiting, of whom one had already established himself in the forsaken chair, exchanged glances. Mr. Quaife himself executed a complex gesture involving both hands and one eye, of which the meaning was not to be mistaken; Gent, spoony, on the square, she's hobbled him. Adare shut the door.

The kitchen was small and hot. It smelled soapy; steam rising from towels drying on their horses clouded its one small window. Susan, for something to do, was wiping this with her hand.

"That's it," said Mr. Adare. "Plenty of light. Turn round now, let's look at you." He took both her hands, the damp and the dry, and turned her. "Different, a little. Your hair is done another way. I like it. Susan, have you remembered me?" She nodded. "Is that all? Remembered now and then? With kindness? Or indifferently? That fellow I ran away from on the night of the ball, that silly young man who talked too much and made me angry. Is that how you thought of me?" She moved her head slightly; do what she would, she could not

*Prad = horse.

look at him full in the eyes. "Not like that? Well, I'll tell you a secret. It isn't the way I've been thinking of you either, away in the bush."

Suddenly she recollected the anger which had been startled out of her at sight of him, and pulled her hands away.

"What is it?" said he, letting her go. "I won't touch you, if you don't want. But I don't deny it's something I've contemplated more than a little these last months. Touch of you; sight of you. I saw you most clearly— here's a queer thing—the night I thought I was dying."

"Have you been very sick? You're thin."

"Very sick," said he gravely. "Sick. Lost. Lonely. It was the devil of an expedition."

"It'll put you off, I shouldn't wonder."

He answered the half-expressed meaning, her fear lest these past unhappy and dangerous months should have sickened him of the country, with an outburst that astonished her.

"Susan, you don't know it, you've never put your nose out of George Street. Sydney's nothing, a makeshift. But the country's great and exciting. Susan, it's country that could feed the world and that you can be quiet in. Put me off! It's got me; I can never leave it now."

"I'd have thought——"

"Don't think. You haven't seen it. You will, though, with me. Come on, and we'll forget all the barbers' shops in creation."

She backed a step away from him, and at last met his

eyes. They were honest and eager, above ridiculous cheeks that did not match. She said, watching for the expression to change:

"I've been out at Woolloomooloo these last weeks——"

"You have?" said he, catching her up. "God bless Lady Hattie! There's a dear, there's a great woman. No wonder you're changed; just a little, just enough to be delightful. I wrote to her, did you know? And asked her to find you."

"She wasn't fair to me. She——"

"Susan," said Mr. Adare with simplicity, "we're together again. We hardly know anything about each other yet. Does Lady Hattie matter?"

She would not give in so soon. Her instinct warned her that anger was barren; told her, too, that he was honest. But she could not yield up, with only this brief parley, her freedom. She said stubbornly:

"She's your sort. Talk, and the way she dresses."

"What's that to do with it? What's the matter with you?" Susan said nothing. "One moment, just before we go on to more important matters, just to ease my mind. Is she keeping off the drink?"

"No," Susan answered, too readily, triumphantly, "she isn't."

"Observe," said he, half-smiling, "the results of schooling. Six months ago you'd have said 'She ain't.'" He was grave again, a young man in earnest, Lady Hattie forgotten. "Six months ago, I was a bit of a fool. I've learned too. If I'd stayed on in this town, coming

here every day for a shave, carrying on playboy fashion—
I don't say, my dear, it wouldn't have been an honest
pursuit of you. But it would have been ignorant; it
would have been the pursuit of a man who was still
running after himself. Look at me."

She obeyed, with an effort that was grievous to something in her, the coltish free spirit. He did not attempt to
touch her.

"I'm not changed. (I still talk too much, you see.)
Nobody changes, even in the shadow of death. But such
as I am, I know and can use myself. Will you have me?"

She held back, still valiantly battling, refusing her own
desire to give and have done. He went on softly:

"You are like the country I have been seeing. It is
sullen, silent; but if its beauty is for you, then there is
nothing to compare, nothing so near heaven."

She said, feeling the nearness of tears:

"You're changed."

"I believe you liked the playboy better. Did you? He's
there still, he's in grain. You can't kill him, thank
God, not with a hatchet." He put a hand suddenly
to the stubbed side of his face, laughed, and rasped
fingers back and forth among the bristles. "Look at me
again. You behold in Charles Adare's visage at this
moment the epitome of his soul. Smooth, the playboy. Rough, the man. Choose which, and choose now.
Ah, Susan, quickly, choose——"

With a queer little rueful smile she came to him,
hesitated; put a hand first to this cheek, then to that; but
at last kissed his mouth.

(xvii)

"Why only two places to-night?"

"That girl's not back."

"Ladyship coming?"

"Oh, she's coming. There's no one else, without you'd ask me to sit down with you, Mr. Flusky." Miss Milly laughed. "There's your favourite ox-cheek pie to-night."

He sat down to wait for Lady Henrietta, dragging from his pocket a newspaper, tightly folded for convenience of handling. When she came in he looked up quickly as if to guess at her mood, and asked:

"Susan not here to-night?"

"She has gone home. It was only a short visit."

He nodded, and began to help the dishes. When their two plates were filled, his with pie, hers with vegetables, he looked at her again, this time long. She answered with a shallow smile and began to play with her food; accepted the wine he poured for her but did not drink it, tilting the liquor, coloured like wallflowers, this way and that to catch the light. It gave her eyes occupation; they were steadier than her hand. They sat in silence until the hot dish, the remove, had been cleared. Then Lady Henrietta said, looking into the wine-glass held with both hands before her:

"Tell me something, Sam, if you please. How long have you known that Charles Adare was alive?"

He took time to answer, and before the words could come she had forestalled them.

"You have known for weeks. Sir Richard told you. I begin—I begin to think you are not human. Did you want, then, to torment me? I have suffered."

He got up, thrust his hands deep in his pockets, and began to walk slowly up and down beside the table.

"The girl, too. She had cause for suffering. Different from mine, but it made her wretched enough."

"The girl!" The word surprised, halted him. "What's it to do with her?"

"She loves Charles."

Flusky resumed his march. She went on:

"I should have explained, but I felt a kind of delicacy— We have not spoken much together these last months; and then, I was not sure you would understand my reasons. It seemed a natural thing, somehow, to take up and comfort the creature Charles had begun to love."

"Natural?" said he, with a jerk.

"Why not? You have done harm there, too, more than you know. I had become fond of the child, and she of me, I think. She won't trust me again."

He seemed not to hear. He was half a dozen sentences behind.

"Me torment you. What did you mean by that? Suffering—why?" He was at the back of her chair, hands on her shoulders, heavily pressing. "Hattie? Answer, can't you?"

She sprang up, lifting against his heavy hands as though

they had been the fringes of a scarf. The glass of wine went over, in the hurry of that unthinking movement.

"You have waited all these weeks to ease my mind. Was it nothing that I have been thinking you a murderer? Did you not care?"

He stood quite still. She caught at his coat, shaking him, enraged by the immobility which seemed to show him indifferent to her distress. "I have not forgotten it for one waking moment. I understood, I did pity you, I was in despair because you had done a horrible thing for no reason. No reason! I had not even that consolation. I could only think that you had done murder because of me, right or wrong, and hate myself, and resolve——" She shook her head; the outburst of strength was failing. She sat back against the table. "All this time you have allowed me to be unhappy. Why? Why did you not tell me?"

Flusky picked up the glass, filled it, and held the wine to her mouth. She shook her head, straining backwards away from it. He hesitated, then emptied the glass himself, and set it down. He said, puzzling it out:

"It was because of me, then? Not because of him?"

The suffering, the drinking, the fantasies, the frenzies— *it* comprehended them all; much virtue in *it*. She answered pitifully:

"You should have known. What do I care for Charles Adare?"

He put his right hand behind her head, pulling it forward and upwards till her eyes were level with his a foot away.

"You was different with him. You seemed ashamed, like, to be yourself for me. Old Quaife's girl—anybody; not me. You couldn't even keep off the liquor for me."

"Because I was no use to you, worse than useless, and I was ashamed. Not of you. Of myself. And so I tried to escape. It was the only way I knew. I'm not very brave."

That puzzled him. Before he could take her meaning she spoke again.

"Give me some water, if you please."

He stood away from her, tumbled some water into a glass and held it out. She put her fingers in it, ran them over her eyelids and forehead, waited a moment. Her pallor, the moisture on her forehead, made her look like a woman dying. Obscurely Flusky seemed to feel this, for he frowned and brushed his sleeve across the drops to dry them. She said:

"This morning, when Sir Richard told me about Charles, I pretended I knew of it. Afterwards, Susan was angry; she thought I really had known. She was bewildered, she accused me. And then she ran away, thinking I had deceived and hurt her, purposely. I said nothing. I let her go. And I lied to Sir Richard, rather than—rather than allow them to suppose you and I were not at one." She paused. "It cost me something."

There was silence. A night bird cried, and cried again, passing the window unseen. Flusky put a hand to her hair; the head was bent, and candlelight showed a silver streak that by day she kept in hiding. She did not speak, nor he, until softly, stroking the silver hair, he asked almost timidly:

"Would he ever marry her, d'ye think? A lord's son——" He paused. His brief laugh implied recognition and astonishment. "It would be like us, only t'other way round."

"With a better chance. Better hope. Both free."

He turned his hand swiftly at that, stroking her above the eyes, round the ears; the movement of a man gentling a timid mare. She leaned her head to the hand, and said, with shut eyes, talking levelly as though in sleep:

"I have always failed. All my schemes have been too big for me. What great things I have tackled, what ugly places I have ridden at, Sam! Too big, at least for me. The first of them all it was that broke my nerve, my brother's death; I never got past that, it was always with me, the memory, even here where nobody knew. I ought to have stayed at home and married a nonentity, some squireen or other, and been safe. Instead, I took you, and did murder and never paid for it, and came out to the ends of the earth, and tried to die—— All too big for me, all a failure."

Above her head he was expressionless, as always when he did not understand and would not commit himself. At the word failure, however, his hand paused.

"If only I had looked different—who was the queen once in Ireland, that had red hair and stood six foot high? That is how Charles saw me. But I could never reign or rule, I can only see and do one thing at a time—not the wisest thing. If I had looked like Milly, perhaps, I should never have tried all these heroics. Your hand makes my head feel cooler."

He pressed the heel of his hand for a second hard against her forehead, then resumed the go and come of fingers lightly over her eyes. She said, as though it mattered very little one way or the other:

"I wonder is it too late? I wonder am I going to die after all?"

He said:

"None of that. I'll see to that."

"Rub me well down, and give me a bran mash." She laughed suddenly. "Young ladies require something more poetical."

"What?"

"Something Sir Richard said. Charles, he meant. But Charles is a difficult sort of poet. He can only work in flesh and blood. He made something of me for a while, only I was not young enough; and then, I didn't love him. She, though, Susan. He may turn her out an ode or, I don't know, a sonnet to Australia Felix."

Flusky halted his hand to ask, in that lingo which best served his thought:

"Are we squared, then? You and me?"

She answered in the same slang of the hulks; the words sounded odd in her crisp speech:

"Fake away."

He continued the stroking movements for a minute or two longer, his eyes fixed upon the cupboard in the corner of the room. She heard him chuckle.

"Sam, what?"

"It's just I was thinking; might as well bury that black fellow's head."

She laughed, a relief from tension. He turned, reached to the cupboard and pulled the thing out by its stringy hair. As he held it a sound caught his attention and he stood fixedly. Lady Henrietta heard too the sound of footsteps on the gravel, whisperings, and a man's laugh. She rose at the laugh, but did not speak. It was Flusky who said:

"Somebody out there."

Then the steps were on the verandah, coming towards them swiftly; like a pair of lovers in a play, Charles Adare and Susan stood in the long window, holding hands. Flusky very quietly, and not looking at the table, put the thing down upon it, and after one glance that identified the newcomers, watched his wife. She held out her arms, saying one word:

"Children!"

They came to her. She put an arm about each, bowed her head between them, and kissed the girl's cheek first, then the young man's. Flusky let out his breath as he had been used to do after watching a horse clear safely some dangerous leap. Adare, as usual, was the first to find words.

"I've brought this toad to make her apologies. She had the impudence to give you some uneasiness, running off in a temper. Do your civility, Miss. You see, she's obstinate, she can't bear to be in the wrong——"

"Let her alone," said Lady Henrietta, and checked the girl's attempt to speak. "That's over. You're happy. Oh, Charles, how foolish you've been, and how glad I am!"

"Sit you down," said Flusky. He brought forward two chairs simultaneously, one in each heavy hand, and Adare, with the insight that sometimes informed him, knew that Flusky did this by way of a gesture of friendliness which yet should dodge the ceremonial handshake. It is not his fault that I am not dead; but I can't detest the fellow rightly, blast his soul. Thus mused the young man, smiling, nodding his thanks.

His illness had left him a small legacy of nervousness; a knock on the door caught him midway to his seat and jerked him upright. But it was only Miss Milly entering the room to clear away, her satellite, the petty thief, following with a large tray held firmly against her waist.

Milly saw Adare at once. She stood in the doorway as in a frame; her mouth opened; then she shut it and came forward, beckoning the woman in, to go about her work. Adare would not have that silence. It threatened. He assailed it.

"Don't take our glasses away, leave them, the evening's only begun. D'you see me, Miss Milly? The bad penny, the black sheep, the rolling stone come home with devil a morsel of moss—no, Flusky, we never got sniff of any gold. Hullo, and there's my White Rose of York, isn't it? Promoted to the parlour. Long may she reign. And Milly too, so long as the Lord will let her. Did you know

I was getting married? Here——" He dashed some wine out into a couple of glasses and held them out. "Toss this down to the health of the happiest pair, and the most improbable (present company excepted) that ever Capricorn threw together. Capricious—to spring about like goats; that's what the word derives from, that's us. Come on, now, haste to the wedding!"

He began to hum that tune, presenting glasses with a bow. White Rose stretched out a hand for the liquor eagerly enough. Miss Milly struck it away as her fingers touched it, with a jerky single movement of the arm, the rest of her body remaining still. She said to Adare:

"So you're back. Well, they've had their warning." She turned to the thief. "Clear this table. That's what you're here for."

"You can leave it, Milly," Lady Henrietta bade her.

"What's your drawing-room for?" Miss Milly retorted. "Here it is, eight o'clock. How'm I to keep this house? Sitting over wine too. A new thing for Mr. Flusky."

"Don't argue." That was Flusky intervening. "If ladyship says leave the table, leave it."

"I hope you've got no fault to find with me, Mr. Flusky. I do my work, and plenty more that isn't my work."

"Yes," said the girl suddenly and angrily, "plenty of that. What did you mean, they've had their warning?"

"I don't pretend," Milly went on, speaking to Flusky, "to understand the Lord's ways, they're past finding out. I said to you months ago all I had to say, with respect to this young man. If you take him back you'll be sorry, you'll go down into the pit, that's what you'll do. And your wife with you."

"Why can't you answer?" the girl badgered. "Go on, say out what you've got against him, without all this Bible——"

Miss Milly disregarded her, turning to Adare.

"It was always the way, from the moment you set foot in this house. Nothing how it ought to be, everything upside down, even to the women in the kitchen."

Adare gave a frankly lewd laugh at that. She went on, trembling with anger, hands pressed together at her waist:

"Yes, you laugh. A mocker and an evil liver, that's you, Mister Charles Adare. This girl don't know what she's getting, but whatever she gets it's good enough for her, and that I go bail for."

The girl had come forward, rejecting Lady Henrietta's hand that implored her to be quiet. She stood by Adare, feet a little apart, looking at the woman who, like a gaoler, carried keys at her waist. Her feeling for the young man, that possessiveness which could not find its way out except brokenly when she spoke to him, took this chance; happiness flowing into cruelty, lacking other outlet.

"He's going to marry me. That's more than you've ever been able to say, or ever will, for all your sermons."

"I don't have to talk to you, Miss——" and the title carried a sneer; like the word 'woman,' used thus in quarrel. Miss Milly turned upon the thief, staring, the tray still pressed against her waist: "You be off to the kitchen."

"Lady Hattie," said Adare, a little alarmed by these feminine exchanges, "don't you think perhaps your drawing-room is after all the place for us?"

Lady Henrietta rose with a look at Flusky, who obeyed it. But Susan did not budge. Mr. Adare's hand at her waist felt a trembling; she took no notice of its gentle persistent pressure.

"Say that again, what you said about him. Say it again, and I'll tell what I know."

"You?" Miss Milly laughed briefly. "What you know won't set the harbour afire." She leaned forward, dropping her voice. "I don't wish you no ill, you're young, don't know no better. You think twice, that's all. I'm only a servant, well, a wise servant shall have rule over a son that causeth shame. And that's what he causes, wherever he goes."

"Who wanted to marry Mr. Flusky?" Susan cried out suddenly, pointing, and beginning to dance like a street child. "Who wanted ladyship out of the way? Who's been planning, and scheming, and waiting to jacket her?* Mrs. Milly Meddler."

At that there was a moment's silence; silence absolute. The tray broke it, dropping with a clang from the satellite's waist; her feet sounded a panic retreat as she fled. Flusky brought his fist down upon the table, and the

*To jacket=to get rid of a person by foul means, in order to take his place.

glasses hummed to it. Lady Henrietta came swiftly back into the room.

"Oh, no, no! Sam, don't listen." She was urgent, her pleading protected not Miss Milly's secret only, but her own. "And you, Susan—Charles, take her away, don't let her be loud and foolish. It's unkind, ridiculous, I can't bear it, I can't indeed. Milly——"

She went towards the housekeeper, stretching one hand in a gesture that said: It is not my fault. I pity you, I have not betrayed you. Miss Milly gave her a stare and moved at last. She put fingers to her waist, unhitched with a single wrench the bunch of keys from her belt, and slashed them down upon the open defenceless hand. Lady Henrietta gave a little gasp, but caught the keys, and turned quickly upon her husband, whose shadow she had seen move forward. He spoke, one single savage word.

"She will go," said Lady Henrietta, pressing him back with her wounded hand upon his breast, the other clutching at his fist. "Don't hurt her, don't speak to her, let her alone. She will go now."

Miss Milly went, not speaking, head erect. Flusky took his wife's hand, and looked at the reddened palm. Adare saw the man's face, and felt the curious discomfort which youth endures at sight of older persons moved by passions properly the patrimony of the young. At once he looked away, and thereby spied upon the table the impassive head.

"Flusky, what do you say? Let's have a wake!" The man's eyes questioned him; he nodded downwards. "This fellow. He ought to have Christian burial. Lady Hattie hates him, he's indecent, and he's been against the law of the land ever since Governor Darling's day. Well, I dare say he mayn't be a Christian, but burial's burial. Let's have up some of the blacks to howl for him."

He was wrapping the head in a napkin as he spoke, hiding strawy hair, sea-blue stains, in linen whitened by Miss Milly's own hand. Flusky said:

"No fear. They'd dig him up and sell him again, and wear the money on strings round their necks."

"You may be right," Adare agreed, busy. "They are mercenary devils, different from us, who only want money for what we can do with it." He finished his task, and straightened, holding the thing up by the napkin's ears. "Farewell to an unknown! Was he a hero? Or a non-entity? Or just a damn nuisance to all concerned, like most of us gentlemen? No answer. No matter. We'll do without the blacks. 'So let me be thy choir, and make a moan Upon the midnight hours——' Will you come, Sue?"

The girl came to him, but Lady Henrietta shook her head as the pair paused beside her. They went out together as they had come, through the window. Adare had taken up a three-branched candlestick from the table, and held this to light them down the path. Their steps sounded crisply at first, then were dulled by the grass. The two left in the room as the light dwindled found themselves assailed by scents from the antipodean garden, stirring memories to which these flowers had no claim, which were the due of lavenders or lilacs twelve thousand miles and twenty years away. Lady Henrietta spoke at last, on a deep breath:

"Perhaps one needs to be born here."

He, for once, answered her thought unerringly:

"It's not the country for your sort. I'm all right here. That girl too; she'll do all right."

"It has beauty," said she, looking out at jacaranda trees showing ghostly through the dark, and stars appearing, suddenly as lamps lit, across the bay.

"I don't know for that," said Flusky. "That's not my lay. It gives a cove a chance."

Then they both sat quietly, listening to young voices downhill, and the pulse of the tide below them.

(xviii)

His Excellency Sir Richard Bourke stood up before a number of gentlemen by profession and one gentleman by courtesy, whose attention was focused upon his boots. To launch the expected oratory a platform had been erected, behind whose bunting rose the skeleton of a building not yet finished with bricks and mortar. This in turn took for its background the oyster-grey dullness, lucent, of a December sky. Said Sir Richard:

"I have not been long among you, but one thing I have observed, one characteristic of the inhabitants of the Colony. You have a strong desire of independence; you are ready, you are willing and able, to help yourselves. Let me say that these are qualities apt to command my most hearty admiration. I am a soldier, I have fought in two hemispheres, and I say, out of that experience, the best soldiers are not always the most biddable. You say: We are at peace now. Long may we remain so! But this is a matter of universal application, and I trust that, should war ever come, you will not let them drill this excellent independence out of you. Each man on his own feet, each man able to maintain himself honestly. That, I believe, is what you would wish as a community for the individuals who grow up and seek to thrive among you. You wish it and work for it. Nay, you are prepared to pay for it; and that is the criterion whereby, in any country, you may find out what it is that the people honestly desire. Mr. Archdeacon, I tread in your preserves, but we have authority for believing that where a man's treasure is there is his heart also. All honour to those who bestow their treasure and their hearts wisely."

The gentlemen by profession swelled their chests, hearing themselves thus extolled. The gentleman by courtesy continued to regard his boots.

"A man finds himself—never mind the circumstances —in this newest of the colonies of our Crown. He works; he does well for himself through natural aptitude and constant labour. One day he rattles the money in his pocket, and he thinks: I had no help to make this money. But I should have been all the better for help. I should have been glad of a chance to study, and learn the ins and outs of a trade. So I will give to others, younger men, the opportunity I have not had myself. With that your respected fellow-citizen Mr. Samson Flusky"—more nods and glances—"says to me: Will you sanction the building of a Mechanics' Institute here in Sydney? A place where young men of the labouring classes may go and be taught letters and a trade. I say to him: Not only will I sanction it, but I authorize you to use for your building some of the labour at my disposal. When you have chosen your site and designed that building, let me know, and I shall make it my business to give it public approval.

"Here I stand, ladies and gentlemen, in pursuance of that promise. Your fellow-citizen is performing a public-spirited action. I believe that this Institute, when the roof is on it and the instructors at work inside it, will do service to your community. Under this stone which I am to lay have been placed, according to custom, three coins: gold, silver and copper. They may stand, the gold for opportunity, the silver for knowledge, the copper for application. I have no more to say, except to hope most heartily that the moral riches, of which these coins are emblematic, may ever belong to the young men of this city, and that these same young men, when they come to handle their riches, will not forget what they owe to Mr. Samson Flusky."

There was dignified applause. A few ill-chosen spectators at the rear of the crowd shouted references to the need of a professorship of prigging, but were hushed down. The denizens of the platform exchanged remarks behind hands while a hod with mortar and a bright new trowel were preparing for His Excellency's hands.

"Confound the fellow, who wants free labourers? We shall have to pay 'em wages. Mark my word, this is the thin end of the wedge, they'll be stopping assignment. I haven't paid a labourer for fifteen years, I don't propose to begin. Still, it looks well, a Mechanics' Institute—progressive, independent. Oh, it *looks* well enough. I don't know which is worse, a Governor with notions, or a Governor without. Ah, but this one, say what you like, can sit a horse. Then, by God, he ought to know better than to cock up the emancipists and currency individuals in this way. Flusky won't make a speech, will he? Won't he? His Excellency's talking——"

"I declare the foundation stone of this Institute well and truly laid."

The platform dignitaries raised a sound that was not exactly cheering, but a sort of decent approving clamour. Their wives at the front of the audience exchanged speculations.

"Her ladyship—absurd it sounds in these wilds—does not appear?"

"Her health—at least, that is the excuse."

"May not this failing of hers be hereditary? 'Drunk as a lord,' you know. There is often some measure of truth in a proverb."

"Oh, we shall soon have her about again. The young man, you know, is back."

"Not——?"

"Yes, indeed, Mr. Charles Adare is back. *And* staying with them in Woolloomooloo."

"Very interesting."

"*Most* interesting."

"My husband tells me he saw them together yesterday in Sydney; she in high good looks."

"And he?"

"Oh, my husband did not observe. Men do not notice other men, you know, unless there is business of some kind. There is your individual getting up to speak."

The ladies, momentarily quiet, studied Flusky, then resumed their prattle.

"One cannot really blame her. Vulgar, gross, the way his hair is plastered! For a lady by birth, on a public occasion such as this! I too should make an excuse, I believe, not to be present."

"Especially if you had somebody more presentable to occupy you at home."

"Hush! He's to speak. Count the dropped h's."

Mr. Samson Flusky was brief.

"I thank His Excellency. We got plenty schools for book-learning. This will be a school to teach hands their job, what this settlement needs, to my mind, more'n books. What we want out here is to think our own thoughts, instead of other people's. This school will do what it can. I thank you for giving it a send-off."

He paused, there was clapping, but he did not sit down. The astonished uniforms heard him say further:

"It's a thirsty day. There's a tent rigged up———" his

hand indicated its whereabouts. "If you care to take a glass of anything, my wife asks me to say you're very welcome."

He sat down, and there was further clapping. Gentlemen sought their wives' eyes, exchanged twitches of the eyebrows and nods. The ladies, inquisitive, yet would not commit themselves. The Governor, they decided wordlessly, unanimously as a flock of birds, must give the cue; and when it was evident from his hand on Flusky's arm that the Governor was to honour the tent, they fell in with the utmost naturalness at his heels, agreeably commenting on the proceedings. So good to take the trouble, quite an impressive ceremony, if only there were a similar institute for cooks, surely not impossible, why not consult—the name twittered agreeably on their tongues—Lady Henrietta? The foremost group ceased its chatter, with interest perceiving that "my wife" was no mere civil formula, it stood for her ladyship in the flesh. They peered forward to catch sight of her.

She was coming out of the tent, a parasol tilted to keep from her eyes the glare of the leaden sky. By her side— the ladies glanced at each other—walked Mr. Adare, so deeply browned that his stock looked theatrically white, and the new whiskers that softened the angle of his jaw theatrically fair. A naval lady surveyed Flusky's expression in preference to watching the advancing couple, as a subtle artist studies his subject in a mirror to get its true proportions; thereby she derived small satisfaction, neither jealousy nor self-esteem could be deciphered.

Lady Henrietta had a smile for Mr. Flusky; indeed the identical smile with which the Governor was greeted reached Mr. Flusky first, and in its full effulgence. The naval lady, cheated of scandal, could only murmur to her neighbour of the Survey:

"Of course, trust the aristocracy to carry off that sort of thing."

Secret lovers, public drunkenness, plebeian husbands? The Survey lady's wondering glance demanded which of these Lady Henrietta might be carrying off under her parasol. But His Excellency was speaking:

"Well, we have made our beginning well and truly. Ah, Charles! You didn't listen to our speechifying."

"It went to my heart, sir, to see you bury that guinea under a hundredweight of sandstone. Too much for me entirely. I kept Lady Hattie company, out of the heat."

Delightful ease, the ladies granted Mr. Adare, eyeing him with the interest that attaches to a careless conqueror. Puppy! thought their husbands, the while they ponderously greeted him:

"Well, sir, what news from the interior? How much gold did you bring back? Any suitable grazing country? Water? You will be having your name on our maps, no doubt. You will be taking up land, I dare say. A change from Ireland! When I was younger——"

Thus the chosen few. In the distance lesser spectators, after wandering about among the piled bricks, and spelling out with their fingers, letter by letter, the inscription on the foundation stone, took themselves off to public-houses. The convict builders had been withdrawn while the gentry made speeches, in order not to affront enthusiasm by their incongruous appearance and dress; they were locked in a travelling cage half a mile from the site, while their soldier guards took an hour off for dinner. The Mechanics' Institute, as yet a matter of brick rect-angles set in the ground, with one imposing sandstone square rising a couple of feet above the courses, remained unattended.

Inside the tent, hotter than the outer air, yet preferred because of its shade, a gentleman with nothing to say, but accustomed to public speaking, had taken it upon himself to propose a toast: His Excellency's health, coupled with that of their respected fellow-citizen. Mr. Flusky made a bow whose clumsiness, had he but known, did something to dispel a current legend: ("My dear, he cannot have been a footman as they say, any butler must have taught him to bow better than that.") His Excellency responded with a smile in the appropriate direction, and reflected that for his part he must often have drunk good luck to a worse man.

"I wish to God, though," protested that side of his mind where the prejudices lodged, "I could get the gaol smell out of my nose when I talk to him. They never quite shake it off. There's the walk; something in the look, too. Why didn't Pitt take Mattra's offer, and colonize this country with loyalist Americans after the Independence? It's no disgrace, I dare say, to have been gaoled. Stone walls do not a prison make, as Charles would say. No, but the imitation of one that they provide is damned convincing where a fellow like Flusky is concerned. What is there about him that could take her fancy?" He saw her face across the crowd. "And keep it, too."

The champagne had been excellent, but it was finished. There was nothing to detain the ladies and gentlemen any longer from their vehicles and, eventually, their homes. They emerged from the tent, looking appealingly up, bending courteously down, parading their gentility before His Excellency's eye. But Sir Richard, accustomed to cast his glance round about on emerging from shelter to air, and more particularly thrown back towards this military mannerism by the fact that the shelter in question was a tent, had found other occupation for his eye; he stopped in mid-compliment. The uniforms, mutely enquiring the reason, saw that he was staring intently in the direction of that stone so well and truly laid half an hour earlier.

"By Jupiter!" vouchsafed His Excellency; the crowd swung to his exclamation. "The rogues! I wonder it hasn't happened before this."

Sydney's most favoured citizens then perceived that the foundation stone had been heaved by main force out of its fresh mortar. They checked their steps to exclaim and to conjecture, then advanced, gentlemen leading, upon the phenomenon. Sir Richard did not hurry himself. He sauntered, rightly conjecturing what would be found. In fact, when the military and naval gentlemen, with gentlemen of bar and bench, arrived at the stone, it was evident that the silver and gold, emblems of opportunity and knowledge, had disappeared; only a penny, symbolizing application, had been left, from which the pop-eyed profile of the third George stared helplessly away from the denizens of his newest dominion.

"Mr. Flusky, if you wish, the ceremony can be repeated. Though I think, you know, that my meaning has already been *taken*."

Thus the Governor. But at his elbow a gentleman of the press noted on a cuff: Outrage at Ceremony, and all about the insulted stone, faces of aides-de-camp, clergymen, justices and gentry stiffened or flexed with indignation, according to the temperament of the wearers, above the collars of uniforms.

(xix)

LADY HENRIETTA spread a letter above the silks upon her knee, with a single glance upwards to thank the bringer.

"MY DEAR FRIEND,—

"It was a great happiness to me to hear of you at last—after how long! I am into the fifth mystery, as the people here say, reckoning by their rosaries, forty-two, and you must be not far off. But there are more agreeable things to be thinking; we will not count the years.

"You have stayed too long in that distant hot country.

Why do you not make a little change, pack your trunks, and come home to some rain and snow? It is blowing very hard to-day, there is quite a stir upon the lake, and the cows grazing have all their backs turned to it. But I dare say what I call a great blow is nothing to you, with your tornadoes and other tropical splendours. Or do you not have these? We know that you walk upside down, that your trees keep their leaves and shed their bark, that your pears are wooden, and your cherries grow with the stones outside. Your winds may be stillnesses for aught I know, and in that case I am sure you would like to see again the stirring of waves upon our lake.

"Charles in his letters says nothing of your circumstances, only that you have been kind to him, and that you are in great beauty. He makes no picture of your house or your life, and I am left to fill in the details with my imagination as best I may. Thus, remembering old days and your predilection for leps and dangers, I have painted an equestrian portrait of you. Is not New South Wales a land of horses? And, I do not know for what reason, in my picture you are always alone. This is nonsense, of course. You cannot be for ever caracoling among the—gum trees, is it? And your husband is by your side.

"I have much to say to you, but my pen is slow, and the ship that bears my thoughts, such as they are, slower still. Oh, for a talk such as in the old days we took so thanklessly for granted! It is a pity that women live so much by trifles, for these show less well upon paper than the important sentiments men have always at command; and though ours sound well enough in talk, yet to arrange them on paper makes us aware that they are nothing, and we ourselves no more than zeros till a man comes to stand in front of us like a digit and lend us meaning.

"You have your digit, bravely chosen. As for me, Charles told you, I make no doubt, that such meaning went out of my life ten years ago. I am not a clever or brave woman, I have neither ambition nor capacity to make a life for myself as you have done. I put all my eggs in two baskets, one has gone, but Charles may be reckoned still as a dozen new-laid. In plain words, he is all my heart has left. And thus I cannot very well describe, without seeming fulsome, the pleasure I had to hear of him safe in your kindest hands.

"My dear friend! Let me write that again, it gives me so much happiness after all these years. My dear friend, the time seems long, you wrote in your message. And yet as I sit here, with the dogs by me as they always used, and everything unchanged (save when I look in the mirror), time seems, not long, but at a standstill. There is a sound of hoofs now, outside. It might be you, come on a visit for the day as you used, bringing your music and needlework pillion in a basket. I know it cannot, but for a moment I allow my heart to play with expectation. Has it not often seemed to you strange, when the scene remains as it was, that the actors should not make their expected appearance?

"I could talk, but cannot write more. God bless you

for what you and your good husband have done for Charles. May He bless you only for being alive, and for not forgetting me. Do, pray, when all your fortunes are made, come home. I promise you a welcome warm as the turf on our hearths. And now, shall I sign myself affectionately yours? sincerely, truly, gratefully? Take your choice, or better still, accept all four; since I am still, without any doubt, your affectionate, sincere, grateful, and true friend,

"ALETHEA ADARE."

A barque, sails spread to a breeze which darkened the harbour water in patches, was moving towards the gap beyond which swung and lifted open sea. Her flags, each with a severely practical significance—departure, has been cleared at Customs, has pilot aboard—made the most of such wind as there was; they struggled in the air from time to time briefly and frantically as fish new-caught. The ship advanced unsteadily, obedient to shoves of the moody breeze, her escape watched and noted by authority in a flicker of signals exchanged:

Fort Phillip:
Where is the vessel that left the Cove?
South Head:
Vessel signalized now off Bradley's Point.
Fort Phillip:
Report movements.

South Head:

Vessel signalized approaching Heads. Vessel has dropped pilot. Is vessel to proceed?

Fort Phillip:

Affirmative. Departure in order.

The barque moved outwards, free.

IF YOU HAVE ENJOYED THIS BOOK, WE SHALL BE DELIGHTED TO HEAR FROM YOU. EVEN A POST CARD WILL BE welcome, if you cannot spare the time to write at length. For your opinions, your tastes and your preferences are important to us. We would like to know, for example, if you have any particular interest in the author of this book, and also which of our writers have won your warmest admiration.

Indeed, we need to know if it is the novel of 'ideas' or of 'escape' which you seek; or the 'crime' story which attracts you; or books of biography, of travel, of art or sport. Have you perhaps an enthusiasm for verse; a taste for reading plays; a liking for essays; a love of any particular periods of history?

You have only to write to us on these points: we will do the rest. We will advise you about the forthcoming books which are certain to please your individual taste. And for your part, you will be able to see them in your bookshop; you will be able to insist that your library produces them reasonably soon. Your communication should be addressed to WILLIAM HEINEMANN LTD, THE WINDMILL PRESS, Kingswood, Tadworth, Surrey, where all our books are made.

THE WOMAN ON THE BEAST

BY

HELEN SIMPSON

"Helen Simpson enjoys an enviably high position among the women-novelists of to-day. That position has come quickly, and it is well deserved. She writes with distinction, she has humour and wit, and she is not afraid to make full use of an unusually vivid imagination. I am not surprised to find it the choice of the Book Society, for it must be one of the most unusual and audacious books of the year."

—*Sunday Times*.

"Smooth unforced brilliance."—*Daily Telegraph*.

"Magnificent story-telling."—*John O'London*.

"As wide a scope as a Recording Angel."—*Time and Tide*.

"To have planned this book is to demonstrate imagination and audacity far beyond the ordinary. We doubt if any living writer but Helen Simpson would have carried it through."

—*Illustrated London News*.

BOOMERANG

BY

HELEN SIMPSON

"The longest, liveliest and most fascinating tale I have read for a long time. A glorious entertainment with a knock-out flick at the end."—*Daily Herald*.

"Truly brilliant book."—*News Chronicle*.

"An original and brilliant book."
—*Times Literary Supplement*.

"In a class by itself."—*Tatler*.

"Helen Simpson has written a good novel—a remarkably good novel; it kept me up into the small hours beside a dying fire and not many novels could do that. There is a luminous quality about this book, a brightness of imagination and a glancing humour which keeps it vividly alive."
—*Daily Telegraph*.

SARABAND FOR DEAD LOVERS

BY

HELEN SIMPSON

"Beautifully told tale, finely conceived and brilliantly written, of star-crossed lovers in which the ghosts of the Bad Old Days walk again."—*Daily Herald*.

"Helen Simpson is a writer who combines a finely direct literary style with great erudition. It is not an ordinary combination. *Saraband for Dead Lovers,* which displays these twin talents admirably, is a historical novel in the top class."—A. G. MACDONELL in the *Bystander*.

"Colourful, powerful and altogether satisfying story."
—*Sphere*.

"Several contemporary writers could have told the story of *Saraband for Dead Lovers* compctently, but it is safe to say that no one could have made as good use of the material as has Miss Simpson with her wit, her liveliness, her imagination and her ability to write a warm and sensitive prose."
—*Spectator*.

THE DESOLATE HOUSE

BY

HELEN SIMPSON

"Miss Simpson suggests the tragedy of Horatio Forster in a moving way; she can create convincing characters and she can feel enough sympathy with the period to give the story unity of tone. The setting is delightful."

—Manchester Guardian.

"A thrilling story of intrigue and falsehood culminating in a really dramatic incident which brings the story to a close."

—Tatler.

"A very fine work of fiction—makes enthralling reading, due in part to a singularly lucid and vivid literary gift."

—Illustrated London News.

THIS LITTLE WORLD

BY

FRANCIS BRETT YOUNG

"Mr. Brett Young's prose is always grave and finely wrought, sometimes lyrical and exalted; his passion for the traditions of the countryside, as well as for its abiding or recurring beauties—the shapes, colours and scents of place and season—deserves the expression at once rich and austere, that he is thus able to give it; and he has few rivals among contemporary writers in his power of sheer description. . . . I expect this to be the most popular of Mr. Brett Young's many and popular books."—GERALD GOULD in the *Observer*.

"It is finely done: a faithful record of country life and a bit of the real England."
　　　　　—RALPH STRAUS in the *Sunday Times*.

"His story is long, but not too long, and we leave Chaddesbourne feeling that we have known, and even wept and laughed with its inhabitants. This is the kind of story people mean when they say they like 'to bury themselves in a good book'."—JAMES AGATE in the *Daily Express*.

PORTRAIT OF CLARE

BY

FRANCIS BRETT YOUNG

"Nowhere, since Meredith's prime, has the spring of love been so lyrically and yet so truthfully painted and the transition into married life is just as beautifully done."

— J. C. SQUIRE in the *Observer*.

"The whole canvas, in its copiousness of domestic detail, its richness in character, in the quality of its climaxes, and even in its blend of obtuseness and tenacity, is characteristically English."—*The Times*.

"The novel is written with a fine, quiet, beauty. The sense of English countryside—Worcestershire and Shropshire—perfumes it like a rainy wind. The intense English-ness of the book, indeed, is one main source of its charm and value. All its people high and low are English to the finger-tips."

—HORACE THOROGOOD in the *Star*.

PANIC AMONG PURITANS

JAMES LAVER

"Mr. Laver writes as a wit and a satirist. His rapier is of the finest Toledo, and he uses the Olympians for some devastating thrusts at contemporary manners. Venus, for example, attends a meeting in a Mayfair drawing-room which is discussing the provision of Homes for Girls, and paralyses the respectable ladies with a speech in favour of Homes for Girls where they may meet their lovers in private. Jupiter succeeds in his advances to a young lady by means of his favourite "rain of gold" trick, and Bacchus plays old Harry with a dance at the Albert Hall. Apollo has a good deal of amusement with some modern poets, and a poor little faun gets run over by a motor. The last scene of all is in the British Museum, where Jupiter assembles the gods and goddesses to hear their report of their experiences. Diana and Venus begin to quarrel, as they have always quarrelled from time immemorial, and only Mars is able to report complete satisfaction with the world as it is to-day. I need not add that Mr. Laver's prose and choice of words are as impeccable as ever."—A. G. MACDONELL in the *Observer*.

"Mr. Laver is one of our choice spirits, an Alexander Pope of our age. His prose is Augustan, and every page has felicities of suave and cultured wit."
    —HAROLD BRIGHOUSE in the *Manchester Guardian*.

ALL HANDS!

BY

H. M. TOMLINSON

"*All Hands* is an extraordinarily fine, plain, simple narrative, which rises in moments of crisis to grandeur. It gives such a description of an ill-starred tramp steamer's encounters with every sort of weather, and such portraits of her captain, passengers, cook, engineers, and wireless operator, as to make the reader feel that he is all the time aboard ship and actively enduring the sailor's lot. It is exciting, moving, and beautiful. In my opinion it will take its place immediately among the classic tales of adventure at sea."

—FRANK SWINNERTON in the *Observer*.

"This is a masterly book; perhaps the best and most satisfying that Mr. Tomlinson has ever written."

—DOUGLAS WEST in the *Daily Mail*.

"The comparison with Conrad—and more especially with *Typhoon*—is here for once inevitable. Mr. Tomlinson's book stands the ordeal well, the narrative touches great heights, not once but many times, and his seamen are neither puppets nor abstractions."—*Punch*.